FATAL BONDS

Mischievous Malamute Mystery Series Book 6

HARLEY CHRISTENSEN

ISBN: 978-1-952252-10-5

For you—the readers...

PROLOGUE

I swore Leah's suitcases were taunting me, all perfectly lined up next to the door. Waiting. They could have ripped my heart out of my chest like a demon in a horror flick and presented it to me with a vicious, demoralizing howl of laughter, and it wouldn't have hurt any less.

"You don't have to go." I couldn't quite bring myself to make eye contact.

"I do. And we both know it," she replied, her voice lacking any of its usual Leah-ness.

After all these years, I couldn't remember the last time I'd felt this crappy—the perpetual pit in my stomach, the pangs of anxiety, and of course, there were the tears. These days, they seemed to appear more and more frequently.

"When will you be back?" I attempted to withhold the whininess.

And failed miserably.

"I don't know." She sighed. "But I will be okay."

"I know you will."

Though she claimed she was heading to Los Angeles to help

the Stantons with an investigation, she'd packed most of her belongings.

"This isn't about you, AJ," she replied after a moment. This time, there was a hint of emotion behind it, though it did little to relieve the feelings of loss, pain, and remorse.

I glanced at her, frowning—we both hated the whole "it isn't you, it's me" cliché—apparently, my facial expressions hadn't improved as we both chuckled, replying in sync, "Yes, it is."

"I just need to feel—"

"Safe," I replied, finishing her thought.

She didn't reply, and I didn't need her to. We both knew the score.

Instead, she pivoted to a recent event—one of too many—that had brought us here. "That was cool of Ramirez…with the cop."

I nodded, knowing that she was referencing my ex-boyfriend slash homicide detective's effort to keep my biological father's true identity under wraps when the crap hit the fan.

"I also appreciate the fact that you didn't divulge the details to anyone…about Jere." Another boyfriend—hers—that had become a casualty of the war that had somehow managed to take up residence in our lives.

I glanced at her. "I said I wouldn't."

"Ramirez assured me of the same, despite the fact he's probably kicking himself for making that promise—always wanting to be the dude to ride in and save the day." She mimicked a guy holding his hat while riding a horse.

"He's kind of like that." I laughed.

"You two been talking?" she asked.

"Not since the hospital."

Her eyes narrowed as she studied me. "Do you…want to?"

I shrugged. "I'd rather have him as a friend than as an enemy."

"Wise choice."

We both chuckled again, and when the laughter fell away, I still felt there was something I needed to address.

"I heard you broke it off with Jere." When she tilted her head, I added, "Ramirez told me."

She rolled her eyes and, after a moment, responded, "It didn't feel right having a secret between us."

"I'm sorry."

"Don't be."

"Will you tell him?" Perhaps I had no right asking, but I was curious if she would tell Jere about his true lineage. I wasn't entirely sure what I would do in her shoes.

She shrugged. "If I do, you'll be the first to know."

"Second."

"Right. Second." She laughed, this time, it sounded heartfelt, which gave me hope. "In the meantime, I have a parting gift."

I quirked a brow. "Shouldn't I be giving you the gift?"

She chuckled. "Perhaps you should review my offering first."

She extended her hand, passing me a slip of paper with a local phone number and a name.

Maria Reynolds.

When I glanced at her in confusion, she continued, "It's about time you started looking into Decker's request to expose her mother's killer. And finally, bring her some justice."

Before I could protest, she added, "It's the name of the woman who used to babysit for Decker while her mother and father were at work." I cocked my head, surely there was more?

My friend did not disappoint.

"But that's not what makes Ms. Reynolds interesting. At least not entirely. She used to serve as the personal assistant—pretty much a glorified housekeeper—of a prominent criminal attorney's wife. On the night Decker's mom was murdered, she allegedly reported seeing this man enter the apartment shortly after dark and emerge twenty-eight minutes later, covered in blood."

"Terrence Edwards," I murmured. "But twenty-eight minutes? Seems pretty exact. Wait—what do you mean by 'allegedly'? She either saw something, or she didn't."

"Didn't," she replied. "Maria Reynolds didn't make the call, and they never found out who did."

I nodded. "I'll admit, that's…odd. But if that's the case, other than working for Edwards, how is she relevant to solving Decker's mom's murder?"

"Because Decker wasn't the only witness to the atrocities her mother endured."

"No…" My mouth went dry, my heart thumping against my chest.

As Leah collected her suitcases, she glanced over her shoulder to reveal the remainder of this parting gift.

"Maria Reynolds' young daughter, Danielle, spent the evening playing in the apartment of her best friend, who lived across the hall, on the same floor. That best friend just happened to be…"

"Kelly Decker," I whispered, as she offered me a single head nod before walking out the door.

I stared down the street long after her vehicle had disappeared—a scene that had played itself out in eighteen seconds flat. I know because I counted. A difficult feat while holding one's breath, but it was a necessary exercise, especially if I planned on retaining my sanity.

My best friend had just walked out of my life.

And I'd let her.

Perhaps I needed to revisit that sanity bit.

There was a lump in my throat and an ache I would not soon forget. I'd felt it before.

When Ramirez left.

What did it say about me—that the important people in my life felt they needed to leave?

Had they been given the option, would they have run, rather than walked?

Would they have left sooner?

I sucked in a breath, puffed out my cheeks, and released it before focusing on the paper Leah had given me. Talking to Maria Reynolds would be beneficial, as it could lead me directly to

Decker's childhood friend, who would be crucial in helping to decipher the murder of her mother.

Question was, now as an adult, would Danielle be willing to resurrect the past and relive what must have been the most terrifying moment in her young life?

As I collected my thoughts and punched the number into my cell phone, I had to wonder why Leah hadn't supplied a direct connection to the friend. Considering how thorough she was in her research, there had to be a good reason.

"Hello?" The woman's voice was hesitant.

"Hello, is this Maria?" I asked, forcing as much cheerfulness into my voice as I could muster without sounding like a chipmunk.

"She's not available." Hesitation quickly transitioned to suspicion. "Who *is* this?"

"My name is Arianna Jackson. I'm a friend of Kelly Decker's. I was hoping to speak to Ms. Reynolds about a matter of mutual concern—"

"Is this about Ellen?" I wasn't sure who Ellen was but never had a chance to ask as the woman continued, "I swear—every time the anniversary of her murder comes up, you reporters turn over every stone and stick your noses where they don't belong. The woman's been dead and buried for nearly thirty years. Can't you just let her rest in peace?"

I was about to respond when the connection abruptly disconnected.

I stared at the phone. The brief conversation—albeit one-sided—had yielded three things. One: Ellen was likely Decker's mother. Two: The woman, while not Maria Reynolds, had some association of her own with Ellen and/or Decker. Three: I needed to get my act together before proceeding any further.

I no longer had the benefit of Leah's crack investigative skills, and had I not jumped the gun making the phone call, might have taken an approach that would have provided some actual results.

Sighing, I shuffled to the kitchen, where my laptop slept on the island. Waking it up, I searched for all Maria Reynolds listed in the metro Phoenix area, as per the area code, and found seven. Letting my fingers do the walking, I was quickly able to narrow the selection by age and, with a few more clicks, obtained an address in nearby Mesa.

It's pretty amazing what you can find on the Internet with relatively little effort.

And a little frightening.

It was also fortuitous that Maria had moved from California to Arizona at some point. After several attempts to contact Maria Reynolds without receiving as much as a voicemail, an in-person visit was next on my list. I wasn't about to let Maria's self-appointed phone monitor stand in my way.

Pausing to glance in the hallway mirror to ensure I was some-what presentable, I noted that the face staring back looked a bit road-worn. Sleep deprivation and stress tended to have that effect on me. At least my hair, which at some point I'd managed to wrangle into a high ponytail, looked somewhat smooth, and my long bangs helped to obscure the dark circles under my eyes.

I pasted on a smile that would have made the Joker cringe. Eh, best not to overdo it on my first visit.

Patting down my shirt to ensure there were no stray Alaskan Malamute fluffies, I noted my jeans and Chuck Taylors' had seen better days, though I gave myself a few points for their cleanliness.

Just then, Nicoh sauntered out of my room, looked around, and shook off. The more I backed away, the faster he advanced.

Sighing when he pressed his massive head into my hip, I gave into his low whoo-whoos and scratched him behind his velvety ears.

"Ready to go for a ride, buddy?" He responded by whipping his curly tail from side to side before trotting to the rack near the door where his lead was hung. "Alright, then, guess I don't need to ask you twice." I chuckled.

As we exited the house, he paused to sniff the ground where Leah had placed her luggage and released a quiet whimper before glancing back at me.

"I know, buddy. I miss her, too."

According to the address I'd looked up, Maria Reynolds lived in an apartment complex off Ellsworth Road and Southern Avenue in East Mesa. After a few wrong turns, I eased my way into a parking spot near the "C" building. I wistfully looked at Nicoh after spotting a sign that read: "NO Dogs Exceeding 50 Pounds Are Allowed. NO EXCEPTIONS."

There was no way I could disguise those extra forty-plus pounds.

"You'll hold down the fort, while I attempt to have a chat with the mother of Decker's friend?" Rolling my eyes when he turned so that his back was facing me, I added, "Great. My wingman has gone from a snarky blond to a passive-aggressive canine. I'm not sure which is worse, but I certainly didn't get an upgrade."

Though it was a cool day by desert standards, I rolled the windows down to an acceptable level, scruffed Nicoh's nose, and made my way to the apartment, which, according to my search, was on the ground floor. I rounded the corner into a courtyard and nearly stumbled over a woman in a wheelchair sitting in the middle of the pathway leading to Maria's.

She was slumped to one side, mouth partially opened and eyes closed with hands carefully folded in her lap. Though the ebony halo of frizzy tufts was graying at the temples, her tanned face showed only the slightest hint of creases, suggesting that her physical condition had betrayed her. I pegged her for at least two decades younger than she appeared.

I approached carefully in an attempt not to rouse her as I passed to knock on Maria's door, but something alerted her to my presence, and she awoke with a shudder. Her eyes were wide as she peered around without moving her head. Finally, her gaze rested on me, though it was difficult to tell if she really saw me.

"My apologies if I startled you. I am here to see Maria. Do you know if she is home?" I gestured toward the door behind her, but her eyes never moved.

I started to repeat myself when a stout woman clad in baby blue hospital scrubs rushed out of Maria's apartment. Her messy reddish-brown topknot swayed precariously as she hustled toward us.

"Mother! What are you doing out here?" Ignoring me, she gripped the handles of the wheelchair, swiveled it around with ease, and began to retreat into the apartment.

"Excuse me. Is Maria home?" I hastened after them, stopping short as the woman pushed her mother across the threshold of the apartment before turning.

"Listen, I told you on the phone. Leave it alone! Can't you see"—she jabbed a finger in her mother's direction—"that she's already been through Hell and back? Have you no compassion? No mercy?" She stepped closer until we were eye to eye and whispered between clenched teeth, "Leave. Before I do something we'll both live to regret."

When I didn't respond, she huffed, turned on her heel, and stomped into the apartment, grasping the wheelchair where her mother sat idle.

"Are you Danielle?" I called after her in a last-ditch attempt.

She spun, her eyes narrowing. "Leave. It. Alone. Danielle is dead." She slammed the door in my face.

The woman had asked about compassion and mercy, and while I had no idea the extent of what their family had endured over the years, I was quite clear on one thing.

The man who had mutilated and killed Decker's mother had possessed neither.

CHAPTER TWO

I slipped a business card into the crack of the door and left another hooked behind the plastic apartment numbers before heading back. I overheard a few of the landscaping crew talking about a giant wolf and hustled to the vehicle to find Nicoh sitting behind the wheel, looking quite pleased with himself as he howled out the window, sharing his tale of woe with anyone within earshot. His shark-like grin broadened when he saw me, and his tail whipped back and forth as he hopped to the passenger seat and popped his head out the window for scratches like he'd been there the entire time.

"Behaving ourselves, I see."

I received a round of delighted whoo-whoos when I gave his head and muzzle my full attention, before settling behind his ears to finish my penance for leaving him behind, though I'd only been gone for less than five minutes.

Nicoh begrudgingly grunted and accepted my scratches, and once he was satisfied, jumped the seat and curled up in the back on the floor, sighing as though the day had been as hard as it was long.

"I hear ya, buddy, I really do," I murmured as I crawled into the driver's seat and retreated, no more informed or encouraged than I had been when I'd set out on this adventure.

I was just about to merge onto the freeway when my cell phone rang. I glanced at the screen, huffing out a breath at the "Unknown Caller." I was in such a mood I decided to answer and was prepared to give the sales bot on the other end a piece of my mind when I heard a soft, almost hesitant, "Arianna?"

The voice was vaguely familiar.

"Yes, this is Arianna Jackson? How can I help you?"

"Oh, good. This is Larissa. Larissa Reynolds? We just spoke…a few moments ago? I found your card and wanted to explain…" Her voice was shaky and when it trailed off, I wondered if she was rethinking the call.

"Okay…" I prompted, not wanting to scare her off or force her to change her mind.

All bets were off, however, if Larissa Reynolds had called me for the purpose of continuing where we'd left off. I was in no mood for another tongue-lashing.

"Can we meet?" she finally managed to blurt out. After a moment of awkward silence—I was still trying to formulate a response—she added, "Somewhere away from the apartment. I don't want to upset Mother. Upset her any more, I guess."

"What did you have in mind?" I asked, trying to keep the sharpness out of my tone. If she had only come to this conclusion about me ten minutes earlier, it would have saved us both time. And frustration.

Thankfully, she didn't seem to notice my attitude. Either that, or she was willing to overlook it.

"I have a shift in a few hours but can meet once Mother's nurse arrives unless that is too soon?"

I bit my lip to keep from spouting a snarky retort. "Not at all. Just tell me where you'd like to meet, and I'll be there." How's that for playing nicey-nice?

"How about the outdoor seating area on the east side of Tempe Marketplace, near the theaters? Say…in forty-five minutes? It's near my workplace, and if you don't mind the scrubs, it should be fairly mellow this time of day."

And public, I noted, though I made no comment. Instead, I had to get something out of the way.

"Sounds fine. What changed your mind?"

Larissa heaved out a long sigh, then another, before responding, "Honestly, you caught me off-guard with your phone call. And then, when you showed up…" I started to apologize when she added, "I overreacted. A lot. I tend to get overprotective where my mother is concerned—call it a habit. Anyway, I'm truly sorry about that first impression. It was not a good showing on my part. But to answer your question, once I met you in person and then found your business card, I realized I needed to calm down, put things into perspective, and give you a chance."

"My business card?" My brows raised, wondering what could be so compelling about a three and a half by two-inch piece of cardstock.

She chuckled. "Anyone who names their business Mischievous Malamute Photography has probably had a few dogs in their life. That simple fact alone tells me a lot about you. Having said that, I'm guessing you're a pretty good human being, Arianna Jackson. And I'd like to hear what you have to say."

Color me speechless. Only Nicoh had words and howled from the back seat, causing her chuckle to morph into full-blown laughter. It also sealed the deal.

I wouldn't have time to drive home, get Nicoh situated, and drive to Tempe Marketplace before the meeting with Larissa, so I headed straight there, nestled into a parking spot, and followed-up with the clients on my current projects. Business had been steady lately, especially with everyone gearing up for the resort season and those out-of-town visitors trying to escape temperatures I couldn't begin to fathom. Just thinking about it made me shiver, despite the sun's warmth through the windshield.

In addition to those seeking refuge from colder climates, wedding season was also on the horizon, which meant brochures and ads needed to be updated and re-shot to reflect the current trends and offerings. Most were in a holding pattern, meaning there was little required on my part until panic mode hit on their end. Fortunately, I was used to it and had learned to plan for such contingencies.

My clientele in the real estate market had also amped up, thanks in part to my friend Charlie Wilson, who had increased the size of his own already sizable portfolio. This was after I'd suggested and then created videos of his more lucrative real estate properties. One included a historic Frank Lloyd Wright-designed estate that had been featured by local media and a few national and international magazines. And while it was quite an honor and a feather in my cap, not to mention a boost in my bank account, it also made me a bit squishy coming from Charlie, as it felt more like a payoff for helping him out of a bind than an act of goodwill on his part.

I glanced at my watch as I pondered that and realized I had used up the extra time. Now I'd have to hustle to not be late meeting with Larissa. After our first go-around, I certainly didn't want her thinking I had blown her off and was no longer interested.

Nicoh didn't seem to care one way or the other as I glanced at him in the rear-view mirror. Instead, he looked bored and chewed on his paw as I gave him the "up and at 'em" command, and we rushed to the outside seating area that Larissa had suggested.

Despite the weather, the outdoor fireplaces were fully ablaze, and the portable patio heaters were strategically positioned around the chairs and couches, where a couple wearing puffy winter coats and Ugg boots hunkered around one while eating double-scooped waffle cones from a nearby creamery. I chuckled and shook my head—only in Arizona.

I heard my name and turned to see Larissa sitting off in a corner, looking only slightly less disheveled than she had earlier, the messy bun a little more under control and baby blue scrubs changed out for navy. There was a sadness in her eyes and a tightness around her mouth as she quickly tucked the remains of a sandwich into a crumpled paper bag and gestured me over.

"Brown-bagging it today. Coming here is a bit more peaceful than my home or workplace, plus the aroma of the surrounding restaurants helps me pretend my PB&J is more interesting and perhaps less pathetic." She shrugged sheepishly as her cheeks reddened.

I nodded, having been there. "Peanut butter & pickle is the usual for me. You ever try it?"

"Gawd, why would I?" She scrunched her nose, then shook her head. "You poor thing. At least I have grape jelly." I fought the urge to chuckle at her disgust as she scooted over for me to sit.

That's when Nicoh's head popped out from behind a table where he'd been scouring for stray tidbits. Having either come up empty or done his due diligence, he wanted to know where I'd wandered off to without him. Mind you, I still had the other end of his lead in hand.

Larissa's eyes widened, and for a moment, I thought she was going to shriek in horror, but she released a tiny giggle and stretched her hands out to encourage Nicoh to advance.

He didn't need to be asked twice. He'd do anything for attention as long as A) it wasn't too strenuous or B) it didn't cut into nap time.

They should probably make a t-shirt for that.

Nicoh whoo-whoo'd as Larissa cooed and nuzzled his neck, embarrassing me as he flopped onto his back and waved his paws in the air, weaving his head back and forth as he impatiently waited for belly scratches to ensue.

Larissa shook her head and chuckled but got down on the pavement and did his bidding until his tail beat a bruise into my calf.

"You do realize he'll be a monster to deal with after this?" I asked.

"I sure hope so." After taking in my expression, she laughed as she returned to her seat and attempted to smooth away the dog flurries that had attached to her scrubs, giving up when she realized it was a fruitless effort. "Based on his size and coloring, I'm guessing he's an Alaskan Malamute and not a Siberian Husky?" She glanced at me, a hopeful look in her eyes.

I nodded and smiled, impressed by her knowledge of the difference, and knew when an olive branch was being extended. "This is Nicoh, my other half, for all intents and purposes."

As if sensing a second opportunity, said beast leaned in for another round of scratches on the head, which Larissa promptly doled out while giving me a knowing smile.

"I see where the 'mischievous' part of the equation factors in."

"If you only knew the half of it," I murmured in a tone that caused both of us to laugh, leaving Nicoh to huff as Larissa's hands left his head to cover her snorts.

Looking from one human to the other, his eyes narrowed, and he curled into a tight ball, leaving his backside to face us.

"I guess we've been dismissed," Larissa commented while still chuckling.

After a moment, she got down to business. "Thank you for agreeing to meet me, especially after the way I treated you earlier. First, I want to apologize for my behavior." When I started to interject, she raised a hand.

"I was brought up better than that, and my mother would have put the fear of the devil in me had she been lucid enough to register my treatment of you." She paused to bite her lip, and her hands shook. "Not that it excuses anything, but my protective instincts kick in where she is concerned. She was never the same after…the stroke."

"I'm so sorry, Larissa…was it recent?" My thoughts drifted to the feeble woman in the wheelchair who had appeared to have aged beyond her years.

She shook her head and closed her eyes. "She's been like that for years. The stroke took her when Danielle left us. Perhaps a heart attack would have been less cruel." She caught me as my eyes and mouth simultaneously went wide, adding, "Better a broken heart than a lost spirit."

I nodded, but it was more of an acknowledgment than an acceptance of her sentiment. "You mentioned Danielle—your sister?"

Larissa sighed and looked off in the distance. "Yes, my younger sister."

"When did she…pass?" I asked, my voice quiet.

Her head swiveled. "What?" I opened my mouth and shut it as Larissa gasped.

"Oh! When I said my sister was dead…" Her voice trailed off as she glanced upward, shaking her head. "I didn't mean dead dead, as in left this realm dead—though with all of those drugs and the things she did to her body—I meant my mother and I were no longer allowing her to infect our lives. We cut her off—financially, mentally, and emotionally."

When I cocked my head, she added, "Admittedly, I was the one who made the decision, but it was only to protect my mother. If I had only been strong enough to act sooner, perhaps she wouldn't have needed to suffer." An involuntary sob slipped out, and Larissa hid her face by leaning over to root in her backpack. After pulling a tissue, she dabbed at her eyes.

I reached over to pat her arm but thought better of it, considering I had only just met this woman.

"I'm sure you did the best you could," I replied, catching her eyes and giving her a sincere nod. "I'm sorry for the way things turned out, but you can't blame yourself for someone else's decisions."

Larissa nodded and sniffed. "My sister was always a bit of a wild child. And yes," she glanced at me, "I know how cliché that sounds, but her 'behavior,' for lack of a better word, started with getting detention for smoking in the bathroom and quickly moved to ditching school altogether for boys, booze and drugs.

"Before long, she transitioned to sex for money to fuel her drug habit, and when we did see her, she was typically acting like a foul-mouthed harpy, fluctuating between raging hallucinations and full-on blackouts." She shook her head. "And the cops…it was a wonder that my mother was able to keep that brat out of juvenile detention and then jail, but somehow she managed to keep our family together, after years of working herself to the bone to just to keep us alive.

"The saddest part was that Mother had finally stocked enough away so that she could slow down a bit and think about getting a small house in the valley when she retired. Danielle managed to destroy it all in one fell swoop. For her finest—and last—performance, she drained Mother's accounts and stole every last possession either of us had and pawned them. This was right before she disappeared for the last time…just like that." She made a "poofing" motion by blowing on her fingers, then shaking them to reveal their emptiness.

"Mother was distraught and rightfully so, but rather than being worried about the money—or the lost possessions—she was worried about Danielle and her soul. Can you believe that?" She wasn't really looking for an answer, so I kept my thoughts to myself.

"Then reality set in, when the bills came due, and there was no money left to pay for anything. My mother worked hard all of her life, never purchased something she couldn't pay for in cash, and would never, ever default on any agreement she'd made.

"And when the landlord came all the way from his fancy office downtown to 'have a chat' with her—basically letting her know that she would need to move out if she couldn't drum up with the money to pay for rent—she completely lost it. Ashamed, embarrassed, and disillusioned upon his departure, she suffered a massive stroke. By the time I found her…" she sucked in a breath before continuing, "it was too late—the damage was irreversible. It was only later I learned that Danielle had been at the apartment earlier that day."

I worked hard to keep the horror I felt from reaching my face. "How did you find out?"

Larissa pressed her eyes shut, her mouth turning down at the corners as she shook her head from side to side. "Later, I noticed things were missing—including the ring on my mother's hand. It had been her grandmother's, and though it wasn't anything fancy, it held great intrinsic value. And believe me, she would never take it off…willingly. I think she hoped to pass it on to one of us when she died, but…" Tears welled up in her eyes as she added, "to have it ripped from her finger?"

A sob erupted, and this time I fought the hesitation and patted her back. "That act…that atrocity? It was the moment I declared my sister dead for my mother's sake, as well as for my own." She lifted her head, wiped away a stray tear, and looked me. "Anyone who could justify that level of evil and is that cold—is already dead inside."

I nodded, though I couldn't begin to imagine what she and her mother had endured at the hands of someone they loved, cared for, and until that moment, had considered family.

"After that, I moved Mother to Arizona, partially because the health care was better and the cost of living cheaper, but it also allowed us an escape from Danielle and her world. For the first time in a very long while, I know my mother is safe when I leave for work—she has a nurse that visits once a day and a companion that sits with her while I'm at work. It's not a spectacular life, but it's decent, and most importantly, it's nowhere near Danielle's reach."

Larissa blushed, perhaps too embarrassed, or fearful, to want more for herself or her mother, but I sidestepped it as gracefully as I could. I had no judgment to pass and certainly did not want her to feel as though I did.

"Where do you work?" I asked, keeping my tone calm as I attempted to lighten the mood.

Thankfully, her face brightened at my question, as she wiped away the last of the tears, she broke into a shy smile, and as she spoke, I realized her voice was filled with pride. And hope.

"At the animal hospital in Tempe. I'm currently a vet tech but would really like to work toward a veterinary degree, specializing in the care of animals with cancer."

"Wow," I replied. "That's impressive and admirable."

Larissa blushed and fussed with her tissue, effectively tearing it to shreds. "Thanks. It's always been a passion but with the rising cost of tuition—" She shook her head. "Guess we'll just have to wait and see."

I patted her on the back. "It will happen, Larissa. Have faith that good things can—and do—present themselves to those who deserve them."

She nodded, and though she would not look at me, responded, "That—right there—is why I knew I could talk to you about…all of this. I just had a feeling…you'd understand. Even though I'm not sure why." This time, she peered at me, her eyes watery and her nose red. "Does that sound crazy, or what?"

I gave her a soft smile and a wink before replying, "You're in good hands, Larissa. I just happen to specialize in crazy."

CHAPTER THREE

"Anyway, I've kept you here long enough. You previously mentioned Kelly and a matter of mutual concern—I assume you are referring to her mother's death." I noticed that she posed no question but took the opportunity to proceed.

"Yes. I'm hoping you can help fill in some of the details surrounding the day—"

Larissa raised a hand, squinting. "Let me get this straight —*you* are helping Kelly investigate?"

It wasn't exactly what I'd said, but I wasn't here to haggle over my word choice, so I shrugged, clearing my throat as I pressed on. "What are you able to recall about that night?"

I figured I didn't need to elaborate, as the night I was referencing went without question. It had not only destroyed Decker's world, it had also impacted Larissa and her family.

She surveyed me before responding, "You know I was like—a child—right?" When I nodded and gestured for her to proceed, she sighed. "If only I had been there."

"In the apartment?" My voice came out more of a squawk, causing Larissa to jump.

"Oh, gosh, no. I meant at home. If I had been there, maybe…" She looked away but not before I caught the tears welling.

"Larissa, look at me. Like you said, you were a child. What happened was not your fault." Her eyes were moist, but she nodded. "If you don't mind me asking, where were you?"

She shuddered, perhaps revisiting what might have happened if she had been there along with her sister and Decker.

"It was my father's weekend, and as much as she hated it, Mother placed me on a bus to Bakersfield, where Father lived with his new wife and family, who I liked to refer to as the step-monsters." She scrunched her nose.

"And your sister?" When Larissa quirked a brow, I quickly added, "Sorry, I don't know how visitation works, but it certainly seems as though it would have been more convenient—for all parties—if you both had the same schedule."

Her hand flew to her mouth. "Oh! Danielle and I didn't have the same father. Please don't think badly of my mother. My father left the minute he knocked her up. Turns out, he was messing around with his ex-girlfriend behind my mother's back and had gotten her pregnant, too. Not sure whether he loved her more or she was just more adamant about having him around, but he divorced my mother so that he could marry her and support their child.

"Of course, there are more than a couple variations to that story, but I was basically my dad's kid for one weekend a month when his new wife begrudgingly allowed me to mingle with their pack of rodents—three of 'em. I grew to loathe them and haven't spoken to any of them, my father included, since I turned eighteen.

"Sadly, Danielle's now on that list, though it wasn't always that way. When she was young, I loved that little bean. God, she was so precocious, even way back then. Of course, paired with her best pal, Kelly? Both were so alive and fearless. The world was there for them to explore and do their bidding. They were not that much younger than me, but looking back, they seemed beyond their years, even though I treated them both like they were nuisances and naughty little pills."

She paused to shake her head and released a small, sad chuckle. "Funny how things change, huh?"

I offered her a tight smile but had to wonder—based on her recollection—had either Decker or Danielle really changed?

Larissa shifted the conversation, snapping me out of my musings, and back to the purpose of the visit.

"By the time I returned on Sunday night, I was already anxious because Father caused me to miss my regular bus over a pool tournament, so I arrived later than Mother had expected. This was before cell phones. Even so, I doubt he would have made an effort to let her know—one of the many side-effects of being a pawn in your parent's war to make the other suffer."

She frowned while nibbling on a nail. "Anyway, I remember pulling into the bus station, sick to my stomach with worry that Mother had been forced to wait for me all that time. Needless to say, I was surprised to find Auntie Mae, a friend of Mother's, waiting for me instead.

"I could immediately tell from her expression that something was off. I almost stayed on the bus, convinced my mother had given her permission to throttle me in her absence. When I finally mustered the nerve to get off, she surprised me by pulling me into a tight hug.

"After a bit, she explained that there had been an accident in our building, and while Mother and Danielle were okay, I would be going to her home while we waited for them. I wanted to ask what had happened and why we couldn't go and get them then, but the look on her face scared me more than the answer.

"By the time she tucked me into bed, it was well after midnight, and Mother and Danielle still had not arrived. I listened for them but eventually fell asleep. When I woke up, Danielle was nestled against me, sucking her thumb. She hadn't done that for years, and from the pinched expression on her little face, I could tell she had been crying and perhaps even sobbed herself to sleep before they had placed her next to me, exhausted.

"I was careful not to wake her as I crept to the kitchen, where I could hear the murmur of voices. Mother and Auntie sat at the table and, from my position, could see Mother's pale face as she gripped a mug, her eyes and nose puffy and red. She bit her lip as Auntie whispered but didn't really seem to be listening. Fear flashed in her eyes when she spotted me, and with my hands tucked behind me, I tiptoed to them, preparing myself for the retribution now that I'd been exposed.

"I reached out to touch her hand and for a split second, thought she might still chastise me for my lateness the night before when she nearly knocked over her cup as she pulled me into her lap. I was too big for such a gesture, but she held me close, rocking back and forth as she whispered, 'My baby, my baby…' over and over in my ear. I was tucked into her chest but caught Auntie as she covered her mouth and stifled a sob. Something told me that when I finally pulled away, our lives would never be the same."

Larissa paused to release a breath. "As Auntie began to talk about the 'accident' that had occurred in our apartment building, Mother hugged me so hard I almost couldn't breathe. I could feel her tears on the top of my head but didn't budge."

She shuddered despite the warmth of the sun. "I don't think I'll ever be able to fully comprehend what happened."

"Auntie took my hand in hers as she told me that Kelly's mom, Ellen, had been injured in the accident late Saturday night. When I begged to see her—I assumed she had been rushed to the hospital—my aunt shook her head and cried as she told me that Ellen had gone to be with the angels.

"We sat like that, the three of us, for what seemed like an eternity until my mother finally managed to utter, 'Ellen's dead, baby. The devil himself came in the flesh and robbed her from us.' I wasn't sure why she felt she needed to confirm what Auntie had said, though perhaps saying the words out loud was her way of wrapping her mind around the truth.

"It was then I remembered that Danielle and Kelly had planned a sleepover. Ellen was going to teach them how to make cupcakes. I remember being jealous about missing out. Mother refused to ask my father for a change in the schedule—it would cost her too much down the road, she'd said—so by pure chance, I missed out on a sleepover that turned out to be a nightmare.

"It wasn't until much, much later that I learned more about what had really happened that night. I won't go into the details. You're probably already familiar with the circumstances surrounding Ellen's murder—that Kelly and Danielle witnessed the attack?" Larissa glanced at me, and though I didn't actually have all of the details as she'd assumed, it was her story to tell, so all I could do was nod.

"Of course, no one came out and told me anything. Mother wouldn't bring it up, and I was afraid to ask. I pieced together bits here and there from hushed conversations among the residents to the late-night phone calls, which typically resulted in my mother abruptly hanging up before hiding her tears behind a closed bedroom door."

"What about Danielle?" I asked, keeping my tone gentle as not to prod too forcefully.

"Somehow she managed to block the whole thing out. She had to be sedated after they found her—and rightly so—which explained her grogginess when she and my mother arrived at Auntie Mae's, but once the drugs wore off, the last thing she remembered about the evening was frosting cupcakes with Kelly and Ellen, which is probably a blessing in disguise."

I nodded, though I had to wonder if those memories had resurfaced over time. If so, had the nightmares they dredged up fed her escape into drugs, alcohol, and promiscuity? Or simply been an excuse for her excesses? Until I knew more about Danielle—perhaps tracked her down and looked her in the eye—I couldn't be sure which devil drove her obsessions.

"And Kelly?"

Larissa frowned, shaking her head. "She and her father never returned to the apartment. After they moved, he transferred her into another school and practically removed anything that could remind her of that night. Not that it mattered anyway."

"Why's that?"

"From what I heard, like Danielle, she'd blocked out everything, too—though I'm not sure whether it gave Max a bit of relief that she couldn't remember, or frustrated him because she couldn't identify her mother's killer."

I cocked my head. "You said from what you'd heard, didn't you see Kelly?"

She looked away, her mouth turned down. I waited her out as she formulated a response. "Never saw her again after Ellen's murder until recently, when she came looking for Danielle."

Recently? "When was this?"

Larissa squinted at me before responding, "It must have been at least a year ago. She also told me they never identified the person who called nine-one-one claiming to be my mother—the one who allegedly reported seeing a man enter Ellen's apartment that night," her voice turned to a whisper, "leaving a half-hour later, covered in blood."

She shook her head and was quiet for a moment. "Mother really never got over that one. She was nowhere near the apartment. And it weighed on her."

"When Kelly asked about your sister, did you know where

Danielle was at the time? Or, more importantly, where she might be now?"

She shook her head, waving a hand dismissively. "Back there. Somewhere. Anywhere. Which is why it's almost easier—even preferable—to pretend she'd died." She must have caught something in my expression, because she quickly added, "After she stole from my mother, she was no longer welcome in our home. Or our lives."

"So she's not aware you and your mother moved?"

She frowned. "I'm sure she figured it out when she returned to the apartment to pilfer through Mother's things and found it was occupied by someone else. But if you're asking whether we left her a forwarding address by way of the landlord? No. I couldn't afford to have Danielle follow us, or bring her trouble with her."

I nodded. "Do you have any way of contacting her?"

Perhaps my tone was too hopeful, but surely Larissa and her mother would want to leave that door open, just in case, if only a crack. Sometimes people changed—Danielle could overcome her addictions and her demons. Or there could come a point where Larissa or her mother needed to reach out one last time before it was too late for all of them.

Larissa bent to scratch Nicoh, responding after a long moment, "There is a post office box."

"A P.O. box?" I prompted, grasping at any crumb I could find.

"It was my mother's, but as we got older she gave us each a key. Once Danielle starting acting out, I begged Mother to change the lock—knowing Danielle would never relinquish hers—but she refused. Later I found out that Mother used it as a means to keep a line of communication open with her—as one-sided as that was.

"She was slipping money, calling cards and meal vouchers into envelopes for Danielle, hoping that she would use it to get some nourishment, pay for a roof for the evening or just to call home, whatever. I knew better. Danielle's grubby little mitts were always willing to take, though I'm betting she squawked about what little Mother had left her, even though it was always more than Mother could afford."

"So, no one's checked it since—"

Larissa shook her head. "Not since we left town. Besides, I gave Kelly my key. I had no intention of returning there myself anytime soon, anyway. I'm surprised she didn't mention it."

My mouth fell open. It hadn't occurred to me that Larissa wouldn't know about Decker's passing, even though it had been recent.

"Kelly didn't really have time to mention…anything," I replied, realizing how flat my tone sounded.

Larissa squinted at me, her brows furrowing. "I thought you said—"

I quickly raised a hand, not wanting her to think I had drawn the information out of her on false pretenses. "I'm really sorry. I thought you knew. I'm here *for* Decker."

"I get that," she snapped. "You said she asked you to contact me, though I'm still not sure why Kelly didn't tell you this herself. So…why? Why are you here? Why don't you know these…things?" Larissa rose, her fists balled as she loomed over me.

I looked away, suddenly stricken by the weight of the task in front of me. "Because she never got the chance." My voice faltered and cracked as I dealt the blow. "Larissa, I hate to have to be the one to tell you this…it shouldn't have had to come from a stranger."

"Just tell me," she growled, closing in on me.

My words sounded hollow, even as I uttered them.

"Kelly's dead."

CHAPTER FOUR

The colored drained from Larissa's face as she collapsed onto her seat, and I relayed the events surrounding Decker's death.

When I finished, she sat for a moment before meeting my gaze. "The people who murdered her. Did they pay?"

I opened my mouth, pausing to frame my response. Just because it wasn't as black and white as it should have been, Larissa didn't deserve an answer that tap-danced around the truth. But she was owed one that was honest.

"The woman who pulled the trigger is dead, and her co-conspirator is in jail, awaiting trial."

She nodded. "This *woman*…did she suffer?"

In all honesty, I didn't think she had, but when I was slow to respond, Larissa nodded and moved on.

"So basically, before she died, Decker bequeathed you the task of finding her mother's killer and bringing him to justice." Not a question.

I shrugged, not wanting to mention that I already had a strong suspicion as who that person might be if Decker was right. My bequeathed task, as Larissa had phrased it, was to secure the proof needed to prove it. Having met the man, I definitely wanted to take him down, as well as wipe that too-white sneer off his smug, entitled face.

Larissa was studying me. "Tall order," she murmured, though I noted her gaze had not drifted elsewhere. "Please don't take this the wrong way, but why you?"

I chuckled. "I have no idea. I didn't know her for that long, but before she died, she told her friend Logan that she had a hunch about me."

"You weren't aware of anything before she…died?" Larissa's tone was incredulous, and when I shook my head, she added, "Well, she must have seen something in you; otherwise, she wouldn't have asked. I trust her instincts and will respect her wishes. And if there is anything you need, other than what I've already told you, just tell me."

"Would you permit me to revisit old territory—talk to former neighbors and friends of your mother's, like your Auntie Mae? I promise to be respectful, and if you'd prefer to call them before-hand to warn them, by all means, please do so."

Larissa surveyed me for a moment, her face unreadable. "Sounds reasonable to me. Is there anything else?"

"Would you permit me to borrow the key?"

Larissa squinted. "Key?"

"You mentioned you had given your key to the P.O. box to Kelly, but I assume your mother still has hers?"

She nodded. "I can do that for you, but you have to promise me something in return."

I didn't see where I had much of a choice and gestured for her to continue.

"When you open the P.O. box or chat with an old family friend if you find anything that disparages my mother's character in any way, you won't share it, unless it's pertinent to the case—which it won't be."

I nodded, it was a reasonable, if not noble request, though I wasn't sure whether I'd have much control what details would come out, relevant or not.

"My mother has had to live with the guilt. Not only was one of her dearest friends murdered, but she also had to endure the judgment cast upon her after Danielle turned out the way she did—the constant whispers of 'what if' or 'if only.'" Larissa's voice cracked as she shook her head. "I wouldn't wish what happened to Ellen on anyone, but she wasn't the only victim that night."

Larissa was silent for a moment, perhaps processing things she'd never said out loud, whether out of respect for her mother or not having had the right platform, I wasn't sure, but it gave me some insight into the world in which she lived. Or, at the very least, one viewed through Larissa's perspective.

"What will you do now?" she asked.

"I'll go in search of answers." I realized it sounded much simpler than it was.

This time, Larissa held my gaze. "Got anyone you can reach out to for help?"

I nodded. "I've got someone in mind."

* * *

Once Larissa and I made arrangements to collect her mother's key, we concluded the meetup even though I hadn't addressed everything I'd wanted to. Our conversation had turned heavy faster than I'd hoped, which made asking about her mother's former employer a risk I couldn't afford. Thanks to Leah's initial legwork, I knew Maria had worked for Terrence Edwards' family, but considering the way things had gone, it wouldn't have been easy to slip into our chat without raising questions.

No, I wasn't ready to toss that hot potato at Larissa just yet. Plus, I needed more than Decker's word as proof. I sifted through my contacts and summoned every ounce of courage that remained before jabbing a finger at the number I'd sought.

"Arianna Jackson. To what do I owe the pleasure?" Logan Piedmont's voice was slow and smooth, like handcrafted caramel sauce decadently drizzled over the top of a sundae.

I got chills just thinking about that lazy grin. It accentuated the scar traveling from the base of his bottom lip to the boyish dimple in his chin. And paired those crystal eyes and sun-kissed locks? Suddenly, I found my stuttering.

In truth, it may have come out as something that sounded more like a baby dolphin's whimper.

"Cat got your tongue, AJ?" Logan drawled in a way that could have melted butter, which didn't help matters, as I continued to struggle forming a response. "Ladies and gents—mark that one down in the history books." Thankfully, he had the good graces to allow me a reprieve to collect my wits, upholding his end of the conversation. "Don't tell me you've gotten yourself into trouble already? Or that you're feeling guilty about something?"

Okay, he may have been generous enough to allow me to brush up on basic sentence structure, but he wasn't letting me off the hook.

"I meant to call before now," I managed to spit out, even though it felt as though someone had rubber-banded my tongue and let a drummer loose in my chest.

"You mean after you ran away from me at the beach." Logan's tone was playful, but my dignity screamed foul, deciding it was time to regain control of the situation.

My brain and my mouth were apparently still missing in action.

"I didn't run—"

Logan laughed, quickly interjecting. "I know, I know. It was a life or death emergency. I'm hoping it resolved itself upon your return unless that detective still has you tied up."

"Yeah," I replied, wincing as I realized his little innuendo about Ramirez was not phrased as a question. "The situation has been handled, but no, the detective no longer needs my assistance. But I need yours," I managed to stammer out.

I seriously wanted to sprinkle salt on my tongue to keep it from flapping about like a slug, and yet, my brain and my mouth seemed to be in concert.

"Ah, the reason behind the mysterious call," Logan replied. "I don't suppose this has anything to do with Decker's request?"

I stared at my phone, open-mouthed. Was I that transparent?

"How did you know?"

"Well, it would probably be a bit of a stretch to believe you called because you missed my boyishly good looks and charming demeanor." He chuckled as I attempted a non-committal response, which turned out to be a series of embarrassing noises.

Was he also a mind-reader?

I managed to compose myself to formulate a somewhat coherent response. "True. There is that. Then again, you do have a pretty awesome canine companion."

"Hmm. Good point. She is quite the specimen."

"How is Mia, anyway?"

Logan had inherited Decker's German Shepherd upon her untimely death.

There was a brief pause before he answered, "Doing real well, though I think she's had more of an effect on me than I could have ever imagined. It's helped me in trying to deal with…well, you probably know what I mean."

"It usually works that way." I agreed. "But let's just keep that little secret to ourselves, shall we? Nicoh already tends to become a bit of diva when he knows he's getting his way."

"Oh, the horror." Logan chuckled. "And I'm sure he's quick to let you know. Those Malamutes always seem to have stories to tell."

I snickered when he faked a series of Nicoh-like howls, before he maneuvered the conversation back to a more serious tone.

"So, what's got you calling me on this fine Arizona day? Stunner like you, I'd think there must be a pretty good reason. Am betting all of your admirers are still licking their wounds after you kicked 'em to the curb."

Okay, I said he'd transitioned the conversation, not that he still didn't have me blushing and forgetting how to use my words.

I managed to clear my throat—my mind was another story, as I blurted out something along the lines of, "Err…yeah, that. I talked to the sister of the girl who witnessed Ellen Decker's murder. Who also witnessed it, I mean. Alongside Decker."

Wow.

Apparently, stringing words into sentences was not my strong suit when it came to talking to Logan.

"Ah. Larissa Reynolds, sister to Danielle, the girl who stayed with Decker. Their mother, Maria, worked for Terrence Edwards' family at the time, if memory serves."

I frowned at the phone, noting a bit of crispness had crossed into his usually easy-going tone.

"You don't sound all that surprised. Or that thrilled."

Logan released a sigh. "Decker spent a lot of time and energy running that angle up the flagpole and came away with nothing, other than a whole lotta regret.

"It's a sad story. Danielle turned out to be a flake, and that's putting it nicely. Maria is an emotional and physical wreck, and Larissa, who wasn't even there that night, has watched the lives of the people she loves fall to pieces.

"Everyone who touched that event was destroyed by it." He was silent for a moment, his voice quiet when he finally added, "So, no, I'm not surprised. Or thrilled. I certainly don't want you feeling responsible for drudging up the worst times in these people's lives, much less walking away with nothing, as Decker did."

Somehow, I knew he meant more than empty-handed, but felt compelled to interject. "What about the P.O. box?"

"What P.O. box?"

I filled him in, detailing how Larissa and I had come to that juncture in our conversation after a false start.

"I wasn't aware," he replied when I finished. "And Larissa mentioned giving Decker her key?"

"She did. I guess it hasn't surfaced yet?"

I realized that sifting through Decker's belongings and her life would be tough, but didn't think Decker would have made it impossible to find for those who knew her.

When he responded in the negative, I added, "I'm sure it will show up. In the meantime, Larissa agreed to give me her mother's key. I've made arrangements to pick it up in the morning."

"Sounds like you've already concocted a plan." It was not a question, though there was an amused, flirtatious inflection in his voice, causing my face to flush, despite the fact he could not see me.

Focus, AJ. Focus.

Yeah, that's always worked out well for me in the past. Of course, why bother breaking a streak?

Before I realized what I was going to say, my mouth took over, and the words blasted out, "I think it's time for a return trip to L.A."

Now that my big mouth had taken the lead, my brain—and my courage—needed time to catch up.

CHAPTER FIVE

After I wrapped my mind around what I'd just committed to, I checked in with all my clients, made the necessary arrangements, and grabbed the key from Larissa. The following afternoon, I entered Los Angeles with my canine companion riding shotgun. I had called Leah to fill her in but upon receiving her voicemail, my enthusiasm for sharing my plans waned, and I hung up with the somber realization that it would be a strange adventure without my wingman.

Logan worked as an officer with the California Highway Patrol and was on shift, so we agreed to meet for a quick bite later that evening.

The extra time should have been a blessing, but after a long day of driving with nothing other than a snoring canine to confer with, I was not only antsy, I was grating on my nerves and slowly driving myself mad.

Biting my lip, I studied the directions I'd mapped out for the trip, bringing up the route to the mailbox store for Maria Reynolds' P.O. box. Logan had offered to go with me the following day, but my curiosity got the better of me. I made my way to an area of Los Angeles that I wasn't all that familiar with, though one online source noted it had among the highest homicide rates in the country for more years running than I had digits on my hands and toes.

Needless to say, I hoped I made it out of there with all of them intact.

As luck would have it, that turned out to be the least of my worries. All of the parking meters within an eight-block radius were covered in shrouds that screamed, "Park here and pay the consequences!"

Gritting my teeth, I looped the block at least two dozen times before determining that there were no meter readers within the vicinity. Surely I could make it into the mailbox store, retrieve the contents of the P.O. box, and sprint back to my vehicle before I was busted?

I eased into a spot, careful not to park too close to the establishment to draw attention, but not out of bounds when it came to my frenzied race against time. I had been a track star—a sprinter —in my youth, after all.

Racing to the store, I was met with a frowny face on the opposite side of the glass as I attempted to tug the door open. The woman's insistence on shaking a massive ring of keys in the air did nothing to deter me.

After my third—okay, it was probably the seventh—attempt at shoving a non-yielding door, the keys were replaced with a large wristwatch on an arm so pale it either belonged to a vampire or someone who was boycotting the fact they lived in a state that was synonymous with sunshine. Either way, they were probably sticklers for punctuality. Thankfully, I was wearing sunglasses as I peered at my own watch, noting that it was just a tad before five p.m.

Frustration mounted after I began tapping my watch, and she mimicked the gesture on hers. I considered retrieving Nicoh from the vehicle and having him strike a pose—whatever that meant.

Frowny Face finally had enough and pointed to a sign just to my left.

The establishment was closed.

After releasing an expletive into the universe and watching a disgusted look form on the opposite side of the glass, I fisted my hands at my side and stomped—yes, very much like a small child —back to my vehicle, just as the fastidiously-uniformed meter reader unceremoniously placed a ticket under my windshield wiper.

I advanced on him, ready for action when he shot me a Dirty Harry look that was so chilling I stopped in my tracks, slowed my gait, and proceeded along my path. I was planning on pretending to be a random pedestrian but as luck would have it, Nicoh employed his annoyingly flawless timing and ratted me out by sticking his large schnoz out the window and bellowing a round of impatient howls as I passed.

Sighing, I looped around the rear of the vehicle, snatched the ticket, thrust open the driver-side door, and plunked myself into the seat, but not before receiving a head shake from the meter reader, who pursed his lips as he stabbed a finger at the covered parking meter.

Giving him a little wave in a feeble attempt at a mea culpa, I started the vehicle and merged onto the street, praying I wouldn't strike out within an hour of my arrival in the City of Angels.

Of course, that desire crashed and burned when I noticed Logan had left me a voicemail. Something must have come up at work, as he apologized for having to put off our get-together until the following day. After leaving him a brief message in return, I headed toward the pup-friendly hotel I'd booked.

I tossed my luggage and Nicoh's supplies on the tiny sofa bed and changed into a light long-sleeve shirt, boyfriend jeans, and maroon Converse Chuck Taylor low-tops.

Nicoh scarfed his kibble and drank from the large bowl of

water I had placed on the bathroom's linoleum so that his jowls wouldn't make a mess on the carpet. It was a pet room, but if I could contain the splatter of drool to one area, I felt I was at least trying to be a good guest.

After tucking the necessities into my pocket—phone, room key, driver's license, credit cards, doggie bags, and treats—we ventured out.

The afternoon was rapidly transitioning into evening, though the overcast of the day had made the passage of time feel seamless. We wandered through an outdoor mall, and I grabbed a couple of street tacos as we traversed the sea of bodies shifting toward the thrumming sounds of music, where a band stood on a makeshift riser performing cover tunes requested by a growing crowd.

Occasionally, a couple would get caught up in the moment and find themselves sashaying onto the impromptu dance floor, as onlookers cleared a path and often joined in. Teens pointed and snickered while furiously texting one another or snapping selfies to that would eventually end up in some social media black hole.

One group of gigglers asked if they could have their pictures taken with Nicoh, chirping that he was the "biggest dog they'd ever seen…like evah," to which I chuckled while shaking my head at their naivety.

After enduring a few requests, Nicoh herded me away from the pomp and circumstance. Apparently, one could only take so much adulation from his fans.

We sauntered from one street to the next. As Nicoh sniffed for stray goodies, I people-watched and took in the sights, snapping a few abstract pics with my phone to use as inspiration for future photoshoots. Before long, Nicoh was at the point he was about to sit and stay, meaning no amount of urging, scratching, or bribing would get his ample frame moving again until he was good and ready.

Realizing his stubborn streak was on the horizon, I began moving us in the direction of the hotel, which seemed to appease him as he kept up my pace. Once the scents became familiar, his curly tail stood tall and swooshed from side to side as he transitioned into a slow jog, his eyes bright and megaphone-sized ears at attention. The concierge gave us a wave and broad smile as we passed through the lobby, and when I returned the greeting, Nicoh added his own "whoo-whoo," causing members of the staff and guests alike to turn and either point or chuckle.

Typically it was my preference to opt for the stairs but worried that Nicoh's burst of energy might be short-lived, decided the elevator was a safer bet. Thankful we were able to have it to ourselves, I leaned my head against the cool steel as the numbers rose, suddenly realizing how tired I was and yet had gotten nothing accomplished since my arrival.

Part of me wanted to throw in the towel, call Logan and tell him it had been a farce—Decker leaving such a request in my incapable hands. If there had been threads, the pros, including Decker and her father—also a P.I.—hadn't unraveled, how could an amateur possibly yield different results?

I'd warmed to the idea as we exited the elevator and was in the process of formulating my well-intentioned speech to Logan as I slid the key card and opened the door, quite satisfied with my decision.

If I made the call now, Nicoh and I could get a decent night's sleep before heading back to Phoenix the next morning. I would be able to return to my more pressing projects sooner than I had anticipated—which would please my clients to no end.

I smiled at the thought, until I noticed my surroundings.

Someone had been in my room.

My bags, which I had tossed on the sofa bed, had been moved —one was on the floor, and the other was on the side chair. Both were zipped but not all the way. I wasn't obsessive about much, but after losing a few primo belongings in the past, had trained myself to be more careful about ensuring my zippers and closures were secure.

After unhooking Nicoh's lead so that he could investigate, or scare the crap out of anyone lurking in the shower, I unzipped my bag. Though nothing seemed missing, items had definitely been shifted around.

Nicoh returned from his search and, after sniffing the couch and my bags, nestled into the opening of the bathroom so that his belly remained cool on the linoleum while he kept an eye on me.

Frowning at my lack of discovery, I quickly scanned the rest of the room, my eyes settling on the desk and the items I had placed there. One was missing.

Maria's P.O. box key.

Squealing, I checked and double-checked before stomping down to the front desk.

Before I could open my mouth and say something that would have curled my late mother's toes, the concierge who had checked us in and greeted us on our return smiled broadly and asked, "Ms. Jackson. Did your sister find you?"

I stopped in my tracks. "My sister?"

He gave me a curious look. "After you departed, she left the room to grab some ice, and when the door closed behind her, realized her key was still in the room. She was quite embarrassed to have to come down to the front desk dressed in a guest robe with her hair wrapped in a towel." He gave me a sympathetic shrug, mistaking my open-mouthed incredulousness for shock. "It happens more often than you think."

I fought the urge to groan and bit my lip before framing my response. "So it's probably helpful when you've seen the person before...you know, so that not just anyone can gain access by copping a robe and towel from the housekeeping cart." Not that I had any experience with that.

The concierge's eyes widened, relaxing only a bit when he saw the quirk at the corner of my mouth. Thankfully, he didn't know me well enough to detect the tone behind it and didn't sense the anger playing at the edges, giving my voice a sarcastic lilt.

"Goodness, yes. It definitely helps that she was with you when you arrived. Of course, she waited over there by the guest couches because the desk was crowded, but I identified her quickly when she gave me a wave and pointed when you were checking in. I do hope the accommodations are to your liking?"

I nodded absently, still trying to wrap my head around the means with which this little thief had so easily bypassed everyone's radar.

"Just like a blonde." I tossed out there, just to see if something caught.

The concierge tilted his head. "Come again?"

"To forgot her keys…just like my sister to lock herself out," I replied, waving a hand as a chuckled. An emotion I was not feeling.

"If you say so," he responded. "Though her hair was dark like yours. Even under the baseball cap and then the towel, I could see the dark roots that framed her forehead and at the base of her neck." Even as he said it, his face reddened, as though he had made a blunder—as in a man should never point out a woman's roots.

Gotcha. "Yeah, well, her hair color changes with her mood. But she was born a tow-head…believe me." I winked.

I could tell the concierge was growing uneasy, so I wrapped it up. "Well, thanks for letting me know. Just like her not to leave a note before she ventures out…or to fess up to her embarrassment." I released a light laugh before spinning on my heel and hastening toward the elevator.

"Wait! Didn't you need something?" He called after me.

I inwardly groaned, realizing my oversight but quickly

rebounded, calling over my shoulder as I giggled and the elevator doors closed, "What? No, just wanted to thank you for your stellar service."

After the day I'd had, who was to say I couldn't feign a moment of my own, blonde or not?

Upon returning to the room, I searched for the towel and robe but mine were present and unused and there were no extras in sight, meaning the perp must have acquired them elsewhere, as I'd suggested to the concierge.

I released a growl that woke Nicoh from his slumber. He gave me a cold glare before looping in the opposite direction as I plopped onto the bed and did the very thing I most dreaded.

"Logan? This is AJ. We've got a situation." Before he could interject, I spouted every last detail since I'd arrived.

I hadn't realized just how frustrated I was until I checked my Fitbit and realized my heart rate was extremely high, even for me. I was in a constant "fat burn" state, which would have normally been good, had I not felt like I wanted to punch a few walls in the process.

After a moment of silence, Logan finally spoke. "First off, are you okay?"

When I responded with some guttural nonsense, he continued, "I think you need to file a report—" When I started to protest, he added, "but I know you won't. I don't want to beat you up more than you are already are, but I really wished you would have waited to go to the mailbox store until we could have gone together."

So much for not beating me up more than I already had been.

"Someone knew you had the key and would eventually make your way there, then followed you from the mailbox store to your hotel. We can deal with the 'who' later, but right now we've got a problem on our hands if she gets to the P.O. box before we do."

I nodded, even though I knew he couldn't see me. "Larissa

said she gave Decker her key." It wasn't a question but Logan remained silent, perhaps waiting for me to draw the connection. "And you now have Decker's possessions."

"Yes, I boxed up her belongings, brought the personal items to my house, put the other stuff in storage, but I don't see—"

"Fantastic!" I interjected. When he graced me with a resounding silence, I added, "Don't you see? All is not lost, Logan, you've got the key Larissa gave Decker, somewhere. We'll just need to find it and make it to the mailbox store first thing tomorrow, before the wretched little thief who stole Maria's does."

CHAPTER SIX

Pregnant pauses were one thing, but when the silence extended into outright bloat, I nearly bit through my lip. Was he deciding between hanging up and forgetting we'd ever crossed paths, or having me committed?

"Logan? Are you still with me?" I fought to keep the squeakiness at a minimum.

My eardrums throbbed. Apparently, I'd failed.

After what seemed like an eternity, he saved me from the brink of insanity.

"Okay, so what are we talking about? Say, twelve or so hours to look through Decker's belongings?" Math wasn't my strong suit, so I murmured in the affirmative. "With two of us, that should be pretty quick work. Then we head straight to the mailbox store first thing, collect the contents of the box and sit back and wait for our girl to do the same. When she shows up, we'll have a friendly chat about the vagaries of breaking and entering, not to mention taking things that don't belong to her. Yeah. We could make this work."

Pleased that he'd ruminated long enough to concur with my

loosely-based plan, I didn't point out that the latter part may prove difficult.

Thankfully, he wasn't waiting on my response. "Anyway, if you're sure you're up for this, I can swing by and pick you guys up in an hour? It'll give me time to grab a quick shower before I head to your hotel. Is that cool?"

"Yeah, yeah…" I stammered. "Are you sure *you're* cool with this?" He'd previously mentioned not being able to involve himself.

I'd purposely left my question open to interpretation, hoping he wouldn't rethink his decision.

"Decker's belongings were entrusted to me, and they're currently at my house. So if finding that key helps her in some way, even if it's just tracking Danielle down and verifying she's still alive, then I think it's worth stepping outside my comfort zone for a bit, regardless of what I said before. So yeah, I think I can muster the nerve to pull my big boy shorts up and help a gal out."

"Bet you get called out for *all* those damsel-in-distress requests," I murmured, a bit louder than I had anticipated, causing him to chuckle.

"You have no idea," he replied, though after seeing him, I was quite sure I did. "In the meantime, grab your stuff—you're not staying there a minute longer. I'd also like to have a little chat with the concierge when I arrive."

"Whoa! He-Man! I can't just check out. What if our little thief comes back?" I heard a scoff on the other end of the connection but pressed on, "If she does, we're gonna need the concierge on our side in order to catch her in the act this time. In Logan-speak, that means you can't just storm in with guns blazing, threatening to rough him up. We need him to give us the heads-up, not force him to tuck tail and run."

"I'm not sure what television programs you've been watching, but we don't exactly 'storm in with guns blazing' or threaten to rough people up anymore," Logan replied. "Besides, just what do you plan on telling him, considering he thinks she's your sister and that you're sharing the room?"

I released a wicked laugh. "I plan on telling him that I've got a little surprise for my 'sis' that requires his assistance—and discretion—to pull off."

Logan groaned. "Do I want to know what this surprise entails?"

"Probably not. Don't worry, it's not illegal," I snorted. "And she definitely won't see it coming."

After negotiating a few minor details—like Logan meeting us outside the hotel, just in case we needed his plan as a backup—I got to work on my sisterly surprise, running to my vehicle to collect a few essentials that I needed.

I lost a lot of time, as I had to bypass the front desk and haul everything up the stairs on the opposite side of the building. After a few trips and a bit of setup—thanks to the bit of schooling I received from Abe and Elijah Stanton of Stanton Investigations—I had everything I needed to catch anyone entering my room in the act. I hadn't changed my room key, so she still had access but this time around, I'd be one step ahead.

Something told me she'd be back.

My phone buzzed—a text from Logan letting me know he'd arrived and was in the parking lot. The clock emoji he'd added three times suggested that he wouldn't be waiting long before he ran with his variation of the plan, so I grabbed what items I couldn't live without and hustled Nicoh out the door.

I made one final stop, letting the concierge know that I had still hadn't connected with my sister—claiming that her cell phone was probably off or the battery had died—and that he shouldn't mention our conversations about her, as I had planned a surprise in our room for her return.

After waving off his offer to have room service deliver some goodies—it wasn't that kind of surprise, after all—I rushed out to meet Logan, hoping I wouldn't see him emerging from some tank with a machine gun and thousands of rounds of ammo in tow. Then again, perhaps I had seen too many Dwayne Johnson movies.

Thankfully, no tank had been commandeered, though the 1969 Pontiac GTO Logan was sporting was an eye-popper of its own.

He waved an arm out the window and looped through the hotel's turnaround when he saw me, a boyish grin on his tanned face.

"Does your dad know you snagged this from his garage?"

Logan frowned. "*Please*. My dad was a Buick man."

"Nice ride," I replied. "You sure you want my drooling beast in the backseat?"

"Only if you want to ride up front with me." He teased, pointing at me before adding, "Besides, perhaps you should check your own drool meter."

I subconsciously batted at my mouth, causing Logan to throw his head back and guffaw as my red face turned a deeper shade.

Flushed, I ushered Nicoh into the back seat, where he promptly sniffed every crevice, likely smelling another canine. One who was curiously absent. Again.

"No Mia?"

At the mention of his new companion, he shook his head. "About that—called my friend—turns out Mia had just launched herself into his pool. Anyway, told him I'd grab her tomorrow, and he was cool with that."

"Hmm. So drool is preferred to pool in the classic car," I replied, a smirk playing at the corner of my mouth as I thumbed behind me.

Laughing, he nodded. "It'd take me longer to get her hosed off and dried than it would to wipe a bit of spittle off the back seat.

Besides, it would have delayed my arrival. And truth be told, I wasn't sure I could trust you not to get yourself into trouble—or do something crazy."

"Seems like I only get away with doing that when I have my best friend riding shotgun," I grumbled.

Noting my tone, Logan gave me a sideways look. "How is Leah doing these days?"

"Dunno." I sighed before filling him in on the latest.

"So, she packed up and left...for good?" He asked when I finished.

"It would seem that way," I replied, chewing a nail.

"Well, I doubt it means she's bailing on you and your friendship—probably just needs a change of scenery." When I shrugged, he added, "She's here, in L.A., isn't she? So why don't you give her a call?"

Fortunately, we arrived at our destination, precluding my response—one which I wasn't prepared to supply.

Logan pulled into the driveway of his condo and, after letting us out, nestled into the garage before escorting us inside.

"Sweet digs," I commented after taking a cursory peek at my surroundings.

Not that I had anticipated frat house sheik, but was surprised by the modern touches and light feel throughout the space with a great deal of attention to color and placement of items, not to mention floors you could eat off.

Logan caught my eye, sheepishly responding, "I pay my cleaning lady well." When I raised a brow, he added, "She also happens to be the wife of a fellow officer who owns a cleaning business."

"Hmm...and your interior decorator?" I teased.

He offered me an embarrassed grin, paired with a boyish shrug. "Another wife of a fellow officer."

I snickered, tapping my chin. "Let me guess, they just happen to have unmarried sisters."

"Something like that," he murmured as his face flushed a deep crimson.

He proceeded to give me a quick tour and, after offering refreshments, hauled several sizable file boxes into the living room. Noting my widened eyes, he nodded.

"I have an entire room filled with these." He glanced away, then murmured, "Just haven't been able to bring myself to go through them."

"I'm sorry, Logan. If you'd prefer—"

"No." He waved a hand. "This needs to be done."

I nodded as he sliced the first box open with a utility knife and shoved it over to me.

"Focus on finding the P.O. box key first and the rest…later?" I asked as more of a final confirmation that he was sure he was ready to proceed than anything.

"Sure." Logan nodded absently, digging into his own box.

It felt odd, rummaging through the life of a person I'd only known for a short while. Logan was having a harder time of it, frowning as he pulled out photos and mementos of his best friend's life.

Every once in a while, he would stop and tell me a story— typically one with a humorous ending—before we moved on. Each box seemed to become easier for him, and by the time the sun came up, we had not only sped up our process, we'd also come up empty.

Logan collapsed onto the couch as I let Nicoh out into the small backyard. "I think we're gonna have to move onto Plan B."

I didn't bother mentioning that this *was* Plan B. Plan A had gotten squashed when I arrived at the mailbox store minutes too late, before the key was snatched from my room, but after twelve hours of digging through his deceased friend's belonging, didn't strangle the point.

"I don't suppose you already have a plan formulated?" I asked, giving him a sideways glance.

Logan puffed out his cheeks before releasing a long breath.

"Well… It's not an ideal scenario." He peered at me from beneath those incredibly—and unfairly—long lashes.

"Just lay it on me," I sighed. "I mean, how much worse could it get?"

"It's nothing earth-shattering; basically, it involves us hustling down to the mailbox store before it opens and keeping an eye out for our thief."

I raised a brow. "Like a stakeout?"

Logan shrugged. "More along the lines of a shadow. We linger. We observe. And hopefully, we snag her in the act."

This time I rolled my eyes. "Like I said, a stakeout."

He frowned. "I told you it wasn't earth-shattering and perhaps not even ideal."

"You mean because we don't know"—I held up a finger for each count—"one: who we're shadowing, two: what she looks like, three: when she might show up, or four: if she even will show up."

"You know, I *am* open to alternative suggestions." Logan huffed and thrust his fists on his hips, and for a moment, I thought I had insulted him.

That was until I caught a hint of a smirk that he'd failed to mask.

Shaking my head, I leaned against the wall as Logan outlined our rough plan. We cleaned it up, and both gave it our seal of approval a half an hour later, which gave us just enough time to get from the townhouse to the mailbox store and get into position before the store opened and our prey could arrive to collect her prize.

Considering her familiarity with me, and my disadvantage where hers was concerned, we agreed I'd surveil the entrance from the vehicle while Logan watched from inside the establishment, hopefully without looking like he was loitering or heaven forbid, getting accused of being creepy.

Given his looks, I doubted that would be much of a problem, especially if the same sales clerk was at her post. Thankfully, Logan wasn't incensed when I injected a caveat into his plan to address that challenge, should it arise.

Just as we were preparing to leave, I noted the overflowing mailbox and reached in to grab it and toss it inside. When Logan caught my gesture, his face contorted as he grabbed me by both shoulders, tilted his head back and released a whoop before kissing me firmly on the forehead and pulling me, with my mouth hanging open, back into the condo.

Nicoh, who was not having any of it, snuffed and collapsed onto the front steps, a now immovable object, positioning his backside in our direction for good measure.

I left him to his mood, my focus on Logan as he rummaged through the drawers of the console in the entryway.

"Ahh…Logan? We don't really have time for spring-cleaning if we're gonna make it across town before the mailbox store opens."

When he ignored me, I bit my lip and shifted from foot to foot and considered injecting some unladylike quip. Just then, he pulled out a stack of envelopes from the deepest recesses of what appeared to be his junk drawer, bound together by ancient twine and crusty rubber bands, and shoved it into my hand.

I frowned. Indiana Jones, I was not.

"Okay…" I stuttered, wishing to deposit the stack into the trash post-haste, preferably before some unfriendly critter popped out, bit me on the hand, and gave me rabies as a special reward for waking it from its slumber.

"It's mail," Logan replied, his tone way too gleeful.

"Um, hmm, I can see that. Am I missing something?"

"It's *Decker's* mail," he extracted his find from my hand, and in the process of removing the twine when the rubber band broke free, bounced off the wall and fell to the ground as he shoved half the stack at me and proceeded to sift through the remainder.

Apparently, I was a bit slow on the uptake, suddenly realizing what was potentially sitting right in front of me.

My hands shook as I shuffled through a plethora of junk mail, magazines, and credit card offers.

"I did pull out the bills and important stuff before I shoved it in the drawer," Logan commented, his face turning red as he focused on his stack.

I nodded absently, pulling a small padded envelope out and pushing it over to him for inspection.

"Decker's handwriting," he confirmed, a smile erupting as he added, "She mailed it to herself."

"She was a smart one," I murmured as he tore one end open, and a small object encased in bubble-wrap tumbled out.

Carefully unwrapping it, we cheered when we were presented with a key—a twin to the one that had been snatched from my hotel room.

Thankfully, the traffic gods had given us a thumbs-up as we made it shortly after the store opened. Logan and I high-fived before he exited the vehicle and slipped inside, the key Decker had gotten from Larissa tucked in his pocket.

As I settled in for my surveillance duties, I suddenly noticed Logan engaged in an animated conversation with the clerk. One maintained an exasperated expression, the other a massive frown, which remained as he exited the establishment moments later, releasing an uncharacteristically loud expletive as he opened the driver's side door and plunked into the seat.

"What?" I managed to squeak out.

"Empty," he ground out, gripping the steering wheel so intensely, I feared his adrenaline would bend it beyond repair.

"Logan, look at me," I said in the calmest voice I could muster, noting his eyes narrowed and the muscles in his jaw vacillated between anger and torment.

I started to rub his arm but impulsively opted to pull him into a fierce embrace, unaware of the gearshift that would later result in a deep bruise on my hip. I gently released him when his breathing slowed, and he expelled a sigh.

"What happened?"

He refused to meet my gaze when he finally spoke, his attempt to appear unruffled betrayed by the cracking of his voice and the immediate slump of his frame as the question filled the space.

"The box was nothing but dust and metal, AJ." He lifted his head, his eyes filled with a mixture of anger, frustration, and sadness. "She beat us to it."

I hated to admit that there was another alternative.

Whatever "it" was had never been there in the first place.

CHAPTER SEVEN

"When I asked the clerk, she said that a girl was waiting outside when she arrived, which isn't all that uncommon. Once she opened the store, she focused on her preparations for the day—opening the register, checking voicemail and email, etc.—so she hadn't noticed which box the girl went to." Logan's voice cracked as he relayed what had transpired just moments before our arrival.

Seeking out the key had cost us—in more ways than one.

"Could the clerk provide a description?" I asked, hoping to gain something positive even though my frustration mounted.

Logan shrugged. "She said there wasn't anything remarkable—a mousy blonde, taller and thinner than she was, dressed in a P coat, whatever that is."

"It's *pea* coat—typically a double-breasted, thigh-length jacket, originally worn by sailors—though it's way too heavy for this weather." But perfect for hiding a stack of mail, I silently mused. "Anything else?"

"Nothing useful," he replied. "Basically, thought she looked like a regular twenty-something, getting her mail and they never exchanged words. And except for the fact I came in asking about it minutes later, she wouldn't have given it a second thought."

"Well," I sighed. "It appears our thief made quick work of the treasure she collected from my room."

"You think she handed the key off to a partner?"

"Maybe. The description didn't match, which means she could be colluding with someone else. Either that or—"

"She's a master of disguise," Logan finished.

"Wouldn't that just be the cherry on top of this already fabulous start to a day," I mumbled and upon catching his wince, patted his leg. "It's okay, we'll just have to come up with an alternate plan."

"I don't suppose you have any suggestions?" He peered at me, tilting his head.

"I was about to ask you the same." When he frowned, I added, "Why don't we head back to the hotel and regroup? We've already spent too much time running this up the flagpole, and it's gotten us nowhere.

"If Decker and her dad were right, we already have a potential *who*, which means we need to stop chasing these breadcrumbs and focus on what we do know and work our way backward, starting with *why* was Ellen killed." Logan nodded and gestured for me to continue. "That's the key to finding the truth. And the key we should have focused on from the start."

Even as I said the words, something tugged at the deepest recesses of my cells. Decker had mailed that key to herself for a reason, which meant there *was* a breadcrumb out there that she had been pursuing when she died. And that she needed it to find her way back if things went haywire.

Unfortunately for Decker, she'd never had the chance.

And now, Logan and I were left to wonder—where had that breadcrumb led her and who or what had been at the end of that path?

We drove to my hotel in comfortable silence—each left to our thoughts. I was grateful that neither of us felt compelled to fill that void.

Logan dropped me at the front entrance, agreeing to bring Nicoh through the back while I checked in with the concierge to see if my "sister" had made another appearance.

A different attendant was on shift but had received instructions regarding my surprise. He confirmed that my sibling had not made her way past his post in the time he had been there. Disappointed, I opted for the stairs so that I could burn off the agitation. Apparently, I needed a few more flights because I was nearing a full-boil by the time I reached my room.

I slammed the key card into the lock, and the second I heard that click and the crimson light blipped green, I punched the handle down with my palm and used my hip to thrust the door open—only to find that my bags dumped on the floor. Clothes, toiletries and shoes were everywhere and Nicoh's food container and the plastic zipped bags holding his dog treats emptied into the trash.

Anger radiated through every nerve as I jumped on the bed, unscrewed the glass protecting the ceiling light, and removed the contraption I had placed there. I pulled a second from the TV stand and the final one from above the door jamb on the hall-side. After tugging my camera from my bag, I plugged them in one by one and watched the ransacking unfold.

According to the time on the first recording, the thief had entered my room just fifteen minutes prior, a key card visible in her grubby little mitts.

She matched the mailbox store clerk's description down to the pea coat, which was unbuttoned, allowing an obnoxious pink T-shirt to peek out, emblazoned with the slang for a female dog in rhinestones across the front, below "SEXY" in blocky black lettering. Her dirty blonde hair hung around her face in a badly cut shag that I was convinced was a wig. Despite being indoors, she wore massive sunglasses that covered almost her entire face, exposing only her tiny, pinched mouth and elfin chin. And though she was just a few inches shorter than I was, I could see that beneath the oversized jacket, she was painfully thin and almost waif-like.

Her movements were anything, but as I watched her dig through my bags and toss them aside in frustration. My own mounted as I swore under my breath that I would force-feed her dog treats from the trash for her transgressions.

Figuring the second video would show more of the same from a different angle, I moved to third which showed her exit, her fists clenched as she uttered several unintelligible phrases and stormed down the hall.

"Gotcha," I muttered through gritted treat teeth when I saw what transpired next.

Tossing the camera on the bed, I pulled my phone out, dialed Logan's number and left him a colorful message when I reached his voicemail, figuring he was wrangling Nicoh, who often pulled the obstinate, manipulative card with new handlers whenever the opportunity presented itself.

I smirked, I had been particularly careful in the wording of said message, leaving out my immediate plans, as he would have surely warned me off. Or, like most of the cops I had encountered as of late, insisted I wait.

The new AJ wasn't big on waiting.

Nope. I was in no mood for that, though I was in a mood. One that would lead me directly to the mangy thief who had the audacity to not only break into my room—twice—but trash my belongings with such careless disregard.

I fumed down the hall, muttering under my breath until I stood three rooms down from my own, on the opposite side of the hall. I covered the peephole with my thumb as I rapped on the door, noting the sound of the metal echoing as I became more incessant.

Finally, the door swung open, and I was confronted with a thin, dark-haired girl whose mouth turned down as she crossed her arms.

I started to give her an extreme tongue-lashing, but she beat me to the punchline and blurted out, "You've got some nerve, Jackson! Where the hell is my stuff?"

CHAPTER EIGHT

I'd never been one to encourage violence as a means when faced with adversity—or aggression—but the millisecond the words came spewing out of her smug mouth, I stepped closer and was prepared to throttle her when her eyes narrowed as they shifted over my shoulder.

"I know you."

Logan was moving swiftly toward us with Nicoh taking the lead, only stopping when Logan released him, and he positioned himself between the girl and me.

Logan's face was unreadable, though it wasn't anywhere near an expression of fondness as he addressed her.

"And I know you, too."

"Somebody had better tell me what's going on," I grounded out, jabbing a finger at the girl. "This…person broke into my room and trashed my belongings. Twice."

The ransacking thief had the nerve to scoff at me as she took an exaggerated step back and thrust a fist on her hip. "Aren't you the pot calling the kettle, you little tattletale."

I glared at her, struggling to string words into a PG-rated sentence. Thankfully, Logan beat me to it.

"AJ, meet Danielle Reynolds."

I squinted at him then turned my full attention to the girl, taking in this new information while fighting back the emotions that I had barely contained since I'd stormed down the hall and banged on her door.

"*Danielle*," I paused. Was that amusement on her face? Or curiosity? "Why in the world would you think I had something that belonged to you?"

She rolled her eyes. "Because you had a key—I saw you—at the mailbox store."

As if that explained it.

"You were stalking me?" I replied through gritted teeth—for all the good it did.

"I occasionally watch the place so that I can hopefully catch someone—my sister, anyone—who has a key, intervene, and get my stuff." Danielle waved a hand nonchalantly.

I shook my head. "That makes no sense. Why not use your own key and get your own 'stuff'?"

She smirked at my overt use of finger quotes, then clucked her tongue and sighed, as though she was being forced to deal with the town idiot.

"Well?" I prompted, not giving her any leeway.

"Lost it," she replied while chewing one of her multi-colored nails—this one was an unappetizing shade of chartreuse.

"You *lost* your key?" I raised a brow.

She shrugged. "My landlord tossed my stuff into the street and by the time I realized it, half of it was gone." Her mouth curled into an unfriendly frown. "Jerk."

"That's commonly known as being evicted," Logan replied, his sarcasm immediately on the receiving end of a snarl.

There was a moment where I thought that Danielle might just be crazy enough to launch herself at him, but she finally released a huff and gave her face muscles and her rigid stance a breather, unfolding her arms so that she could refocus on her nails.

"He had no right," she commented after selecting a digit that was the color of Pepto-Bismol. My stomach seized as my brain broadcast that tidbit to my other body parts.

"Did you pay your rent?" I winced as she spat what remained of the Pepto polish in my direction.

Apparently, I'd hit a nerve.

"Not all of us were born with titanium spoons in our mouths," she snapped.

"No, we weren't," I replied, quickly adding before she had a chance to interject, "So you lost your key, but that doesn't explain how you knew who I was, much less that I had a key…to *your* P.O. box."

"Hell-o… Is this chick for real?" Danielle cast an exasperated glance at Logan.

I tapped my foot, even though Nicoh was sitting on it, which cost me a bit in the effect department.

Danielle huffed and shrugged, still too animated for my liking.

"Decker, of course. I just didn't know that she'd gotten sloppy and hired an associate she hadn't checked out. And who also turned out to be a thief. You *did* steal my stuff," she growled when I opened my mouth.

"But what pisses me off the most? Is that after all that build-up about finally bringing her mom's killer to justice, she goes MIA? Won't return my calls? Is nowhere to be found? That's crap." She swiveled her head toward Logan. "Seriously dude, I know she's *your* friend and all—and though she and I had fallen out over the years—I would have never thought Decker would turn out to be such a flake. How hard is it to return a call to someone who you've asked for help? Is she out of the country or working undercover or something?"

I glanced at Logan, my stomach dropping when his brow

furrowed as he worked his jaw. I tossed out the first thing that came to mind just so I wouldn't have to endure his response.

"When was the last time you actually spoke to Decker?"

She frowned, though she did seem to be considering my question as opposed to annoyed by it.

"Dunno, maybe a few weeks ago? A month? Last time was a text, letting me know that she had someone helping her out on her mother's case. Described you down to that judgey expression you're giving me. How else would I know what you looked like?" She shot me an annoyed look.

Something wasn't adding up. It still didn't explain how she'd known that I'd gotten hold of the P.O. box key…one that I had not gotten from Decker.

I put a pin in that when she added, "Either way, I'm surprised that Decker wouldn't want someone more…suitable helping her out in a manner that was this serious, or personal."

I couldn't help myself. "You're one to talk."

"I should report you for the fraud you are," she snapped, nodding. "Decker needs to know *exactly* what type of people she has working for her."

"Good luck with that," I murmured, careful not to look at Logan, though I'd noted Nicoh had moved to his side.

Traitor.

Still, I didn't think it was my place to tell Danielle that Decker would no longer care what she had to say. Plus, I selfishly hoped her belief that Decker was still alive could help us. Perhaps she would be able to reveal some relevant details, either to what Decker had requested of her or what she had witnessed. Or, better still, what the P.O. box had contained.

Logan seemed just as eager to tackle that subject as he skillfully shifted Danielle's attention back to him.

"Why are you so hopped up on getting this 'stuff' of yours anyway? What were you hiding in there? The GPS coordinates of

Hoffa's grave? KFC's extra crispy chicken recipe? Wait…don't tell me… You're a double agent." Logan tapped his chin, his tone layered with maple syrup-like sarcasm as he added, "Russian? North Korean?"

"You wouldn't be so blasé about this if you knew what's in there—scratch that—what was *supposed* to have been in there." She shook her head. "And I doubt…considering…Decker would appreciate your sarcasm. And yeah, I caught that." She shot him a look that would have made most men wither and retreat. Not all men were Logan, though, whose arms remained crossed as he offered her an Oscar-worthy stare.

I swore he had an uncanny ability of not blinking on command.

"Enlighten us, then," I interjected, careful to keep any hint of judgment out of my voice as she seemed particularly sensitive to it.

Despite my efforts, Danielle shook her head, and I feared we'd made a serious misstep where her boundaries were concerned, but after a moment, she surprised me.

"Since it seems Decker failed to fill you in before she went MIA, I guess that leaves me to do her job for her," she huffed, frowning before adding, "Seriously, I can't believe she would leave something of this magnitude up in the air without a net."

"What…something?" My mind whirled, hoping this dance was finally leading somewhere.

If I truly dissected the situation, given what Danielle had just said, even knowing what I did about Decker and her recent departure, to have left such a detail to chance was completely out of character. And leaving it in Danielle's care? Unfathomable.

Lucky me, my thoughts must have translated to my face, as Danielle narrowed her eyes and scoffed. "Welcome to my nightmare."

After a prolonged silence—perhaps Danielle was rethinking

her position, she added, "This could take a minute, mind if we go somewhere and sit down? Have a drink?"

She scoffed after gauging our expressions. Mine was probably a mix of exasperation and surprise, Logan's was more an irritated head shake.

"Fine. Let's just continue loitering in the doorway of my room. No worries that my leg is falling asleep or that some of us might actually need to use the facilities." She paused to look at Logan pointedly before adding, "As long as you two are comfy, we should be good."

I made a waving gesture this time, to which she responded by rolling her eyes again, but the annoyance didn't quite reach them this time. If I hadn't been glaring at her, I would have missed the shift, but it was there. I recognized it immediately.

Fear.

I know, because I'd seen it looking back in the mirror more times than I could count.

I shuddered, just as the emotion flashed like a firefly, and disappeared.

"You both know what happened to Decker's mom, so I won't rehash old territory. As I'm sure you're aware, Decker and I were in the apartment when the attack occurred, though neither of us remembers diddly—the pros chalk it up to P.T.S.D." She waved a hand. "Whatever. The fact still remains that we were witnesses to the darkest of moments one can experience. To quote one of the gurus: 'a crime beyond the bounds of cruelty, in which a killer still roams free, unrepentant, unapologetic…'

"And, until a switch flips in either my or Decker's skull and we can recall the details, he'll continue to live his life, while Decker's mom remains condemned to a cold, hard grave."

She was preaching to the choir, but we let her continue. She was either a really good actress, or there was a teaspoonful of decency and humanity that still remained in this being.

I was still on the fence, but it leaned pretty heavily to one side. There was too much about Danielle that just didn't measure up, regardless of what I'd been told beforehand, the girl before me presented one version to the world, while the other she tucked away.

My mind snapped back when Danielle shifted, and I caught her surveying me. "Anyway, as time passes, it's less likely that these memories are just going to show up." This time, her voice caught and when our eyes met, she glanced away.

Was it possible Danielle was remorseful about the path her life had taken after that day? The set of her jaw and the blackness of her soulless eyes said no. But still, there was something that rumbled below the surface.

She released a breath before continuing, "Of course, there *is* another path we can pursue. One, thanks to Decker, that recently popped up, though I'm still floored that she hasn't been around to follow up on it. Not after coming this far."

I glanced at Logan, but his expression hadn't changed. Perhaps this was yet another of Danielle's schemes—only this one had been concocted to weasel her way out of her current crap storm.

Then again, if that were true, then why had she stayed in the hotel? Why not cut and run once she had realized her efforts to retrieve her "stuff" turned out to be a bust?

As if sensing my inner dialogue, Danielle pressed on, this time ensuring she had my full attention, almost daring me to look away.

"During the investigation, there wasn't anything that tied the killer to the scene, absolutely no hint that he was ever there." She saw the quirk in my brow and added, "Until now."

"Are you suggesting evidence has recently come to light?" Logan's voice caused me to jump, he had been quiet for so long.

"Not just evidence," she replied. "The smoking gun, as you cops like to call it. DNA evidence."

"Whose?" My throat must have been dry because it came out as a croak. "Sorry, whose DNA?"

Danielle shook her head, the scrunch of her nose and the purse of her mouth suggesting she'd either smelled rotten eggs or that I had just uttered the stupidest question ever posed. "The killer's, of course."

"Who. Is. The. Killer?" I ground out.

"Well, now that we no longer have the evidence—that 'stuff' that was supposed to be in the P.O. box—I guess we'll never know, " she huffed. "And before you ask, I know because I put it there."

CHAPTER NINE

As Logan and I spouted questions, she held up both hands and gave a sharp whistle before growling out, "First off, I said it *was* in the P.O. box. Second, I do happen to have first-hand knowledge that it directly ties the murder scene. Third, yes, I realize that it is currently missing."

"How can you be sure of any of this?" Logan snapped.

"Like I said…I put it there." She shrugged nonchalantly, though she avoided eye contact with either of us.

If anything, twisting the ends of her hair seemed high on Danielle's current list of priorities.

"Yeah, you've already said that, yet you've been light on the details. While you've got our attention, and what remains of our patience, I recommend you get a move on with it," Logan demanded.

When he caught my single head shake, he relaxed slightly, shifting back on one leg and unfisting his clenched hands. His facial expression—one that mirrored sucking on a particularly sour lime—refused to waver.

As Danielle watched our silent interaction, a tiny smirk

crossed the corner of her mouth and then evaporated, but not before I'd caught it. If I'd read her right, she believed she'd finally gotten Logan where she'd wanted him. I wasn't an expert on the subject of all things Logan, but I thought she'd missed the mark. If anything, he was more skeptical of her now than he had been.

She feigned disinterest a while longer before offering a response. "I put it there for safekeeping. I was moving around a lot, but once I knew what I had, realized the value it could have, and wanted to keep it close."

I didn't much care for her reference to value, especially where a human life was concerned, but pushed my feelings down as I waved a hand in the air.

"Whoa! Wrangle the cattle back into the corral, Danielle." When I received a blank look, I added, "Please, go back to the beginning. *What*, specifically, are we talking about here? And, *how* did you come into possession of whatever it was before the whole P.O. box debacle occurred?"

The emptiness transitioned into a glare as she scrunched her nose. It wasn't a good look—making her look even more impish that she already appeared. If she felt as though I was challenging her, that had not been my intention.

Sighing, I raised my hands in surrender. Finally, her face slackened, and her frowny-face turned neutral.

"The item in question belongs to me, or at least it did. When I was…a child, it was an old dirty teddy bear, about this big." She paused to show us the toy's size using her palms, which spanned about ten inches, before adding, "He was blue with a red nose and beady black eyes that looked like Junior Mints—ugly little thing —but I loved it. Took it everywhere. I had it with me the night… uh, you know…"

Danielle's eyes misted as her voice caught. It was the first real show of emotion she revealed. I still didn't trust her as far as I could throw her, but the sentiment behind it and her reaction to having to say the words out loud seemed genuine.

I glanced at Logan but he was focused on Danielle.

"I lost track of Buddy—that was the bear's name—after that." She shrugged. "I grew up. I moved on."

"This bear, Buddy, *was* the evidence?" I prompted.

Danielle nodded. "Decker thought so."

"What evidence did she think this…bear possessed?" Logan finally spoke, though he couldn't quite bring himself to utter the stuffed animal's name.

"DNA." Her voice cracked again as she added, "The killer's."

"DNA…as in blood?" My voice sounded squeaky, even to me.

She nodded. "A few drops."

"Even if it was blood, how could you be sure it was the killer's? It could have just as easily been Ellen's." Logan wasn't buying, and neither was I.

"Or another type of stain altogether," I added, realizing my commentary wasn't all that helpful where Danielle was concerned, though Logan's antagonistic tone wasn't much better.

Danielle pressed her lips together and shook her head. "I *know* it. I just know it was his."

"But you couldn't remember what happened that night. Neither of you could. How could you be so sure now?" Logan's voice turned sharp.

Thankfully, Danielle's mind seemed elsewhere as she bit her lip, and when she finally spoke, I noted that she chose her words carefully.

"I don't. Remember. And though it seems unlikely that I ever will—pharmaceuticals being what they are—" she hacked out a rough laugh before continuing, "I'm not sure I'd want to remember, no matter how much Decker wishes that we could."

I released another involuntary shudder at the mention of

Decker in the present tense but didn't dare venture a glance at Logan. We'd tackle that hurdle down the road, if and when it was warranted, or became necessary in helping us get what we wanted from her. From my perspective, we owed nothing to Danielle. She'd offered us little in the way of information that expanded beyond her imagination.

"Then how?" I prompted, keeping my tone calm despite the fact my nerves were a constant reminder that I was anything but.

"I had this weird habit when I was young. Actually, Decker reminded me and we had a good laugh about it. Mom used to say it was nervous energy, called me her 'fuzz bug' because I'd go around and collect things off the floor—lint, dust bunnies, bugs—you name it, I found it.

"Since mom's job was as a cleaning lady for the richie types, she thought it was amusing, especially when her three-year-old would hand her bits of whatever she found from God knows where—always the good little helper.

"Of course, the older I got, the older it got and mom grew tired of telling me to throw the items straight into the trash. After a while, the habit showed up less and less but typically popped back up whenever I got stressed—or scared." Danielle paused to swallow, pressing her eyes closed.

"Like that night," I murmured. "What did you collect?"

Danielle's mouth turned down, and she crossed her arms, rubbing them. "Hair. His. Sometime during the incident or maybe after—I don't know—I grabbed something he dropped, picked the hair off, probably out of nervousness—gross, I know—and then absently stuffed it in a ripped seam in the back of Buddy." When she caught the incredulous glance I cast Logan, she added with an exasperated huff, "That was another weird habit I had…stuffing odd crap into Buddy's seams."

"Still, how could you be sure it was his…hair? Much less came from the murder scene?"

Danielle and I both jumped at the sharpness of Logan's voice and while she glanced at him, I didn't care to see what expression was behind the terseness of those words. It was a side of him I hadn't seen, and though Danielle was certainly testing both of our limits, it was a cause for concern.

Her brow furrowed as she contemplated him, but whatever she saw, she chose to continue.

"The blood I mentioned came from the hair I stuffed into the bear." When Logan started up again, she tossed him a frosty stare. "The hair was his. Decker's mom struggled. She fought. And when she did, she pulled a nice big patch out from that monster's murderous roots."

Logan exploded, and this time, no icy looks were holding him back. "You expect us to believe that you had the wits to do something like that, right after your best friend's mother was brutally murdered, and then stuff it into your mangy teddy bear? Come on, Danielle! Let's not forget that you'd previously forgotten the entire event. Yet now, with a little prompting from Decker, everything is clear and all of this"—he waved his hands around animatedly—"suddenly makes sense?"

"What more did you expect, you moron—I was a freaking kid!" she screamed, before stumbling backward and slamming the door in our faces.

CHAPTER TEN

I wasn't about to allow the little twit to have the last word and guessing by Logan's colorful commentary; he wasn't either.

"You're honestly suggesting that Decker actually bought this little fantasy?" Logan shouted through the door. "Get real, Danielle. It's one thing to concoct this farce to drum up attention or scam something off someone, but to use the violent murder of your best friend's mother to do it? That takes one twisted mind."

"Bought it?" She hollered back, surprising us both. "Decker's the one who figured it out."

"You're saying she came up with the story and suddenly after all these years, not remembering squat, convinced you—out of the blue, for whatever reason—that it was true?" You could have cut Logan's sarcasm with a plastic picnic knife.

Finally, Danielle opened the door, leveling a glare at him that could have melted ice in a snowstorm.

"I'm saying no such thing. Besides, once I found the bear, I confirmed it." Danielle smirked, thrusting a hand on one hip.

"Convenient, now that the evidence is missing." Logan's tone was haughty, but it only drew a disinterested look from Danielle.

I attempted to redirect. "How did you acquire the bear, after all of these years?"

"Someone…probably Mom…left it for me." She shrugged, her eyes never shifting away from Logan.

"Left it for you?"

"In the P.O. box." When she caught my furrowed brow, she added, "It was probably the only way she figured she could keep in touch with me. There were years when I was…difficult. I'd ditch school so that I could hang with my friends and do what I wanted to. You know…typical teenage stuff." She shrugged again —a habit that was starting to annoy me—much like the nail-snacking she'd started in on again. The victim this time was a thumbnail painted in traffic cone orange.

"Okay, how did your mom know you'd check the box during these difficult years?" I prodded.

She laughed but there was no humor in it. "You mean what would possess a teenager with a busy social life to bother checking her family's mailbox?"

I nodded, offering a small smile. "Something like that."

"Old habits die hard, I guess. I always loved having a mailbox that was separate from where we lived. As a kid, I thought it made us special—that maybe we were like the richies or something—to be able to afford our own special place, even if it was just to pick up our mail." Danielle shrugged.

"Of course, life has a nasty way of knocking you back into your place and reminding you how silly the kid stuff is. The truth of it was, our slumlord was too cheap to replace the mail traps in the building when they got damaged. And Mom, being the responsible person she was, paid money she couldn't afford so that she could ensure that she'd receive bills, notices from our schools, stuff like that. Not so special, after all, huh?

"Anyway, because of the hours Mom worked, cooking, and cleaning houses, she assigned either Larissa or me to collect the mail from the box after school. Larissa was older and it cramped her style, so she paid me part of her allowance to grab it on her days." She chuckled at the memory. "It was easy money for me because I didn't care.

"As an added benefit, when Mom realized I'd taken over the mail collection duty, she would leave little treats for me when she could, using her key. The surprises weren't anything big—a pretty hair clip, a figurine, a pack of cards to play Crazy 8's, stuff like that—but it was *our* secret." Danielle paused, smiling as she shook her head at the memory.

"When I got older, I still checked the box on occasion, out of habit. Later, I did it to get away from my friends and all of their drama." When I tilted my head, she chuckled and added, "Someone always had something tragic going on, and after a while it was too much to handle. I don't know. I guess I wanted a sense of normal…something that tied me to this world."

"And the bear?" I prompted.

She glanced at me. "Yeah. The bear. Mom probably figured it a was a last-ditch effort to stay in touch with me—only this time around, the surprises usually came in the form of scathing notes from her or the school, threatening expulsion for ditching. Stupid stuff. Of course, I ignored them and left them where they were. Dumb kid—thought I was making a point." She snorted before frowning as she continued, "Then one day, someone had put Buddy in the mailbox."

"Your mother," Logan replied.

Danielle nodded absently, not catching the sideways glance he'd cast me. "I assumed so. Later, I learned that they had moved and left me with no forwarding address or phone number. I thought it was her way of saying goodbye. Or just cutting ties with me once and for all. She'd threatened to do it before, but I thought maybe she'd finally had all she could take." She frowned, biting her nail as she scraped a toe across the threshold.

"When was last time you saw Larissa and your mother, prior to their move?" Logan asked.

I was curious to know too, as she hadn't mentioned the stroke, nor seemed to be aware of it.

Danielle blew out a breath before responding, "It'd been…a while."

"Why was that?" Logan continued to push her.

"Dunno. Don't remember." She shrugged but hesitated just long enough to make me think she wasn't entirely truthful.

Logan caught the movement, too. "Come on, Danielle. Surely there was a reason you didn't return home for such a long time."

Danielle pursed her lips. "Fine. The last time I saw Mom… and probably Larissa, for that matter, we got into it. It got…bad."

"What did you fight about?" I asked.

She sighed. "I don't know. Drugs. Booze. Boys. Men. Not necessarily in that order."

"Nothing more specific comes to mind?" I gave Logan a single head-shake, as his tone had been on the confrontational side.

Thankfully, Danielle hadn't seemed to notice. Or just didn't care.

"Nope, that seemed to be the range of topics we usually fought about, 'Danielle is a screw-up, and a slut' was an ongoing theme. I dunno. It was a long time ago. Things were said that can't be taken back."

"By you?" I asked.

"By all of us." Danielle's eyes bore into me. "Listen. It's water under the bridge. We've all moved on. Though I guess, some of us more literally than others.

"And, for the record, we wouldn't be talking about this if the first place if Decker hadn't tried drumming up the past. It all seems pretty stupid to have banked everything on a stupid stuffed animal. And now that it's disappeared, like Decker, it doesn't really matter, does it?"

I shot a look at Logan. The glare he was leveling on her pretty much summed it up. That "stupid stuffed animal" made all of the difference in the world.

To top it off, it'd started looking like a recurring theme, as we were rewarded with another door slammed in our faces.

CHAPTER ELEVEN

Despite our attempts to draw her back out, Danielle had finally gone silent.

I couldn't speak for Logan, but I needed a mindset shift—one that did not include either A) utilizing my super ninja skillset to kick her door down or B) hurling newly-crafted expletives into the universe at the top of my lungs. The latter was far more plausible. I realized I was in desperate need of sleep and suddenly retreating to my room to rest my weary bones—and mind— sounded like a dream.

And weary I was.

Bone. Tired.

Yet, thanks to Danielle, I was feeling too frustrated, agitated, fussy, and discombobulated for rest. My trip to L.A. thus far had been a bust. I had not only accomplished nothing, but I had also wasted time in the process and was nowhere closer to reeling in a killer.

The hamster on the wheel in my brain was burning oil as I huffed and gave Logan the head nod—it was time to retreat.

As I stomped the short distance, I pondered what information we'd actually gotten out of Danielle, other than a couple of raging headaches.

Perhaps it was better to chew on the things that Danielle hadn't mentioned.

Though she claimed to have been in contact with her, Decker had not shared the name of the man who had murdered her mother—a man who Maria had not only known but worked for. Now, with Decker dead and Danielle's mother in no physical or mental condition to assist, we were running out of ways to track Edwards' trail to Decker's mother.

Other than her husband's profession as a private investigator, his documented disdain for the man and his connection to a woman he'd known since childhood who lived in the building— how had Ellen Decker and Terrence Edwards crossed paths?

The brutal murder of one's wife as revenge for his interference into the man's affairs would have been a stretch, even for a narcissist like Terrence, so something else must have put her on his radar. Lust? Jealously?

"Ellen did know Edwards," Logan murmured.

I spun on my heel, realizing that I'd actually spoken that entire inner monologue out loud.

I shook my head. Not having one's best friend at the ready seemed to do that as of late.

"How?" I managed to stammer out as I shoved my key card into the lock and kicked the door with my foot so hard it hit the spring on the backside and nearly pummeled me in the face on its return trip.

Nicoh tucked tail and disappeared into the bathroom while I growled out a curse and slumped on the edge of the bed.

Logan ignored my outburst and calmly shut the door before sitting down next to me. Brave man, I thought to myself.

Or very dumb.

"Decker told me that between her other jobs, Ellen was going to school to get her court reporter's certification. One of her female professors took a liking to her—saw a lot of herself in Ellen at that age—and became her unofficial mentor. I don't recall all of the details, but she was able to get approval for Ellen to gain some on-the-job training in an actual court setting and get credit toward her certificate in the process. On one of those occasions—"

"Let me guess. Terrence Edwards sauntered in, representing one of his low-life clients charged with racketeering."

Logan looked like he'd been sprayed by a skunk. "Worse. Trafficking."

"Okay…That's pretty bad, too, but when it comes to Edwards, you'll have to explain why that's worse," I replied

"Human. Trafficking," he enunciated through gritted teeth. "Young girls. And boys. You need me to expound?"

This time, I was the one who puckered up.

"Does Edwards seriously have no boundaries when it comes to choosing his clients?" When Logan shot me a disgusted glance, I murmured, "Right. This is not a normal human being we're talking about."

Terrence Edwards was anything but normal.

I kicked the edge of the bed with my heel, which turns out, was crafted from some sort of composite material constructed to shatter bone.

After releasing a Borax-worthy expletive that left Logan temporarily speechless, he continued, "According to Decker's conversation with the retired professor, despite being married, Edwards was notorious for zoning in on fresh meat, so once Ellen was in his sights, he was a hungry panther on the prowl."

I scrunched my nose, and though I could have done without the visual, I urged him to continue.

"The teacher could only verify what happened in broad daylight, under her watchful eye. Not that I find it acceptable, but what she alluded to didn't extend beyond overt comments about Ellen's physical appearance to both his male counterparts and directly to Ellen."

"Wow. Poor Ellen. And Decker. It must have killed her, hearing as an adult, how her mother had been grazed over by that monster. I can't believe she didn't just take him out."

Logan nodded, frowning. "I'm surprised her pops didn't either, but both of them were determined to take the killer down by the book, whoever he was. And if that meant Edwards, they didn't want their…feelings about him getting in the way."

"Right. Nailing Edwards, given his knowledge of the criminal justice system—and slimy ways— would have been an undertaking. Even with all of one's ducks in a row." Something else occurred to me. "Wait—Decker's father *knew* about Edwards' advances on his wife?"

Logan shook his head, sighing. "Decker learned about that a few years before he passed. Max had gotten himself all riled up about something and was rambling—he was pretty far into his sickness by that point. Once she got him calmed down, he revealed that her mother had been forthcoming about all of it from day one. Mind you, she wasn't doing so to get a rise out of him. She simply found Edwards' behavior deplorable and didn't like people thinking she was going along with it."

"Full transparency," I murmured.

"Decker got that trait from her mum, I guess. Good or bad. You always knew what was what," he replied, his eyes hooded by the darkness of the room. "Guess in the end, it got them both killed."

"You can't put the blame on them," I ground out.

Logan jerked his head in my direction. "I didn't mean—"

I put up a hand. "Sorry, just tired. I know you didn't. I'm just angry. About all of it. Such a waste."

"Sounds like Decker got under your skin, too."

"Like a freaking rash," I replied, chewing my lip as I reflected on my short tenure working with the private investigator.

She was a force. That was for sure. And if anyone could have nailed Edwards for her mother's murder, it was Decker. Sadly, her life had been cut short. She was too young and vibrant to have left this world so soon.

Sighing, I returned to the subject at hand. "So, Decker's mom...did she ever get her certification?"

Logan frowned. "Took the test. Scored higher than any other student. Her father found the notification in the mail the day after Ellen was murdered."

"That's harsh," I murmured as he nodded, staring at his hands, giving me the opportunity to study him.

During our discussion with Danielle, he'd revealed a side I hadn't seen.

"So, are you always so...intense when you go into cop mode?"

He raised a brow. "Cop mode?"

"Something in you changed when we were talking to Danielle. Is that your typical M.O.? Or, is it Danielle herself that gave you an edge? Truth be told, it was kind of unsettling."

His gaze shifted ever so slightly when I mentioned Danielle, and I knew I had latched onto something.

"How did you end up crossing paths?"

Logan shrugged. "Not much to tell. I arrested her a few years back."

My eyes widened. "Okay, wow. That explains it, I guess." It didn't, but I could tell that was all he was willing to share about the specifics, so I shifted tactics. "Did you tell Decker?"

He nodded. "Sometimes, I wish I hadn't." When I tilted my

head, he added, "It's what gave her the idea to get Danielle involved. Up to that point, she'd had a hard time tracking her down. Danielle wasn't really putting down roots anywhere and the friends she bummed a couch with typically ended up kicking her out, getting evicted or overdosing."

"Yeesh. I could see why you'd want Decker to steer clear. Still, we both know she was more than capable of handling herself in tough situations. It makes me wonder—knowing Danielle's path—why she felt that was her only route?"

"It does seem a stretch, doesn't it?"

"I take it Decker never explained her rationale?" I asked.

"There wasn't really time before…" Logan gestured with his hand.

I nodded and cast my eyes down.

I didn't need to relive that moment and felt a pang of angst over pursuing this conversation with her best friend, when he added, "You are right though, it's beyond me why she chose to turn to Danielle. Though, I really wish I knew."

"So, where do we go from here?"

He chuckled. "I was going to ask you the same."

"Well, I, for one would like to know how Danielle knew who I was, not to mention why I was here."

"You think Larissa alerted her." It was not a question.

I shrugged. "Maybe. If she did, someone's got some serious explaining to do."

I proceeded to call Larissa and, after receiving an automated message, left a terse message that said a few syllables more than 'call me back' but still gave the impression I expected a return call, post-haste. As I pressed "End" on the connection, I noticed Logan giving me a cautious glance.

"You really think she can give us any insights that will help us identify what Danielle is really up to?" His tone spoke volumes—

he was doubtful—but there was something in the way he said it caught me off-guard.

Perhaps he'd thought I'd lost my marbles and was turning out to be a wildcard like Danielle.

"I doubt it, but at this point, it'll go a heck of a long way toward unloading some of this frustration," I growled. "Even if it's short-lived, giving her a piece of my mind will make me feel a whole lot better."

"Remind me not to get on your bad side," he murmured.

I hacked out a laugh. "What? That was nothing. I haven't started unleashing the wild beastie."

Logan's eyes widened. "That's what I was afraid of."

I proceeded to cast him a devilish grin so mischievous that we were both forced to laugh.

After a moment, I got back to business. "Danielle was more 'with it' than I would have expected. She surprised me."

"How do you mean?" Logan asked, his tone curious as he zoned in on my overt use of finger quotes.

"I got the impression she was far more educated than she was letting on, and I'm not talking about education in a street smarts kind of way." When he tilted his head, I added, "Think about how she phrased things. Not like a girl who'd barely shown up in school or hung out on the streets doing whatever she wanted. It was almost like she was…"

"Acting," Logan finished.

I nodded, "But had been taught how to do so in a way that yielded the results she was going after. Look at how she played us."

"Playing to an audience," he replied, nodding. "Interesting."

"Decker never mentioned anything about what Danielle had been up to since leaving home?"

He shook his head. "Not sure why it would have come up. But it doesn't mean she knew, either."

"Maybe she even used those skills to play on Decker's sympathies when Decker reconnected," I suggested.

"Seriously?" he asked, frowning.

"No, you're right. Danielle was a means to an end for Decker."

"And now?"

"Now, we just have to figure out why."

CHAPTER TWELVE

Logan opened his mouth, but I never got a chance to hear his thoughts as my phone's ringtone filled the room. I tilted the screen so that he could see the caller's name and he gave a single head nod before moving toward the window and glancing down into the city, now buzzing with activity.

"Larissa. Thanks for calling me back."

The timbre of her voice was crispy. "Given the tone of your message and its brevity, I didn't feel as though I had a choice."

"Touché. I'll get right to the point then," I ground out, matching her in kind. "Did you warn Danielle that I'd be coming for the contents of the P.O. box?"

There was a moment of silence as I braced for an outburst and was surprised when none came. The snappishness was replaced with confusion. "I'm not sure…what you mean."

I offered her a brief rundown of our interactions with Danielle, starting with her tailing us to the mailbox store and ending with our awkward conversation at the hotel.

When I finished, there was another awkward pause, followed by, "You're saying that Danielle is there? In person?"

"That would be correct."

"How…how does she look?" Her voice was hesitant, almost pleading that I wouldn't reveal the worst.

"Fine, I guess. Considering it was our first introduction, I have nothing to compare it to, but Danielle *appears* okay." I didn't mention that her attitude could use some work.

"That's…good to hear." I heard a sniffle as Larissa's voice cracked.

I didn't respond, opting to allow her to answer my question.

After an awkward silence, she continued, her voice weary and filled with a resigned sadness. "I did not warn Danielle. As I mentioned before, I haven't seen her since…before we moved to Arizona." She released a shaky breath before adding, "Besides, you were the one who came to me. Remember?"

"I do, but how did she know? And who accessed the P.O. box, let alone put the bear there in the first place?"

"I have no idea. Mother's little treats to Larissa are news to me, but it sounds like something she would have done. Having said that, she was nowhere near any condition to have been able to do so for quite some time before we actually moved, so if someone was communicating with her, it wasn't either of us."

I believed her, but it didn't help our current situation. Given Logan's frown as he caught my eye, he'd gotten the gist from my side of the conversation.

Larissa spoke her next words so quietly I almost missed them. "You said Danielle was there. Could I possibly…talk to her?"

"You want to talk to Danielle?" I glanced at Logan, who shrugged, then pointed at the door. When I nodded, he strode past and went to retrieve her from her room.

"If I can, I would like to, though I'll be honest, I'm so nervous, I wouldn't know what to say. Where to even begin."

"I'm sure something will come to you, just be yourself. She won't bite."

She squeaked out a small chuckle. "We are talking about *Danielle*, right?"

I managed to cough out a laugh, but it sounded more I was choking. Perhaps I was.

"True."

I was about to add some quip when Logan returned, frowning and shaking his head.

"Hold on just a sec, Larissa," I said as I placed her on mute. "What?"

"Danielle's gone."

"Use your words, Logan. Define 'gone.'"

Mussing his hair as he used the other hand to talk, they came out rapid-fire with a kick of gasoline tossed in there. "Cleared out. Housekeeping is turning her room over as we speak, said she did the express checkout."

"So, she bypassed the front desk?"

"Looks that way." He nodded, this time both hands scruffed his head. "How could we—I have been so stupid? I should have glued myself to her door. She would have eventually come out. I could have tailed her. Now…" His voice trailed off as he gave his hair a rest and thrust his hands into his pockets.

"Well, crap." I bit my lip, mulling over the likelihood we'd be able to track her down again within the timeframe we'd need her when I realized I had a more immediate issue to address.

Her sister.

No sense worrying her unnecessarily. "Sorry about that, Larissa. Logan just told me that Danielle went to grab a bite. It's been a long day. Want me to tell her we spoke?" I carefully omitted the "when I see her again" part.

She sighed, almost sounding relieved that the conversation had been delayed. "Sure, if you wouldn't mind. You could also give her my number if you want. Maybe then she'll call?"

"Maybe." I kept my tone even but knew that reconnecting

with Larissa or her mother was the furthest thing from Danielle's mind. She'd popped out of the woodwork again, and it wasn't for a family reunion.

I took a chance and tiptoed in a direction I hadn't intended going with her. "Before everything went…south with Danielle, did she express any interest in her plans…what she wanted to do with her life, what she wanted to be when she grew up, anything like that?"

"Again, we're talking about Danielle, right?" she laughed, but it fringed on the worn side. "Problem was. Danielle was too smart. School was actually easy for her. Everything from English to math to chemistry, she blew past everyone. Could read when she was three. Wrote when she was four. Mastered algebra and how to balance mother's checkbook at ten. But there was one thing she excelled at above all else, despite her attempts to hide it."

"Hide it?"

"Oh yeah, Danielle was also quite manipulative and could wrap nearly anyone around her finger. Most people underestimated her and never saw it coming."

"So…you could say she was quite the little actress." This drew a stare from Logan.

"Give that girl a prize. Boy, was she ever. Even Mother fell for it."

"What about you?"

"Sure, until she used it to drive a wedge between Mother and me. She'd make up stuff, especially when I was away at my dad's house." She paused to reflect. "Yeah, I could tell she used *that* time to her benefit. Of course, it helped that Mother favored Danielle anyway. Man, was she a charmer, but she was also a sneak and played quite dirty."

"Did she ever consider acting as a career?"

"As in school?" she asked, snickering when I replied in the

affirmative. "Now that you mention it, it would have suited her—considering her antics and desire to be the center of attention. Danielle wasn't one who liked to be told what to do, though. It's really too bad she didn't choose to apply herself—a kid that smart. I would have killed to have had the opportunities she did."

"How do you mean?"

"As I mentioned, Mother did the best she could, but money was tight. My father did an okay job of paying his due—he wasn't always on time but he was by no means a dead-beat dad—and considering he had his own family, there wasn't going to be anything left over for college. Danielle was another story.

"Her father set her up nicely. Though Mother would never tell us who he was, in a moment of frustration, she told me she felt like a high-priced call girl, and at the end of the evening, her services paid in full. It turned out, that amounted to a one-time payment that covered Danielle's expenses for eighteen years. It also included a college fund that would have paid for both under-grad and master's courses at an Ivy League school with enough leftovers for plenty of extras.

"And while I doubt Mother was worried that Danielle would follow her down the same path in her choice of professions, I don't think she believed Danielle would just bail, either."

I blew out a whistle. It was a wasted opportunity, for sure. But my focus wasn't on Danielle. "Your mom never alluded to this man's identity?"

"Oh, heck, no. When I asked her, she not only recoiled from the question, she seemed…afraid. And now…well, his secret is forever held safe, serving only as a memory that haunts her mind."

"That's terrible," I murmured. "And Danielle, she was never aware of her biological father's…investment in her future?"

"No. It was part of the deal. The money resided in an account that only my mother could access until Danielle turned eighteen.

At that time, the money transitioned into a fund managed by a third party responsible for ensuring that Danielle's choice of schooling would receive payment and that she would never have direct access to it.

"Of course, Danielle left home long before that happened, so she was never aware of her inheritance or that she could have chosen any school she wanted. I'll admit, when mother told me, I was bitter. It took me years to be able to afford to pay for classes, and even now, I can only do so part-time while working a full-time job."

"And taking care of your mother," I added.

"Yes, of course," she replied. "I didn't mean to sound ungrateful. My mother worked too hard and often missed our big events, but look at her now. Look at our lives. I hate to say it, but sometimes I think that Danielle got off easy. Then again, maybe she proved she was the smart one. I've often wondered what it would be like to have that kind of freedom—to do what you wanted when you wanted. Without responsibilities or repercussions."

Having met Danielle, I doubted that her life had been as free as Larissa believed, and bet that there had been far too many repercussions. And fiddlers to pay.

I didn't share my intuitions and elected instead to follow up on something Larissa had said. I knew the answer, but it was the first time she had brought it up and previously hadn't wanted to point her in a particular direction. "You mentioned your mom working hard, missing your events, stuff like that?"

Larissa hacked out a harsh laugh. "She was treated more like an indentured servant by an up and coming attorney and his entitled, rich wife. She liked the woman, somewhat. The husband, she…tolerated. Said he had a real chip on his shoulder where money and success were concerned—always something to prove, even when no one was watching. From what she'd alluded to, he was willing to do whatever it took—including murder and theft—

to get it. Though that last part was more tongue-in-cheek, I'm sure."

Or perhaps not, I shuddered.

I'd met Terrence Edwards years later, long after he'd established himself. The man was arrogant, and while that chip may have been gone, I still doubted he'd let anyone get in the way of something he wanted. Or someone.

Knowing any of that wouldn't help Larissa, I focused on the topic at hand.

"Is that why Danielle was staying over at the Decker's that night—because your mom was working? You already mentioned that you were staying at your dad's. Maybe your mom was required to work late, and the sleepover was arranged as a result?"

"I'm...not sure. I honestly never really thought about it. I came home. Kelly's mom was dead. Kelly and her dad moved. And life...was never the same...afterward. But I never really thought about Mom. Other than she lost her best friend. And Danielle and I lost ours."

"Your mom...her job...she worked there a long time?"

"Until around the time both of us were out of school...or when Danielle would have been out of school."

"So, there was no falling out between your mom and this woman or her husband?"

"Not that I know of. Why do you ask?"

"No reason," I murmured. "Just curious, after all those years of servitude."

"I guess it just...made things a bit easier, as it was a job that was closer to home..." She faded for a second and I heard a muffled voice in the background before she responded. "Sorry, just got called back—you'll let me know if you hear any more?"

I agreed and released a sigh of relief that she had not asked me about having Danielle contact her again. I doubted that would be in the cards and didn't want to have to tell another fib that I'd probably come to regret later.

Logan was staring at me expectantly, so I filled him in on the side of the conversation he hadn't heard.

"You believe her?" he asked when I was finished.

I shrugged. "She has no reason to lie. Plus, as she reminded me, I reached out to her."

"True. There is that." His tone suggested he wasn't convinced.

"But…" I prompted.

"Someone was going to show up eventually. Ask about Decker's mom. Decker, for all of her strengths, couldn't have been the only one to draw a connection between Maria's employer and her mother's murder."

"It's hard to say his name, isn't it? Terrence Edwards."

"You've met him in the flesh. Need you ask?"

"Good point." I scrunched my nose. "Anyway, that convo with Larissa led us nowhere. I think we give Danielle a breather—even if she was in our line-of-sight, she sucks too much energy."

"Agreed," he replied, bobbing his head once though no confirmation was required on that particular subject. "Next steps?"

"Dunno. Talk to neighbors. That Auntie Mae gal. Without the benefit of the DNA evidence, or knowing where it is, we're at a stalemate on that front."

He nodded. "I think I've got the address in my phone somewhere." Logan proceeded to pan through his contacts, pausing as he caught my tilted head. "What?"

"I thought you couldn't get involved."

He shrugged, focusing far too intently on his phone as he continued to scroll. "Must be all that optimism you're projecting—suddenly, I'm feeling like a believer."

He tried to mask a smirk as I mock-punched him in the arm, feigning surprise and injury once the blow was dealt. "You're quite tenacious when you want to be." I offered my own smirk in response as he squinted at something behind me. "What's that?"

I turned and looked at my bag, its contents now sprawled across the hotel's floral comforter, turning back to face Logan. "Officer Piedmont, if you want to know what secrets I've got hidden in my purse, just ask."

I meant it as a joke, but his face turned serious. "No. That." He poked a finger at a pile of envelopes and junk mail that had toppled to one side.

I squinted then groaned, registering what I had done.

"I am so sorry. I must have grabbed Decker's mail as we were leaving your place." I bent to collect it, suddenly feeling the weight of Logan's hand on my forearm.

"No, AJ. *Look.*"

He used his other arm to grab one of the larger items from the stack. "I recognize this logo." He nodded at the top left corner of the envelope. "It's one of the labs we use at work to process our evidence. Our *DNA* evidence." When my mouth formed an "o" he added, "It was also one of the labs I suggested to Decker when she asked for a recommendation."

"Did she say why she needed it?" My voice sounded hoarse as I glanced from Logan to the manila envelope.

Logan shook his head as he released the grip on my arm, carefully extracting the parcel from the pile. "I guess we're about to find out."

CHAPTER THIRTEEN

Logan pulled out a pocketknife and sliced the top of the envelope, casting a tilted head in my direction. Dancing from one foot to the next must have given him ample go-ahead, as he proceeded to carefully slide the document out. It wasn't a tome, but it still had a bit of girth to it, given the way he cradled it with both hands. As his eyes skirted from side to side, he offered a nail-biting variation of frowns, pursed lips, head shakes and nods before flipping to the next page.

Despite my effort to remain calm, I gnawed at my lip, and before long, it became so tender I was forced to dab at it with my fingers. Sighing when they came away blood-free, I realized that even this temporary distraction had done zilch in the way of alleviating the anxiety that continued to surge throughout my body.

Finally, my impatience won the battle.

"Logan?" I pleaded, forcing his attention away from the document.

"I'm not sure." He shook his head. "Somehow, Decker was the one who ended up with that bear." Noting my raised brows, he quickly added, "At some point, she snagged it and shipped it off to the lab for testing before…" His voice trailed off as he squinted at the document, frowning as he continued to read.

I swallowed. This should be *good* news, shouldn't it?

The mystery of the missing stuffed animal had been solved. We now knew where it had ended up, how it had gotten there, and considering Danielle's constant transient status, it was easy to see how she might have missed an update from Decker.

Still, there was something about the tightness of Logan's jaw and the wrinkle forming between his brows as he continued to span the pages, flipping from one to the next with more force than the thin paper warranted. I worried this new information just opened up a whole new can of stink where there had previously already been plenty.

"Care…to share?" When he glanced up, his eyes softened ever so slightly. "You okay? You seem…" I paused, shrugging as I waved a hand at him. "I don't know. I thought this could be good news or at least provide an answer that would either close a door or put us on the right track for a change."

"It does do that," he replied, "just not in the way we'd expected it to. Here, read for yourself."

He pushed the document at me, but when I got an eyeful of the long paragraph blocks spanning the page coupled with a severe lack of white space or visuals, my mouth went dry and my hands were clammy as I shoved it back.

"Um, perhaps you could provide the LogansNotes version?" I replied, quietly blushing as he caught my gaze.

"LogansNotes?" His mouth curled up on one side.

"Err, they're like Cliff's but without the blinding yellow and black psychedelic cover."

"Are you suggesting I'm just a pretty face?" He squinted at me then pressed his hand against his chest, feigning a stumble as though he'd been mortally wounded.

I coughed out a laugh. "Uh, no! Not unless 'pretty' translates to a two-day shadow, rumpled kind of look. I simply meant that I'm way too exhausted to attempt to decipher *that*, especially when you're coply eye has already given it a look-see." I nodded, more to myself than Logan, satisfied with my off-the-cuff comeback.

"Chalking it up to exhaustion, huh?" He shook his head as he extracted the paper from my hand. "Well, the least I can do is put my 'coply' expertise to work." He faked a sniff before adding, "It's always nice to be appreciated for more than one's looks, especially when the other party admits to being too exhausted to bother noticing."

He paused to cast an eye roll in my direction, possibly attempting to mirror something he'd caught either Leah or me engaging in at some point. "Yeah, quite a feather in my cap, not to mention a blow to my obviously over-inflated ego."

On that note, there was something in his gaze I couldn't quite decipher.

Unfortunately, it caught me at a loss, and I suddenly realized that, unlike my usual wingman, Leah, I didn't honestly know Logan all that well.

"I didn't mean…"

"No, no." He waved a hand. "I know *precisely* what you meant."

When I released an exasperated huff, he covered his mouth with a fist in an attempt to hide a chuckle.

"Can we get on with it?" I growled, tossing a pillow from the bed at him, missing him by a good foot or two and causing him to finally burst out in a round of guffaws that soon had me laughing too.

After catching his breath, he sat down beside me. "Well, for starters, the sample the lab tested did come from the bear that belonged to Danielle, which Decker extracted once she retrieved the key from Larissa." He paused and when I offered nothing more than a bland expression, then retorted, "What? I just wanted to ensure we were on the same page—one that gave us a good jumping-off point."

"Consider my parachute prepped," I replied, gesturing for him to proceed.

Logan offered a quick nod and got down to business.

"As you might expect, there were a lot of samples to work with—apparently, Decker must've had to sell a bike or two to get such a quick turnaround."

"No…seriously?" Logan nodded when my gaze shifted from the document. It was obviously something that had meant a great deal to her.

"Anyway, the results are good…and bad. Lots of samples but then again, lots of fingerprints, DNA, yada yada to extract, review and find a match for, hoping that someone who had been in the vicinity of the bear transferred something onto it," he paused to blow out a breath.

"Okay, I get that." I nodded. "After all that time, the quality and quantity of the evidence, how it got there, and all that stuff, it would've been difficult and time-consuming but not impossible, right?" My voice sounded weak and took on a pleading tone that was starting to grate on my nerves, so I could only imagine what it was doing for Logan and nipped it in the bud by waving him on to continue.

"I understand where you're coming from," he replied, launching my whole mental meandering and assumptions about him off the ledge and into the Grand Canyon. "There was a lot to tackle, but all was not lost. We got the info that we—that Decker was looking for. *But*, before you get too excited, I need to explain a few things. Believe me, if you allow me to walk it through, it will not only make more sense for you but help me get a grasp on things."

I nodded and swallowed. If an experienced law enforcement

professional needed a moment to digest the information, an amateur like me probably needed the *Pop-Up Video* version as he relayed the specifics. Oh, how I missed that show.

I prompted him to continue, and after he flipped through the pages a final time, he proceeded to lay out what secrets they revealed and how a childhood comfort might confirm a killer's identity.

"As mentioned, there were *a lot* of samples—both DNA and fingerprints." When I open my mouth to inquire how one might collect fingerprints from faux fur, he cut me off as though reading my thoughts.

"Smeary, but on smooth surfaces such as plastic eyes or nose or even a tag, as well as the various items Danielle had tucked inside the bear for safe-keeping, they were still intact. Of course, they were degraded and not of optimum quality, but they were still present. Anyway, according to this, many of the samples tested were from saliva or sweat secretions, blood..." I blanched at the thought of the implications.

Logan continued to focus on the document though I could tell he wasn't reading from it. I wondered if he was even referencing it or merely using it as a convenient prop while he collected his thoughts or reined in his judgment on the findings.

"Anyway, as expected, there were samples present from Danielle, her mother and Larissa. Decker also managed to obtain some samples from the original crime scene that were later identified as belonging to them, for comparison." He paused and glanced at me, his frown deepening as he shook his head. "I seriously have no idea how she came into possession of the evidence, though I have to wonder if her father had actually been the one who acquired them and when he passed..."

His voice trailed off, and I felt compelled to finish the thought. "She found them among his things and had them tested again, in case more could be gleaned this time around with the advancements in technology. DNA testing would've been in its infancy at the time of the murder. Maybe her father called in a favor and had one of his buddies on the force snag it and then sat on it, hoping technology would catch up and be able to identify his wife's killer."

"That would be my best guess, too. I just wish she would have shared all of this with me." Logan frowned and glanced away, focusing on nothing in particular.

Perhaps he found himself evaluating his friendship with the person he believed he knew. A person he would have put his life on the line for, had he been given the opportunity.

It wasn't the time or place to reassure him that, had she lived, Decker would've done the same.

After a long moment, he released a breath and moved on. "Of course, there were other samples, many of which can't be attributed to anyone, meaning anyone within a criminal record or logged in any government system. But, there was one clear sample tucked in the bear that differentiated itself from the others."

My eyes widened. "So, there *was* a sample that belonged to the killer." Perhaps I was surprised that Danielle had actually been telling the truth.

"Mmm…yeah, but it wasn't identified in the way you'd expect."

I frowned. "Um, you've lost me."

Logan shook his head. "Sorry. Still trying to work through it myself and based on the look on your face, doing a poor job of it. Let me try to explain it this way—it was actually *Danielle's* DNA that tied everything together."

I squinted. This wasn't helping and Logan grimaced as he took in my expression. "Okay, okay… Let me back up. Danielle stuffed evidence into the bear that she claims came from the crime scene. Right?" I nodded, and he did the same before continuing.

"That evidence produced two specific sets of DNA. One came from Decker's mom and the other from the person believed to be her killer."

"Terrence Edwards," I responded, both anxious and frustrated he wouldn't just say it.

"Yes."

"So, we've got that pompous jerk, like flies on dog doo!" I pumped a fist in the air. In Logan's frown deepened and it wasn't because of my disturbing analogy. "Come on!" I growled. "You can't tell me you're not ecstatic about the results."

He shrugged. "I was, and then the more I read, the more unsettled I became."

"Well, are you gonna tell me? Or am I gonna have to get the alphabet soup out and piece it together, one painful letter at a time? Geez, Logan, how bad could it be?" I snapped.

He cast me a dark look. "Bad."

I released an exasperated sigh and collapsed onto the edge of the bed, and though he didn't join me, he didn't speak until he was sure my eyes had dialed into his.

"Yes, a sample of Edward's DNA was tucked inside the bear, along with the other samples. It was *how* they identified his DNA that gets…interesting," he paused and seemed to be struggling with a way to frame whatever "it" was he was about to divulge. "When Danielle was born, there were challenges. There was talk about the possibility of needing a transfusion, so blood was taken from both parents as a precaution."

"Okay…" I squinted, not sure where he was going with this as we didn't know who Danielle's father was, but wanting to encourage him, I was prepped for the ride, *wherever* it took us.

"It's because of those records that the techs were able to tie him to the scene. They already had Danielle's and Maria's, but when Danielle snatched that evidence from the crime scene and stuffed it into her bear, she not only condemned Decker's mom's killer, she confirmed the identity of her biological father."

Realization kicked in as I struggled to shove out my two least favorite words.

"Terrence Edwards."

CHAPTER FOURTEEN

"Well, this isn't turning out like I'd expected," I murmured after we'd both had a moment of silence to digest that bombshell.

"You didn't expect any of this to be easy, did you?" Logan cast me a quick sideways glance.

I shot a look back that suggested he should refrain from asking questions of that nature in the future. He immediately raised his hands in surrender, so I doubted he'd make that mistake again.

"Now what?"

"Now that we've had about as much drama as either of us can take, we move ourselves to a drama-free environment," he replied. When I raised a brow, he added, "We're getting you out of this place."

I thrust a hand on my hip. "And just where do you suggest I go?"

Logan offered me a broad grin. "My place. And I won't take no for an answer."

"Okay…" I briefly mulled it over, before adding, "On one condition."

"Just one?" He quirked a brow.

I wondered if he realized what he was in for.

"I drive my own vehicle," I replied after a pregnant pause, though it was more for effect than anything.

His brow creased, but he nodded. "Deal. While you collect your stuff and check out, I'll take Nicoh, grab some necessities, and we'll meet you at my place?"

I nodded. That was easy enough. "Do you think there's any chance we could get more out of the hotel staff regarding Danielle?"

Logan shrugged. "You can try, but I gave them a pretty thorough shakedown."

"Yeah, they'd probably be more responsive to you," I murmured, trying hard not to let him notice me giving him a once-over.

He caught the look and snickered. "Ah, so we're back to that pretty face mumbo-jumbo."

I raised my hands. "Hey, you said it, not me. Whatever's been working for you, might as well stick with it."

"Mmm, hmm…" he chuckled. "On that note, I'll attempt to gracefully make my exit."

"I shouldn't be that far behind you, and perhaps, if you linger a bit grabbing those necessities, I may actually beat you to your place."

Logan nodded. "Sounds like a plan."

"Probably the only one so far that might actually work," I replied.

Famous last words.

I was able to pack and get checked out twenty minutes after Logan left with Nicoh. Before leaving, I cast a glance at the room Danielle had occupied but knew that even if she had returned, it would only result in more frustration and lost time.

I tossed the thought and was in the parking lot, digging in my bag for keys when someone grabbed my elbow.

My head snapped up, surprised as I took in the sizable frame of a barrel-chested bouncer-looking type, dressed in an all-black suit, complete with shades that only emphasized the egg-shaped cap of his skull. He had no facial hair on his deeply tanned face, though there were tiny frown lines at the corners of his mouth as I sized him up, down and up again, and an unhappy face of my own formed.

"My employer would like to have a word."

"*Which* word?" I snarked, but before I could utter another syllable, he efficiently propelled me away from my vehicle, toward a gunmetal-colored SUV.

Well, crap. This day was just getting better by the hour, wasn't it? Where was Leah when I needed some comic relief? Heck, where were the margaritas?

Considering the company I was about to find myself in, I would have requested a pitcher. Large.

After being thrust into the back of the SUV, I scrambled to sit upright while salvaging the contents of my bag, only to find myself face-to-face with the devil himself.

"Arianna, my dear. It's been too long." My companion raised a champagne flute in my direction before indulging in a languid sip.

Childishly, I hoped all those bubbles went to his head and exploded in a Wile E. Coyote vs. Acme fashion as I took him in.

He looked the same as he had at our previous meeting. His hawk-like gaze perused me in a way that made me wish for an acid bath, his too smooth, tanned skin pulled into a snake-like grin, exposing teeth that were even brighter this time around. Every silver strand of his perfectly coiffed hair was slick in its place, matching the expertly-cut suit and tie.

My observations, had I spoken them aloud, may have made it seem as though I'd morphed into a green-eyed monster. I was anything but. In reality, I viewed the man across from me as a slimy, gelatinous toxin, oozing arrogance from every pore.

So yeah, I would have preferred death by firing squad to having this man's overinflated ego invade my personal space.

Satisfied with my reaction, he tipped his glass toward his minion—also known as the Thuggy who had forcibly placed me in this narrative—who casually refilled his employer's flute from a magnum-sized bottle of what I expected was the highest quality stuff.

I did not respond, as I was not particularly saddened by the time that had passed since our last meet and greet, nor was this my party.

Smug as ever, Terrence Edwards simply sat and watched.

And still, under the awkward and squishy weight of his gaze, I did not take the bait.

Finally, he nodded, set the glass on an invisible ledge where it was collected by his associate, and leaned back in his seat.

"You shouldn't have wasted your time coming to Los Angeles. Though I'm sure it seemed well-intentioned at the time, you and your officer friend are heading down the wrong track and are both going to end up getting hurt."

I leveled a glare at him that would have melted ice in Antarctica. "Is that a threat?"

Edwards hacked out a chuckle that ended with a sneer, exposing gums above those pearly-whites.

His eyes glistened as he spoke. "Not at all, my dear. Just offering a bit of wisdom, having been down that path myself."

"I can't imagine," I murmured, and truthfully, I couldn't.

"Simply speaking from experience, my dear." He tossed it back precisely as I would have expected, making me wonder, who was the cat and who was the mouse?

"Mmm…hmm." I focused on biting my non-existent nails for a moment, just to be a nuisance. "If you aren't going to invite me to join you for refreshments, perhaps you could at least have the courtesy to tell me the real reason you got me here." I stopped my nibbling and deadpanned.

Edwards surveyed me for a moment, but even my blatant disinterest failed to wipe the entitled sneer from his face. "Nothing will come of this little venture you're on, Arianna. Nothing positive." He paused to take an indulgent sip before adding, "Sometimes our drive to seek something becomes so strong, we fail to account for the outcome once we find it."

"Meaning?" My tone was droll.

"Meaning, my dear, that when you find what you are looking for, be prepared for the fact that the knowledge, once exposed, may do more harm than good. Can you live with that?"

"I don't recall appointing you my moral compass. Or my life coach," I replied, staring him directly in the eyes.

A tiny smirk played at the corner of his mouth, and after a long stare-down, he clucked his tongue but never diverted his eyes. "Then I don't think you need me to remind you that your friend Kelly is dead. No matter how much you want to believe it —or are compelled by this false sense of obligation to proceed— you, the world, owe her nothing more."

"Says you," I snapped. It wasn't my best comeback, but it was the best I could muster without launching myself across the vehicle and knocking that smirk off his face. I would have given myself bonus points had I knocked a few of those blinding fangs out.

"She gets feisty when you amp her up." Edwards laughed and glanced at his minion, who didn't respond—rather rude considering the dude was his boss—but instead chose to stare me down from behind his shades.

"*She's* sitting right here," I ground out, glancing from the minion to Edwards. "And now that you've said your piece, I think I'll be going." I shifted toward the door, but the minion, despite his size, swiftly barred me with his arm. "Apparently, he doesn't speak." I gave him a frosty look before adding, "Man of action, huh?"

Edwards clapped, but his amusement faded quickly. "I'm not sure the message has been communicated…effectively."

"Oh, I heard it loud and clear," I replied, crossing my arms as I settled back into my seat. "Though I think as we've come to an impasse on the subject, there's clearly nothing more that can be said and therefore, nothing more to be gained by this…get-together. Buster here said you wanted a word." I tipped my head at the minion, who I could only assume was mentally shooting lasers at my head, before returning my full focus to Edwards. "Consider your word shared."

This time the minion remained stationary when I gripped the handle and thrust the door open. As I stepped out, I fought the urge to turn and unleash a few choice words on Edwards—but if he was anything—he was always on-point and beat me to the punchline.

"You and your friend Kelly appear to have had one thing in common before she left this world." My blood ran cold, and despite the fact he could not see my face, nor I his, I could hear the sneer in his voice as he uttered, "Your mothers. It's interesting how they both met an unfortunate and untimely death. Let's hope, like Kelly, you don't follow them down that path."

CHAPTER FIFTEEN

I walked as calmly as I could to my vehicle, collected my luggage, tossed it in the passenger seat, jumped into the driver's seat, casually putting it in gear as I pulled away. I even managed to conjure a toothy grin as I offered Edwards' minion a finger wave when I passed his hulking frame.

He did not reciprocate.

I exited the parking lot, drove several blocks while looking in my rear-view mirror before pulling onto a side street and into a public parking lot. Once safely tucked into a spot between two massive SUVs, I turned the vehicle off. Trembling with fear as an undercurrent of anger vibrated, I pummeled the steering wheel while my emotions were shaken like a Bond martini, without the satisfaction of knowing that first heavenly sip was on the horizon.

I stopped torturing the poor steering wheel, only because my hands throbbed in pain. I was silent for a moment as I listened to the beating of my heart, as heavy and rapid as the sound emitted from a bass drum. A bead of sweat trickled down the side of my face, and though it stung, I let it drop into my lap, forming a blotchy spot on my somewhat clean jeans.

Hysterics got the best of me as I burst out laughing, despite my frustration. Even to my ear, it sounded crazed and maniacal, but it was better than the alternative.

I had faced Edwards down. Alone. And we'd both lived.

I smirked, reaching for my phone. I knew one person who would revel in the tale of my adventure. Leah. But when I received voicemail, a pang of sadness and guilt washed over me and plucked at my heartstrings. I hoped she was merely busy—doing Leah-type things—and not avoiding me altogether.

Dismissing that thought, I started the vehicle and made my way to Logan's, testing my sanity as I attempted to focus on the busy roadways instead of rehashing my chat with Edwards, as one-sided as it had been.

I approached the condo and was surprised to find his vehicle missing as I pulled in front. Surely, given my delay, he should have made it here before I did? Had he doubled-back to find me? I was in the process of dialing his cell number when he pulled up behind me.

Logan surveyed me as he approached, frowning at what he saw. "What's up?"

"Edwards," I grounded out, causing it to sound more like a dirty word.

"I think we're gonna need adult beverages for this one," he replied solemnly, collecting the bags from my vehicle and striding toward his condo.

Once settled in—canine with food and water bowls filled, humans with adult refreshment in hand—I relayed the events that transpired after he and Nicoh had left the hotel. When I finished, I looked up. Logan's brow was furrowed as he balled his hands into fists. He didn't seem to notice my gaze and jumped when I spoke.

"Well?"

"Well, I'm pissed for one."

"I get that." I nodded at his hands, causing him to look down and then place them on his thighs. "But…"

"But I'm also not surprised. Typical Edwards' tactics." When I tilted my head, he huffed out a breath. "This isn't the first time he's used intimidation—or I suppose, his unique power of persuasion—to elicit the results he wants."

"Go on…" I gathered there was more to his statement than mere speculation.

Logan frowned, but proceeded to relay instances of the man: hiring ringers to blindside the prosecution, dredging up skeletons in the star witness' past at the last minute and employing heavy-handed tactics to deal with problematic witnesses and even judges, prosecutors and their staffs were among them.

It seemed there was nothing or no one that was out of bounds for Terrence Edwards. I wondered if it wasn't as much for him as it was for his clients. Even though their wallets were seemingly limitless, they were only surpassed by their lawyer's ego.

Logan finished things off with one of his personal interactions with the man. I was disgusted but again, not surprised.

"And, in case you hadn't gotten a clear picture of the man's character," he paused to shoot me a wry look, "my partner and I witnessed a situation considered common practice by Edwards—one that fell under the category of 'encouraging' unreliable witnesses," Logan continued, using finger quotes for emphasis.

"A few years ago—actually, I was still wet behind the ears then—I was working in West Hollywood. My partner and I pulled a double and got called to check out some suspicious activity in the alley behind one of the seedier dives on Santa Monica Boulevard. Turns out, one of the bartenders was selling the bar's liquor to minors out the back door whenever the manager went to have a quickie with his honey." Logan caught my expression and shrugged. "Hey, just quoting what the more reputable wits on the scene told us.

"Anyway, this barkeep was also offering the minors a quickie of their own for a quarter-hourly rate. Girls were not much older than the boys themselves." He grimaced and shook his head. "As it turns out, one of them was the property of a notoriously vicious businessman, who was unaware that this bartender was double-dipping."

"Double-dipping?"

"This businessman also owned the bar."

I winced. "Ooof. Harsh."

"It would have been a lot harsher for the bartender, but we rounded all of them up and hauled them to jail before the businessman could intervene to dole out his form of punishment."

"But what about the girl—wouldn't she have been in just as much trouble as the bartender, where the businessman was concerned? I mean, and I can't believe that I'm saying this, but if she *belonged* to him? Surely, she knew the rules. And by putting herself in the situation—"

Logan put up a finger. "Hang onto that thought for a minute. I was getting to that part." I gestured for him to proceed by making a zipping motion across my lips. "To answer your question, you would have thought it would have played out that way, but when we arrived at the station, we were immediately confronted by the businessman's high-powered criminal defense attorney."

I groaned. "Let me guess, Edwards?"

"Almost as bad." As I presently considered no one on this planet to be "almost as bad" as Edwards, I twisted my mouth into what probably looked like a cross between The Joker and Billy Idol, causing Logan to cough into his hand to mask a chuckle before he continued. "No, he sent one of his minions to do the job."

"Hmm, apparently, the client wasn't *that* important," I replied. "Wait—by 'minion,' you don't mean the thug from the impromptu SUV shakedown?"

"No, the guy was supposedly an associate of the firm. Apparently, they've lowered the bar, no pun intended, on who they hand licenses out to these days." He shook his head. "I honestly don't know why a person who had a legitimate interest in law and justice—and who'd endured the rigors of law school—could throw all that and their morals out the window to work for someone like Edwards."

"I can think of one big reason."

"Yeah, *that*." He shook his head, frowning. "It's still pretty disappointing, though."

"The world can be a pretty disappointing place, Logan. If we allow it to be."

"Touché. Long story short, this lawyer and his entourage prevented us from entering our station, thrusting papers and spouting legal jargon at us just as the media circus erupted out of nowhere, adding to the chaos. The higher-ups attempted to control the scene, but the whole thing was a well-scripted act."

"Let me get this straight—the circus was staged by Edwards' firm." I didn't pose a question because I already knew the answer. Logan's pursed his lips and shrugged. "So what, you had to let them all go?"

"Not all of them," Logan murmured. "Just one."

"Let me guess. The businessman's property…err, girl?" I released a frustrated breath as he nodded. "Convenient."

"Yup, especially when you consider the identity of this property."

The way he said it gave me pause.

"What am I missing here, Logan? *Who* was she?"

I sucked in a breath as he uttered the name.

"Danielle."

CHAPTER SIXTEEN

Perhaps I had a delayed reaction to Logan's bombshell, but it explained the strange feeling there was more to their history than he had previously alluded to, and I said as much. I tilted my head when Logan offered a sheepish nod.

"Geez, Logan. You didn't think this was worth mentioning before now?" I clucked my tongue when he shrugged, causing him to glance in my direction before quickly averting his eyes.

Another moment passed before he responded. "I honestly don't think she remembers the incident. There were probably others in her past that were similar—actually, I know there were." When I shot him my best frowny face, he returned one of his own.

"The Danielle we encountered today was nothing like the girl I hauled in years ago. No matter how much she wants to try to maintain that illusion."

An illusion for who? I thought. For us? Or for herself?

And who, exactly, was Logan trying to convince?

I let it pass, tackling the prior part of his statement instead. "Whether Danielle remembers it or not, being used as a commodity is as much of a crime as anything. Against her boss at the very least."

He nodded. "You would think. Of course, in the underworld, they don't play by the same laws."

"Doesn't seem like they'd trouble themselves with something as contrite as the notion of laws," I replied.

Logan gave a so-so gesture with his hand. "You'd probably be surprised. They have more than you'd think. Then again, most of them fall on the scale of life versus death."

I didn't doubt it, but my interests were elsewhere. "Hmm....so Danielle?"

"What about her?"

I nailed him with a glare. Tap dancing didn't suit him, but if he wanted me to take the lead, I was more than prepared.

"It's quite a coincidence, don't you think? Her mother worked for Edwards' family. Danielle is associated with one of his clients. Both lead back to Decker's family." Logan nodded but wouldn't look at me. I grabbed his sleeve. "What? What aren't you telling me?"

He looked at my grip on his shirt, making no move to break free. "Nothing."

I increased my grip, this time connecting with his arm. "Listen, Logan, you need to be straight with me. Right. Now. Is there anything I need to know that you're not telling me with regards to Danielle? Or Decker's request? 'Cause it sure feels like you're holding out."

He sighed. "I didn't tell you about Danielle because it wasn't relevant. Or, at least, it didn't appear to be, but when you connect the dots and add in Edwards showing up to issue a "suggestion"? Yeah, it's starting to get too close for comfort."

I didn't mention that everything prior to that had been too close for comfort, and yet he hadn't deemed it necessary to tell me until

I'd called him out. I let it pass. I needed time—away from him—to think about all of this, decide where I wanted to go with it, and whether I trusted him enough to continue accepting his involvement.

Unfortunately, that mental detox would need to wait, as Logan, still present and accounted for, transitioned the conversation. "So, what's the plan?"

I chewed a nail. "Well, barring any other impromptu sidebars, we'll proceed as previously discussed and give a go at tracking down people who knew Decker's family. There's probably not many left in their apartment complex, but perhaps those that are could give us a lead or two, or help us to locate some of the other former residents.

"There's also Auntie Mae, who may be our best bet when it comes to identifying an Ellen-Edwards connection. If anything, she should be able provide insights on the personal side of some of these people's lives during that time."

Logan nodded. "You never know what people remember now that may not have been relevant at the time. Once you collect all the threads, they start taking on the shape of something recognizable."

Unless that shape took on the form of a big tangled ball of string, I mused but kept my thoughts to myself. Logan's spirits seemed higher than I would have expected given the current state of things.

"If we're going to make short work of this, perhaps it's best to divide and conquer. I could track down Mae. You could do a run-through on the remaining residents at the apartment building and see where that leads." I had my reasons for wanting to separate from Logan.

He surveyed me for a moment too long, making me wonder if his coply senses tipped him off. What did he see when he looked at me? I held his gaze, and finally, he nodded.

"I think you're onto something. Either way, I'm not holding

out hope for a brass ring."

"Even grabbing a tarnished one would be better than nothing," I reminded him.

"So it seems."

"Do you think we should call first to make sure these people are even home or will even see us?"

"No." His tone was sharp, but he quickly added, "Doing so will give them too much time to consider and allow them the opportunity to change their minds."

"Or filter what they remember."

"Exactly," Logan replied. "In my experience, hitting them out of the gate gets the freshest recall."

"And perhaps the most honest," I murmured.

We hammered out the specifics over takeout Thai and decided to start fresh the next morning. As we wrapped up for the day and Logan showed me to the guest room, I asked about Mia, as he'd made no mention of returning to his friend's to collect her.

I'd noticed Nicoh cautiously sniffing around but never messing with anything that clearly belonged to the formidable German Shepherd. Finally, he chose a spot to rest, and before long, was snoring softly, his paws flopping as he chased his puppy dreams. And possibly, a beauty names Mia.

"She'll be fine," had been Logan's response before changing the subject.

Not that I thought there was anything was wrong with Mia, but it was another mystery that Logan held close. Each one stacked on top of another intensified my curiosity. My spidey senses also told me to keep my eyes peeled, so while Logan harbored secrets, I felt compelled to push him away and keep that watchful eye.

Something was amiss, and until I figured out what, I needed to keep him at arm's length.

As it turned out, he was easier to evade than I'd anticipated.

The next morning I awoke, confused by my surroundings. Lack of sleep hadn't helped matters as I tossed and turned. At some point, Nicoh had made his way to the guest room and was now sprawled against the bed, preventing me from exiting unless I hyper-extended my legs to leap past his snoring frame. I have long legs, so that should say something.

Wandering into the kitchen, I noted how neat and tidy Logan kept everything and was a bit annoyed that a bachelor with a dog could keep his place in better shape than two grown women with one dog. Then again, even after Leah had moved out, things had not improved, so he'd bested me on equal footing.

The smell of coffee snared me in its trap and drew me in like a mouse to deliciously stinky cheese. Attached to the pot, Logan had a left a note: "Had some things to take care of. Will tackle the residents at the apartment complex, as discussed. Key is on the counter. Let's compare notes over dinner. 7 pm. Your choice."

I absently poured a cup as Nicoh nudged my hand, reminding me that although we were out of town, he still had canine needs. I collected his lead, grabbed the key, and walked him through the neighborhood as I plotted out my day, sans Logan. I had already mapped Auntie Mae's address and figured I'd head that way, even though I had no idea whether she'd be home.

Larissa had mentioned that she had moved from L.A. to Newport Beach years earlier and had provided her address. And though she'd admitted it had been a while since she'd touched base with the woman, she had not mentioned on whose side the lapse had fallen. Then again, Auntie Mae had been her mother's friend first, and perhaps the conversations became difficult after Maria's stroke.

After collecting a few necessities for the trip, I checked my phone for messages one final time before Nicoh and I piled into the vehicle and hit the road. With decent traffic, we'd make it to the beach community by noon.

I'd wanted to take the time to enjoy the sights—I hadn't been on a road trip by myself in a long time—but before I hit the city limits, my mind was already wandering to other places not on the path to my destination. More specifically, to people and the questions swirling around them.

Why hadn't Leah called back? What was she doing? How was she doing? Did she miss talking to me as much as I did her? Would she ever forgive me? And if she did, would she come home?

Ditto for Ramirez. Nearly as painful as losing my best friend, only on a completely different level.

What was Martin, my bio-pop up to these days? He'd been unusually quiet—even for him—in the days since I'd last seen him and I could have used some fatherly advice after Leah had departed, but those messages, like Leah's, had fallen on deaf ears.

That led me to my present predicament, which I owned. I had placed myself here.

What was up with Logan? He had been firm about not wanting to be involved in bringing Decker's mother's killer to justice at the start, but the minute I put things in motion, he was front and center, almost directing the action. Why was that? And why had he been evasive about previously knowing Danielle?

And let's not forget his erratic behavior—not picking up Mia, talking off without notice. I sighed. I hadn't really known him that well, and on the occasions we had spoken, he'd not been forced to show his true colors. If this was the section of the color palette he played in, I wanted no part of it.

Where was Danielle? Why had she shown up, only to bail? How much of what she said was carefully crafted for our benefit?

Lastly…why, Decker? Why me? What was it you saw that compelled you to charge me with this task?

If you couldn't bring your mother's killer to justice, how the hell could I?

CHAPTER SEVENTEEN

I hadn't been to the Newport Beach community to spend any length of time for years, and for as much that had changed, just as much had stayed the same. Sure, new quaint shops, wine bars and micro-pubs had popped up, but the easy-going vibe of the locals remained.

I watched as people strolled, hand-in-hand, and laughed as their pups darted in and out of the water, attempting to fetch a bit of stray seaweed. No sooner had one come away victorious, the other snatched it, running to his humans to show-off. Before long, the episode started over and the victors swapped places.

Looping through the neighborhoods, I rechecked my GPS before pulling up in front of my destination.

Mae Santini had done well for herself in the years since she had moved from L.A. Larissa hadn't mentioned an occupation, other than to say that Mae was self-sufficient, alluding to the fact she had never married.

Her residence, just a short walk from the beach, was a lovely cottage nestled among several in a string along the street. Surrounded by a white picket fence, framed by rose bushes with a cobblestone walkway leading up to the curved archway, Mae's home was something straight out of a fairytale. Even the healthy-looking cat licking its paws on the step guarding the door looked whimsical, as though cast for the part. It paused to give me a cursory once-over as I opened the car door. If it sensed Nicoh, it gave no indication, returning to its leisurely grooming.

"Stay here, buddy," I murmured as Nicoh huffed and whimpered upon spotting the feline.

I rolled the windows down a notch as I got out and shut the door firmly. He huffed before turning around so that he could stare out the opposite window.

"Point taken." I chuckled, smoothing down my ponytail as a proceeded up the walkway, suddenly nervous.

I hadn't decided what I would say but figured directness and honesty would be the best route.

Sidestepping the cat, who'd been too busy to bother with the likes of a human, I was about to use the extravagant brass knocker when the door opened.

"Alabaster, where have you—oh, my!" the woman exclaimed, placing a hand to her chest.

If she had been friends with Maria, Mae Santini would have been well into her sixties. But either the woman had Raquel Welch's bloodline, or she had paid for the luxury of looking like she could give women half her age a run for their money.

Her auburn curls bounced loosely on her shoulders, framing her unlined, heart-shaped face. Her eyes were a luminous shade of green, set off by dark, pillowy lashes I would have killed for. Her nose was pert and the angel's bow of her lips formed a permanent upward curve.

Mae was nearly my height and lean in a fit, toned way. She looked comfortable, yet somehow elegant in her white beach-combers and sandals that were paired with a vibrant green three-quarter t-shirt that matched her eyes. Other than a single horse-shoe pendant she wore around her neck, she was devoid of any other accessories or makeup, as though she was the focal point of her own masterpiece.

Quickly, I stuck out a hand. "Hi, I'm Arianna. Arianna Jackson." Only after the words came out did I notice how shaky they sounded.

Her mouth quirked at the corner as she shook my hand. Her grip was firm. "Well, hello, Arianna Jackson. What brings you to my door this afternoon? I don't see any cookies, so I take you're not trying to ply me with sweets. And, I'm pretty sure I already provided my census data." She paused and, after taking in my expression, chuckled.

"Come on in. And don't worry, I don't bite. But he might." She winked as she nodded at the cat, who was content with ignoring me. I knew better, however, than to turn my back on a feline, and gave him an "eyes on you" gesture before Mae glanced over her shoulder.

"Can I get you anything? Iced tea? Lemonade? I apologize, but I don't have any coffee. The weather is just too warm to bother brewing a pot."

After taking in the cottage's interior, I had to close my mouth to prevent myself from drooling before answering. She chuckled before gesturing me to follow her through the house. Like its owner, it was casual, yet elegant with an upscale beachy feel. Though it wasn't ostentatious, I had seen similar pieces of furniture in some of the higher-end shops in Scottsdale and was pretty sure the artwork was original as well.

I must have murmured something to that effect out loud because Mae patted me on the arm and laughed. "Thank you, dear. I think my style rocks, too."

I was sure my cheeks were a deep shade of red as she led me to the patio on the back of the house. Of course, I exasperated the situation, gasping as I walked through the door before quickly glancing over my shoulder. Had we teleported to another world? For as Hansel and Gretel-ish the front of the house was, the back opened up into an experience in and of itself.

If I left with nothing more, the view of the ocean was worth the price of admission. Just off the patio was Mae's garden backyard, a marvel of twisted vines and foliage with a small gate leading to the beach below.

Mae smiled broadly as she waited for me to settle into the freshly painted wicker furniture, only distinct because the scent of turpentine and acrylic cut through the brininess of the salt air.

"How can I help you, Ms. Jackson? I assume this is about Kelly's mother, Ellen?"

My gaze tore from the scenic view and before I could speak, she quickly added, "Larissa called to let me know that I might be receiving a call from you." She offered a pointed glance.

"Uh, yeah, well…I needed some fresh air and figured I'd get as far as I could, then phone you." My excuse sounded feeble even to my own ears.

"Ah yes, as an old biddy, I'd be sure to be bundled up, talking all by my lonesome to my herd of cats until the mailman or grocery delivery person happened by."

"I think it's called a clowder."

Mae squinted. "Excuse me?"

"A group of cats, that is. Or a glaring, if there is uncertainty among the group."

"I see. And what do they call a grouping of cats that encounter that massive canine that's drooling all over the front seat of your vehicle?" She nodded toward the front of the house.

I muttered a curse. Darn dog knew better than to sit in the command chair. That was reserved for the captain…me. He'd just been downgraded from first mate to swabby. "That would be called a cluster. Add your own flavor to the end of that term, if you like."

Mae tilted her head back. The sound of her laughter blended into the breeze like tinkling chimes. "Larissa said you had spunk."

I waved a hand. "Nah, my best friend's the one with all the spunk. Me, I'm just prone to a stubborn, obstinate streak as of late."

She gave me a curious look, but I shifted the conversation before we got too far off-track.

"How much did Larissa tell you?"

"Just the basics of what you were up to, that you might be calling." I dipped my head in apology, having sidestepped that common courtesy, but she waved a hand. "She also asked me, pleaded with me actually, to help you in any way that I could in the name of justice."

"How well did you know Decker's...err, Kelly's, mom?"

"Oh, as well as anyone, I guess. Never saw her much, between work, school, her family, and me doing my thing. We were, as they say, passing ships. Don't get me wrong, she was nice enough, and everybody liked her, but the fact is that I saw more of that little pumpkin than I ever did of her mom, as much as those kids were over at my house or running in that pack like they did."

I nodded, having been part of a pack like that myself when I was younger—Leah and I either spent our time at my house or hers and our friends typically followed suit—our parents easily accommodating our requests, as it gave them peace of mind that we were safe, just kids being kids. Then again, we'd been at each other's houses, not at the home of a random adult. As if sensing the question, Mae promptly intervened.

"As a friend of Maria's, I was a natural choice. Plus, everyone knew me from the neighborhood or had grown up themselves at my place." When I raised a brow, she added. "In a neighborhood where most people lived the apartment life, we had a house with a yard and a fully-decked out basement, complete with pool table, pinball machines, a commercial popcorn maker, and a fridge filled with sodas."

"Wow…" was all I could manage, though my expression must have said it all as she chuckled.

"My father was considered an institution in our community. It was natural for kids and adults alike to gravitate toward him." She chuckled, but a hint of sadness filtered in.

"Was he a teacher at the school, or a coach?" I asked.

She shook her head, chuckling again. "Oh, nothing like that. He worked for one of the local baseball teams in various roles throughout his career. He was always big on getting kids and families involved in the community, and getting them down to the ball field to take in a game was one way he thought he could promote that.

"He was known for doing random stuff, like rounding up a group of kids doing nothing or likely up to no good and either giving them tickets or loading them all into his truck and taking them to a game himself. He'd also give tickets to families—many of whom couldn't have afforded such luxuries otherwise. Before long, kids would show up after school, offering to mow the yard, trim the bushes, whatever, in exchange for a round of pool in the basement, or just a much-needed reprieve from the stresses of home life.

"Same went for the adults. He'd host barbecues and end up offering counsel to either the husband or wife or both. He saved more than one marriage over the years, not to mention kept a lot of kids out of trouble and probably more out of jail."

"He sounds like quite a man."

"He was." Mae's eye cast down. "Quite a man."

"And a great father, I would imagine," I added, catching her off-guard as her eyes snapped up, squinting as she focused on mine.

"What?" Her brow furrowed as her face and body language

transformed from mirroring her surroundings to something that was dark and filled with rage. And dangerous.

I bit my lip in an attempt to collect my wits and my words, before managing to utter, "Um, I was just saying that a man with that disposition would probably be an equally good father."

Whatever it was, it slipped away as easily as it had arrived as Mae shrugged, focusing on the ocean. "The community *was* his family."

The crispness of her tone suggested that the subject was a sore one, and as I was here by her good graces, I decided not to press her further.

"I get that, having a house that everyone gravitates to," I replied after a moment.

She nodded absently. "Yeah, when we grew up, the tradition continued, for a while, anyway. I mean, when we were kids, Maria, Max and the rest of us all hung out here and we turned out alright, so why not pass the benefit onto our kids?"

I didn't point out that she was lacking on that last part, but was interested in a nugget that I had not known. "So you and Maria grew up with Kelly's dad?"

"Oh, sure. Sorry, I figured someone had already mentioned that to you." She scrunched her nose when I shook my head. "We were basically raised in the same crib." She paused to chuckle, a wide grin crossing her face. "And if you think I'm exaggerating, I'm not. Pretty sure Kelly inherited the one we'd all chewed the paint off at one point or another. Of course, Ellen repainted it, but you get the gist."

I nodded. "Must have been like having one big extended family." When she nodded, I added, "Did you all go to the same school?"

"For the most part. There were times when someone would phase out—the family would move, or the parents got divorced and the kids were shuffled back and forth—but Maria, Max and I made it through together."

"Your dad must have loved that, having a built-in family," I murmured.

"He did, especially considering Max was the son he always wanted…" A tiny frown escaped the corner of her mouth as the words faded out.

Had I noted a touch of disapproval in her tone? Jealousy? Or something more?

Rather than allowing her to dwell on something that could potentially distract her from the matter at hand, I quickly redirected.

"It definitely seems natural, that the children of the people who grew up so closely would follow in their parent's shoes."

She shrugged. "It was a natural transition. As much as neighborhoods can feel like a wool blanket that keeps us comfy and safe in a winter storm, they also evolve as time passes and the world outside changes. Businesses close. People move away. New faces appear. Sometimes, it seemed safer to stay in the confines of that blanket rather than risk getting an unexpected and unwelcomed case of frostbite."

I mentally questioned the sincerity of her comment. If it were true, why had each of them left its comfort? She, by her very presence here in Newport Beach, was a divergence from that sentiment. So why had she left? Had it been an attempt to escape her father's legacy? Had its safety and comfort ended up smothering her?

The questions were endless, but I rounded back to the matter at hand.

"What do you remember about Larissa, Kelly, and Danielle—over the years?" When she tilted her head and shrugged, I added, "Not a play-by-play of every time you interacted with them, but what stands out the most? Considering they spent as much time as they did with you, it must have seemed like you were all family."

Though I was curious why she hadn't married and had a child of her own to add to that equation, I didn't mention it as it wasn't my place. Perhaps she enjoyed a child-free life but delighted in having them around on a strictly temporary basis, assuming the crew went home at night.

Until they didn't.

I thought about Danielle, who had left the nest to seek out solace in drugs and prostitution. Had the breakup of their little group after Decker's death created a fracture that never healed? If so, Larissa had seemed to weather the storm until it took its toll on her mother. How long had they suffered, though, before escaping to Arizona?

Decker lost her connection to the group when her father moved her from the environment where her mother's murder occurred. It seemed like a kind, fatherly gesture, except when you considered his lifelong obsession with finding his wife's killer, and how that obsession had transferred to his daughter.

And now, she too was dead.

One could say the two weren't even remotely related, but Decker's father's choice of professions had rubbed off on her and sent her down that same path every time she threw herself into a new case. It was almost like she had been trying to appease her father while solving other people's challenges or saving their lives.

It was something she couldn't offer her father. Or her mother.

And, unfortunately, in the end, it had led to her demise.

"You've heard about Kelly's death." It was not posed as a question because I already knew the answer but hoped she would expound without prodding.

Mae did not disappoint, nodding as a frown clouded her face.

"I did. Words can't seem to appropriately express how…

pained I was to hear about the circumstances surrounding…" she sucked in a breath, and looked toward the sky, before she continued, "how she passed. Tragic that it ended like her mother's did—in violence." She paused, biting her lip, her eyes focused on her hands, which seemed unsure if they wanted to remain folded or not. Finally, she unlaced them and stretched each across a thigh, exposing long, slender fingers.

"If Max was still alive, it would have surely killed him. Don't get me wrong, the man was as strong and as stubborn as a bull. Kept most things bottled up. I'm sure you know the type." She released a sad chuckle when I nodded. "Though he worked hard to make sure Kelly was okay—or as okay as a traumatized kid could be after losing her mother—he was really never the same after the murder." She paused, and her fingers twined together as she stared at them, frowning. "I mean, how could he be…okay? How could anything ever be right in the world again…after something so tragic?"

The question was not for me, so I remained silent, allowing her to proceed when she was ready.

"To cope, rather than expressing his feelings emotionally, he became obsessed with finding Ellen's killer, and eventually, it encompassed everything he lived and breathed. If that's how you were conditioned, was it any wonder that Kelly grew up the same? If anything, she must have felt compelled to join her father in his mission, believing it was her destiny to do so. Perhaps she thought she owed it to both him and her mother, especially at the end, when he was no longer physically capable of continuing on. Whatever…it's obvious she ran with that torch, right up until the day she…left us."

Once again, it seemed as though "death" was a word that Mae couldn't bring herself to utter. I bore no judgment but wanted to tuck it away for future reference.

"It's hard to wrap your mind around. Here was a child who

lost her childhood to the darkest form of evil, yet became an adult who was consumed by it, until it devoured her. Hardly seems fair, does it?"

"When was the last time you saw Kelly?" I asked, after contemplating whether to pose the question.

Mae's eyes widened. "Wow, I don't know. It was probably a month or so before she died."

"How did that come about?" I pressed.

She shot me a wry smile. "Pretty much the same way you showed up."

Before I could offer up another lame apology, she waved a hand and continued, "Mind you, she was a little less polite than you were about it, but being raised by Max and not her mother, she did tend to take on some of his brashness. Not much patience for the small talk."

I nodded and shrugged. Decker was what she was—forthcoming, blunt, and unapologetic about it.

"Basically came right out and stated her intention to bring her mother's killer to justice."

"She...said it just like that?" I withheld a chuckle. It did sound like Decker.

"Yup, I would have figured she would need to identify who the killer was first, but something told me she already had her mind wrapped around that one."

"Did she say who?"

"You didn't need to be a rocket scientist to figure out who she'd set her sights on, but I was hoping she'd put her ducks in a row before she went down that path."

"She didn't...make it that far."

"Well, obviously." Mae pursed her lips. "The whole world would have heard about it. Even all the way out here." She rolled her eyes, flipping a hand in the air. "Anyway, it's probably for the best that she didn't."

I frowned. At the cost of Decker's life? It was the only thing that had kept that train from moving forward. I didn't care for the quip but elected to move on.

"You have doubts?"

She shrugged but said nothing. The firm set of her mouth said she probably wouldn't. Another thing I had to wonder about—Edwards was a powerful man, but offering commentary about his innocence or guilt to a stranger seemed innocuous enough, and posed Mae seemingly little threat.

"Did you know that Kelly was trying to track Danielle down before her death?" I finally asked.

Mae shook her head. "She didn't mention it, though I'd heard they lost touch."

I mulled that over and continued. "Were you aware of Danielle's…challenges? How she changed after the murder?"

"Of course, though she always was high strung. So it's hard to say whether she would have turned out that way regardless."

"Regardless of being present when a woman was brutally murdered?" Though I hadn't intended it, words came tumbling out.

Mae frowned at me. "Well, I'm sure the child was traumatized, as was Kelly, but it certainly didn't transform her into the little twit she became afterward." She shook her head. "Nope, sometimes no matter how well you tend to the hens which supply them or the impressiveness of the stock they come from, they just don't produce good eggs. That…in an eggshell, is Danielle."

It was an interesting, if not odd, analogy, and I wondered whether there was a double meaning behind it. Considering how tight-lipped she'd been about the prior queries, figured this first go-around was not the time to press it. One thing was clear: there was no love lost between Mae and Danielle.

"So, I take it that you've not seen nor heard from her for some time?"

Mae shook her head. "It's definitely been a while. Before they moved. Maria was pitching a fit about her behavior. Had kicked her out."

So, before Maria's stroke, I thought.

"Anything specific driving her frustration on this particular occasion?"

She waved a hand. "Oh gosh, Danielle was always threatening something. Or someone."

"And this time?" I prompted.

"If memory serves, she was threatening to go to her father, tell him about the atrocities her mother had forced her to endure."

"I thought Danielle didn't know who her father was?"

Mae shot me a dark look. "I wouldn't know about that. Then again, Danielle was always quite the little drama queen, like some other people we both know."

Something about the way she said it sent chills up my spine and made me wonder if she wasn't all that disappointed that none of the people from her past were no longer part of her world, or no longer alive to remind her about the role she'd played in it.

CHAPTER EIGHTEEN

I might have missed it had I not been looking right at her, but after her heated delivery of that comment, Mae bit her lip. Had she said too much?

I decided to take a stab at whatever *it* was. "You're not suggesting Maria's condition is—"

She waved a hand to cut me off and shook her head. "She probably did have an episode, brought on by stress…whatever… but I was just saying that Danielle would take liberties with the drama whenever she felt it benefited her cause. Or when she thought she could get a rise out of her mother. As if Maria didn't have enough of her own challenges."

I could think of one big one. "How'd she get the job working for Terrence Edwards' wife?"

"Huh, I would have thought that either Kelly or Larissa would have filled you in on that." I shrugged and used my hand to encourage her to continue.

"My father, as I mentioned, had a certain amount of clout in our community. At first, he only knew Terrence Edwards as a passing acquaintance, but as Edwards gained momentum at his firm, he started showing up around the community, making sure his name got out there, and he was seen by those whose word mattered."

I didn't really take Edwards as a man of the people, but if it was important to those he worked for, then he probably would have held a stinky baby if it put him in the favor of potential future clients, especially the ones with influence, like Mae's father. The image almost made me laugh.

Almost.

"Anyway, back to the job Maria was hired for. After having a succession of kids over the course of a few years, the young Mrs. Edwards' decided she'd had her fill of mommy duty and wasn't about to waste the remainder of her youth changing dirty diapers." When I arched a brow, she offered me a nod, followed by an abrasive chuckle.

"Rumor has it that the former debutante insisted on adding more people to her ever-expanding staff, which already included two cooks, a housekeeper and a nanny for each of the children. If she was to be seen on the arm of a rising star, after all, she needed additional support in the home so that she could tend to her own affairs. Big emphasis on 'her' if you get my drift."

I nodded, returning a tight smile. I'd encountered the type.

"Anyway, Pops happened to be at the ribbon-cutting of a new park that was part of a neighborhood revitalization project Edwards' firm spearheaded. Such involvement helped them keep a finger of the heartbeat of the goings-on in the community, which is precisely the way their 'clients' liked it." She paused to tap a finger against the side of her nose.

"Pops and Edwards had seen each other at a number of other community events and got to chatting, realized they knew some of the same people, frequented the same places, that sort of thing. On this particular occasion, Edwards mentioned his wife's desire for additional help around the house—presenting the job as it as a light housekeeping role with a particular focus on his wife's personal needs."

"Personal needs as in someone who could pull out each of her handbags and talk to them on a daily basis?" I joked, causing Mae to cover her mouth to mask a snicker. "Okay, so Mrs. Edwards hired a personal assistant."

"Oh no, from what Edwards told Pops, his wife was way too suspicious of those who worked for her, even though his description of the position was precisely that. Apparently, the missus has quite a sense of entitlement, with an ego to match."

Much like her husband, I mused.

"Pops knew Maria was looking for another job, and given his rave recommendation, the deal was sealed before Maria even had the opportunity to interview for the position."

"When the job was discussed, did Edwards ask your father if he had a recommendation? Or did your father just pull Maria off the top of his head and suggest her as a potential candidate?"

My question must have caught her off-guard because her eyes flashed to mine, and her mouth opened and closed before she responded, "I'm not sure. Why do you ask?"

Was that a hint of sharpness I detected?

Though her bristling interested me, I played it off with a casual shrug. "Just curious."

"Umm-hmm...." I felt the intensity of her gaze as she continued. "Anyway, the rest, as they say, was history. Maria was ecstatic when Pops told her about the 'opportunity.'" She exaggerated her finger quotes, stabbing at the air.

I murmured an appropriate sound, something between shock, interest, and distaste before asking, "Once she took the job, did she enjoy it?"

Mae shrugged. "It was as you said...a job. She needed one, and it dropped into her lap. What do you think?"

"I think working in those circumstances must have

been...challenging, but if it kept a roof over her family's head and ensured her children had food, clothes, etc., then I would say it was a necessity that couldn't be avoided."

"A necessary evil is more like it," she scoffed.

"I can imagine working for the rich and entitled had its challenges." When Mae frowned, I winked and added, "Believe me, I'd have trouble ensuring the shoes were sorted by the proper color, especially if I was expected to discern beige from tan. And if asked to dust a husband's clothing with the appropriate scent to keep other women away, I'd be tempted to pull out my handy can of insect repellent and spray him down instead."

Mae snorted and rolled her eyes, the tension easing from her face as the firm set of her lips transitioned into a small smile.

"If you only knew the half of it." She shook her head and chuckled, though it was not filled with humor. "Woman looks like a mouse—and plays the role well—but safely tucked behind the walls of that McMansion, she's all rat—fierce, snarling and downright evil...meaning, she'd gouge your eyes out before it got that far."

"According to Maria, of course." It hadn't escaped my notice that she seemed awfully close to "Maria's" story.

Her eyes snapped to mine and narrowed. "Of course."

I pressed my lips together, meeting her eyes as l contemplated my next segue.

"And that's why you feel responsible." It was not posed as a question.

There was a moment of quiet as she focused on the ocean before responding, "If I hadn't been so insistent that Pops use his connections to find Maria work, perhaps she would never have crossed paths with...those people."

"You can't blame yourself for trying to help your friend. I'm sure she appreciated it at the time." I paused to glance at her. She caught it and shrugged, though the frown had returned. "Had the situation been reversed, Maria would have done the same." When she shuddered, I realized my misstep and quickly added, "Helped you find a job, if you desperately needed one."

She relaxed a bit, but the mood had shifted—a sign my welcome was wearing thin. Hedging my bets, I bit the bullet, deciding I had nothing to lose by throwing the last nut at the elephant in the room.

"So...exactly how did Ellen play into this scenario?"

"I don't know what you mean," she snapped, her eyes narrowing.

"Somehow, she and Edwards crossed paths, yet she wasn't close to you or Maria. That leaves Max, who would have never recommended his wife for anything Edwards was involved in. So, how did they cross paths?"

"I have no idea. That...situation had nothing to do with Pops, Maria...or me...so our consciences are clear."

I hadn't suggested anything otherwise, though she'd quickly jumped on it. Obviously, something I'd said had gotten her all bristly and brought out the claws.

"Just seems like quite a coincidence is all," I replied, leaning back in my chair and folding my hands in my lap.

Mae surveyed me, and for a moment, I thought she was about to boot me out. Finally, she looked away.

"However Ellen became acquainted with Terrence Edwards was of her own doing."

"So you have no idea—"

She raised a hand. "Listen. Whatever you might have heard? Leave it alone. It's in the past. And that's where it will stay."

Her directness might have surprised me had I taken Auntie Mae at face value based on Larissa's memory of the woman. But having met her in the flesh, I'd witnessed snippets of inconsistency in a very short time. Perhaps they'd been lurking in the shadows all along, and my line of questioning had brought forth the very thing she feared.

The truth.

We were interrupted as a man emerged onto the porch.

"Mae?" His voice was breathless, and as he was clad head-to-toe in the most impressively-coordinated charcoal exercise ensemble that I couldn't have pulled off without a pit crew.

Sharp gray eyes peered from Mae to me and back, a deep frown causing only minute creases around his otherwise unlined face. I gauged him to be about her age—both looked much younger than their years—but either he'd had an exceptional surgeon, or his genes were superb, and even the slight graying at the temples of his amazingly lush full head of raven hair seemed to be placed simply for effect. He was about my height, with the lean build of a gymnast. Everything about him was screaming to be noticed. Even his tapping foot suggested he expected Mae to have rolled out the red carpet in preparation for his arrival.

"Mas, by all means, join us." Mae started to introduce us, but he waved her off, animatedly thumbing over his shoulder as he spoke.

"My God, Mae. There is a massive wolf out there. Just sitting in the driver's seat of someone's vehicle." I winced and was about to interject, but Mas ignored me and continued. "I passed by and I swear, the…beast…lunged at me from the window…drooling…snarling…"

"Probably rabid, too," Mae replied dryly. "He didn't bite you, did he?"

Mas' eyes went wide. "You don't think?"

She caught my eye and though I'd been biting the inside of my cheek, once she started laughing, I couldn't keep myself from joining in, which caused Mas to sputter and toss his hands up.

"This…is funny? And who the hell are you, anyway?"

Though he'd seen me, he hadn't acknowledged my presence,

and now that he had, he looked as though he'd smelled bad eggs after perusing me from head to toe. I think he actually sniffed, too, but Mae and I were still chuckling and I found myself withholding a deep desire to produce a poopie bag from my pocket.

It was empty, of course, but Mas didn't know that.

Mae interrupted my thoughts, pausing her laughter long enough to respond. "Mas…manners. This is Arianna Jackson. She's here to chat about Kelly Decker, who was a friend of hers before she passed."

If Mas was aware of the story, he feigned disinterest, as his interest was elsewhere. "And the dog?"

"Mine." I extended my hand to him, but he took a step back. "Don't worry. Shots are up to date." Mas offered me a doubtful look, though it was hard to tell because his face didn't move much. "For both of us." I nodded toward the front of the house where the beast wreaked havoc on the neighborhood, according to Mas.

His brows raised, and his mouth formed an "o" that was somewhere between shock and mortification. Mae shook her head and chuckled.

Scoffing at Mae's reaction, he smoothed his outfit and crossed his arms before turning his attention to me. "Well, you should do something about him. He *looks* menacing."

"He's not much into masks." I winked at Mae. "We tried at Halloween. Turned out to be a no-go on Nicoh's part." I deadpanned at Mas. "Something about costumes only being appropriate for *Cats* on Broadway.

Once he realized I was having some fun with him, Mas huffed and gave me a hard stare.

"You really shouldn't leave strange dogs alone in the vehicle."

"He's not strange. He's an Alaskan Malamute," I rebutted.

Mae shook her head, chuckling, intervening as Mas' lip curled. "Arianna couldn't bring him in because of Alabaster. I think it was very considerate of her to proceed without her canine when entering a new environment. That could have proven a real disaster, and I think you know it."

I gave her a nod of appreciation, but Mas' eyes never left me, and unless I was mistaken, the glare only intensified. It was hard to tell about the frown. That only seems to translate to the surface so much, though his ramrod composure suggested his hackles were raised.

It was my cue to leave.

Mas obviously thought it was his place to get the last word in. "As I said—"

I raised a hand. "Yeah, yeah, yeah…the dog looks menacing."

He attempted to pucker his lips as he narrowed his eyes. "*Well?*" He drew out the word as though doing an impersonation of Ted Knight's Judge Smails character in *Caddyshack*, though I doubted he'd ever seen the movie.

Even if he had, he was too far above mimicking catchphrases. Doing so would offend his ego.

"Don't we have a right to be concerned?" he snapped.

I thought he was using "we" a bit freely since Mae seemed more amused than distressed. I rolled my eyes and retorted, "Only at dinnertime," before giving Mae a final nod of thanks and making my dramatic exit.

CHAPTER NINETEEN

There was significantly more drool than I'd anticipated on the steering wheel when I returned. It amused me that Nicoh had retreated to the backseat and was now pretending to be asleep.

Of course, he'd had plenty of warning when Mas decided to trail me out and loudly slammed Mae's front door on my backside. Considering it wasn't his house, he had some nerve, but I was guessing that it gave Mae a bit of added amusement and I'd take the points to be in her favor any day.

After using my sleeve to clean up the mess, I slid behind the wheel and tugged the door shut. In my side mirror, I caught a glimpse of something—no, someone—familiar, but by the time I wrenched my head around to get a better look, he, she or it was gone.

And though recent events had made me question my sanity, my gut told me that I needed to watch my back. Before pulling away, I glanced at Mae's house, but no one was peering at me from beyond the cottage shutters, so I figured that Mas was back on the patio giving Mae an earful. Or perhaps, more interestingly, vice versa.

On a whim, I swung a U-turn and headed in the direction I thought I had seen my tail, with the hope of catching him at his own game and thought I spied a familiar vehicle turning onto a residential street a couple of blocks ahead.

I sped to the corner of the street and peered to my right, noting the vehicle was still in view. Did I follow it and risk being seen? Or worse, end up freaking out some soccer mom who would end up calling the police and get myself arrested for being creepy?

There was also the chance that I was wrong—Logan's other vehicle, his daily driver, was pretty common—and I'd end up wasting more time that we didn't have.

Turning the opposite direction, I released a laugh that was just diabolical enough to rouse Nicoh, as I saw an eye pop open in the rear-view mirror. I laughed again.

There was more than one way to find out if Logan had been the one following me.

* * *

A few hours later, I pulled in front of an apartment complex that had seen better days, even in this part of L.A. I gave myself a high-five for having the foresight to take notes when talking to Larissa. I would have never found her childhood residence otherwise. A man I estimated to be in his 70s was watering the yard with a hose that appeared to have a kink in it as he yanked it from side to side, cursing when a gush of water spurted out, drenching his front.

I jumped out of the vehicle and barely managed to untwist the kink before it snaked up and cracked him on the head. Once under control, he gave me an appreciative nod as he squished his way to the faucet, grumbling as he turned it off. Tossing the offending hose to the ground, he shook his head as he appraised the situation, which had left him a wet mess.

"Much appreciated, Miss. You saved me a bit of embarrassment from the wife, who delights in reminding me that I'm getting too darn old for this."

I nodded as I wrapped up the remaining coil of hose, though I doubted his appearance would go unnoticed by his wife.

The man chuckled as he glanced at me. "Believe me, having her witness the aftermath is much more tolerable than…that." He waved a hand at the now innocuous-looking hose. "Ben Jennings. Ben." He reached out a hand, and though it was wet, I grasped it.

"Pleased to meet you, Ben. Arianna Jackson."

"You as well, Ms. Jackson."

"Arianna, please…or even better, AJ." He squinted as he took me in then offered me a toothy smile. "AJ, it is." He looked at me then at Nicoh, who stuck his head out the back window and tongue flopping in amusement. "What's his name?" He tilted his head in my canine's direction.

"Nicoh," I replied, which caused said canine to emit a low whoo-whoo at the mention of his name.

"Well, you best fetch Nicoh and come on over and tell me what brings you here. I'll just pop in and get changed while you do, before the wife gets home and finds out I've been having fun again." Ben thrust his hands on his hips, which made him look like an urban scarecrow as he tilted his head toward the vehicle.

I did as he requested, and Nicoh, happy to stretch his legs, complied, leaning in for head scratches when Ben ventured out in fresh clothing.

He chuckled as Nicoh urged him closer with persistent grumblings. "He's got quite a personality on him, doesn't he?"

Nicoh swished his tail as the man used both hands to scratch his massive head.

"That he does." I smiled. "I'd like to say he was well-behaved, but honestly, it depends on the day."

Ben nodded, offering me a toothy grin. "Probably something to do with the breed."

"That too." I laughed.

"So, AJ and Nicoh, what brings you two all the way from the fine state of Arizona to our humble dwelling on this brilliant day?" Ben was not only polite, he was quite astute, having noted my license plate, even at the angle and distance he was standing from it.

I made a mental note to keep that in mind as I progressed. He would likely spot an omission, but some details were not for me to tell.

"I'm doing some background work for a friend regarding the murder of Ellen Decker several years ago. Are you familiar with the case?"

Ben squinted, gesturing for me to sit in one of the two plastic lawn chairs he had pulled out. "I am. Are you a private investigator, or a reporter?"

I took a seat and waited for him to do the same before responding, "No, nothing as exciting as that. I'm just a private citizen, trying to track down some of the residents that used to live here around that time, see if I could ask them a couple of questions that could help clear things up for my friend."

"As for the residents that were here, you're looking at it. Well, me and my wife. All the rest have either moved on. Or passed on. More on the latter side, I'm afraid, though I try my best to keep in touch with everyone who is still above-ground." He winked. "Before we go any further, I've gotta ask—if your friend has a curious streak, then why isn't he here asking the questions himself?"

Though I was there asking questions on behalf of Decker, the male pronoun caused me to stutter, as I remembered Logan was supposed to have already completed this task.

I paused to collect my thought before responding. "It's a she, and unfortunately, she's not in a position...." My voice wavered, causing Ben's brow to rise. "She's not able to be here. Believe me, she would if it were at all possible."

Ben pressed his lips together, surveying me for a moment before nodding. "I'll take your word for it. What would you like to know?"

"First off, I apologize for drumming this up again after so many years. I'm sure you were asked again and again by the investigators, and that it's been well documented, so I'll try to avoid being redundant on every question. At the same time, if something I ask sparks a memory, feel free to speak up, no matter how inconsequential it seems. You just never know." I shrugged.

"That seems fair. And truth be told, it was a long time ago, back when my brain was much sharper, so even if you asked me the same question a hundred times, I'd probably be lucky to remember you'd ever asked it." He winked.

"Good to know I won't need to wipe your mind when I leave," I teased, causing him to chuckle.

Once the laughter had died down, I proceeded. "Were you and your wife here that night?"

He shook his head, frowning. "Back then, it was our bowling night, followed by some cocktails with friends. By the time we returned, all hell had broken loose. Bill Saunders, the apartment manager back then, before I took over—he's deceased now—was the one who found her...them." He turned his head and gazed out into the distance.

"What made Mr. Saunders go to the apartment that night?"

"Someone called, said that there was some noise coming from the unit, a possible domestic disturbance."

"Another resident?"

"At the time, Bill said no, that the person wouldn't identify themselves. He didn't recognize the voice either, and before you ask, he wasn't sure whether it was a male or female." I nodded, thankful that Ben's memory was better than he had implied.

"Not that I would wish it on anyone, but the wife and I were always thankful that we hadn't been there to witness it. It haunted Bill for years. Man had fought in wars and said that night was the only thing that gave him the sort of nightmares they did."

"I can't imagine it ever gets easier to witness that sort of violence, whether in war or otherwise."

Ben frowned, shaking his head. "Bill said it took pure evil to have done something like that, but it wasn't Ellen's murder that kept him up at night—it was finding those girls stashed in the closet. Little Danielle was hysterical once they got her out—they had to sedate her to keep her from hurting herself. Kelly, on the other hand? He said she just looked…lost. Like she'd woken up and the world had changed."

"It had." He offered me a solemn nod. "In the days prior, was there anything that stuck out to you? Any unusual events, conversations, occurrences? Any people or vehicles in the vicinity that seemed out of place or deliveries or service workers?" To each, Ben shook his head.

"How did the residents get along?"

"What you mean to ask is—how did the residents get along with the Decker family?" Ben was sharp, and all I could do was shrug and nod before he continued.

"I hate to sound cliché, but they were pretty normal, as far as people go. The wife was quiet and kept to herself, but was always very polite and gracious when addressed. Some might have been a bit green-eyed about her—she was almost too good to be true. It didn't help that she was incredibly and unknowingly beautiful. You almost couldn't help but look." Ben cast his eyes down as his cheeks flushed.

"What about Mr. Decker?" I prompted.

He scratched his head absently. "He was a bit rough around

the edges but noble to the core. Many of the residents—who were older—liked having a cop-like presence in the building, even though he wasn't in law enforcement. It made no difference. And I think he liked it too. He always kept a watchful eye on things around here and made sure everyone in residence was safe and secure."

"Except on that night," I murmured.

"Except on that night," he repeated. "If memory serves, he was working a case. I don't think he ever forgave himself for that, or for not finding Ellen's killer. He passed recently, you know."

I nodded, then shifted the subject away from Max. "I'd heard the girls typically stayed over at one another's whenever a parent was working late.

Ben chuckled. "Probably even more than that. Bill threatened —teasing, of course—that they were wearing a path in the carpet from one apartment to the next. Danielle's older sister was thankfully away that night, otherwise…" He shook his head and the smile shifted into a grim line. "Another child's life…damaged."

I didn't mention the toll it had taken on Larissa and the guilt she continued to endure as a result of the events of that night.

"What about other friends—from school, church, whatever?"

"Not that I remember. Three of 'em were thick as thieves though, at least until that night." Ben was quiet for a moment, absently scratching Nicoh. "Do you mind if I pose a question of my own? Outside of your *friend's* inquiry?" He paused to study me.

I noted that he had placed emphasis on "friend's" but tried not to relay that I had noticed, simply gesturing for him to proceed.

"You said that you weren't in law enforcement or a P.I. So, exactly what is your chosen profession?"

I smiled. "I'm a photographer. A sole proprietor of Mischievous Malamute Photography, aptly named after my cohort here."

He chuckled. "That makes sense. And while I can only

assume the name is fitting, your profession comes as no surprise to me at all."

I tilted my head, "Why is that?"

"Well, like law enforcement or private investigation, you have to really listen to people, deduce things that others don't, *see* what they can't."

I nodded slowly. I hadn't thought of it that way.

"I wish you and your friend much luck. If Ellen's killer is still alive and kicking, then I hope you find him and do whatever it is that you plan on doing to him."

"He will be brought to justice."

"There are many definitions of justice, AJ." He tilted his head, and for a moment, I thought he would continue.

When he didn't, I offered him a single nod and leaned in to shake his hand. After thanking him for his time and allowing Nicoh another round of scruffs, I started to leave but remembered what had inspired me to drop by in the first place.

"Thanks again, Ben. I truly appreciate you helping me out, especially considering all of the people who probably stop by, asking the same questions over the years."

He waved a hand. "Pfft. Nobody's been by here in a while. Nobody except Decker's daughter, Kelly. The one who..." He gestured toward the building as I nodded.

"Anyway, come to think of it, she hasn't been here in months, which isn't like her. Typically, she stops by every so often to check up on the wife and me. Though, she never once went back into that apartment, much less cast a look in that direction. She's someone you should talk to." He rattled off Decker's cell number, and I guiltily jotted it down. "Anyway, if you do happen to come across her, please pass on how much we miss her?"

I nodded, though my eyes couldn't quite meet his. I didn't have the heart to tell him about Decker, even if it was the right thing to do. I made a mental note to follow up with him in the near future and come clean. Today, however, was not that day.

Plus, I was not in the frame of mind to divulge such news. Right now, I was ruminating about what Ben had told me. And wondering why, after inserting himself into my amateur investigation, Logan had chosen to lie?

CHAPTER TWENTY

Of course, just as I was cursing Logan, I noted that I had missed a call from him. He'd left a voicemail, which I hoped would mitigate the anger that was quickly burbling to the surface, but all he had to offer were brief apologies for having to dodge off to work.

Perhaps I needed to stop by and have a quick chat with Officer Piedmont. As far as I was aware that "work" didn't include following me.

I must have ground my teeth all the way to my destination because my jaw ached, though I'd drummed up at least three new phrases to toss at him. Each one had been carefully crafted and was worthy of getting my mouth washed out with soap, so I'd have to choose wisely.

I grimaced as I pulled into the parking lot where my trusty GPS informed me that Logan was stationed. Snapping at Nicoh as he impatiently huffed, I snugged into a spot, gave him a stern lecture about commandeering the captain's chair while I got out and thrust my phone in my back pocket before slamming the driver-side door shut.

Of course, in my frothing, I'd overlooked the fact that while this was Logan's home base, a lot of the work occurred in the field. Not in a mindset to be deterred, I decided that if it turned out to be the case, I could probably, at the very least, get a line on his current location.

I was wrong on all counts.

No sooner than I connected with the desk sergeant did I wrap my mind around the full extent of just how far off the range I'd traveled.

"Officer Piedmont is not here, ma'am." I noted that he hadn't even referenced any sort of schedule—digital or otherwise—before responding.

"I see," I replied, attempted to keep my voice calm. "Do you know when he is expected back?"

"No, ma'am," he replied. His tone was flat, revealing nothing, though he did grant me the courtesy of looking me in the eye when he said it.

"He'll have to check-in before his shift ends, though, right?"

The officer shook his head, saving me, thankfully, from another "ma'am." I wasn't fond of it.

"Officer Piedmont isn't on shift today."

There it was. The thread of a lie I had driven out of my way while frothing to obtain. Still, I had to be sure.

"Well, I know he wasn't *supposed* to have been on shift, but then he was called in for some sort of emergency—"

Another head shake. "Not to my knowledge."

"Excuse me?" Not so calm or hopeful this time around.

"He's on leave."

"Since when?" This time, I tossed a bit of snark tossed in there. For effect, of course.

"It's been a few weeks now."

Since I'd last seen him, after Decker had died.

"I see. Did he say when he would return?"

"He did not." I didn't think I would get much more from him, but he either felt sorry for me or wanted to get me out of his hair. "It's an indefinite leave."

I fought the urge to curse. "Well, that's…interesting. And unfortunate."

"Is there someone else in his department that you'd like to speak with?"

I shook my head. "It's a personal matter. I'll just have to catch up with him later."

"Yes, ma'am." I wasn't sure which of us was more uncomfortable as we would have tied in a fidgeting competition.

After several seconds of awkward silence, I tucked my tail, thanked him for his time, and retreated before every inch of me turning a blistering red.

As I stormed across the parking lot, I extracted the cell from my pocket and punched in Logan's number, muttering under my breath when he picked up on the first ring. Why hadn't I just done this in the first place?

Because I wanted to pin him in the corner where the apartment complex was concerned. And I didn't want him to have anywhere to run.

"Hey AJ, what's up?" Logan's voice was smooth, and for a split second, I forgot why I had called.

Oh, yeah.

Shaking my head at my nincompoopery, I laid out the cheese for my trap.

"So sorry to bother you *at work*," I paused before proceeding, "but I just wanted to find out how things went at Decker's old apartment and see if there was anything you needed me to follow up on with regards to the residents?"

"I'm afraid it was a dead end. Nobody remembered much, probably because most of them moved in after the fact, and by then it was all hearsay anyway," he replied in the same velvety tone.

"Hmm, that's…disappointing." I had to work hard—too hard—to keep from unleashing my wrath on him. "But if you're sure."

"I am. We just need to move on, find other avenues."

"Guess so."

"So, based on your mood, I take you had no better luck with Mae, then?"

I stared at the phone and reined my "mood" in before responding. "Nope. I can fill you in later. Unless you think your shift will run over?"

There was a brief pause before he responded. "What? Oh, no…that sounds like a plan. I'll bring takeout home." His tone was distracted, rushed even, and I was about to respond with something less gracious that was warranted for his hospitality when he added, "AJ, can you hold on for a second?"

He didn't wait for my response before placing me on hold. I considered hanging up but decided to sit and seethe for a bit longer. When I finally let him have it, I wanted it to have maximum impact.

I waited for what seemed like an eternity, but according to my cell, it was only three minutes and thirty-eight seconds before he returned, though perhaps my phone was slow.

"AJ, where are you?" His breathing was labored as though he was jogging or in the middle of an intense workout.

"Talking to you, Logan."

"I didn't ask *what* you were doing, I asked *where* you were," he snarled.

I wasn't prepared for the shift and stuttered my way through a response. "I'm sitting in my car…err, in a parking lot. I'm in the vicinity of your condo, I think." Not a lie.

His tone eased but not by much. "And you were with Mae in Newport Beach prior to that?"

"Yes," I replied, rolling my eyes, as he should have known that if he'd been following me. "I just got back."

"Okay, okay, that's good," he mumbled. "I need to think about this."

I frowned at the phone. Had he forgotten we'd been having a conversation?

"Logan! Dude! What is going on?" I growled.

"Terrence Edwards was attacked. They're not sure he'll make it."

CHAPTER TWENTY-ONE

"What? When?" I gripped my phone.

"I don't know all of the details, AJ, but there's a video of the assailant leaving the area around the time they believe it all went down."

"Oh, that's good, right?" I realized I was matching every inflection of Logan's panicked tone.

"Not really," he replied. "Especially when they've put a BOLO for a female whose description could be a dead ringer for you. God, AJ. I take my eyes off you for a brief time…what have you done?"

Before I could utter a syllable, he did the last thing I'd expected.

He disconnected.

I used up all three newly-crafted and finely-hones curses in one fell swoop.

Sure, I'd been with Edwards, but that had been a day earlier and I'd already told Logan about it. So…what was with the sudden judgyness on his part? He was the one lying behind those kissably-smooth lips and perfectly straight teeth, after all.

I groaned, still pondering whether to give him the benefit of the doubt when my phone rang. For a split second, I hoped it was Leah, popping in to offer some sage commentary, until I noted the call was from an unidentified caller.

"Yes?" I'd said it a bit more tersely than anticipated and immediately noted it was not your standard greeting, no matter where you were from.

"Arianna?" The voice had a hint of familiarity, but I couldn't quite place it.

"This is Arianna. How can I help you?"

"Uh, we talked earlier. In the hotel?" I could sense the hesitance but was surprised, given the first impressions I'd made. And assumptions.

"Danielle?" I said through gritted teeth while feeling a strange sense of relief.

"Before you hang up…I know I came off acting like a complete twit," she replied, the words jumbling together as she forced them out. When I said nothing, she continued. "I can't apologize for what I've done, but I can do something to make up for it."

"Go on," I replied, my mind running through the options of how she might propose to accommodate that.

"I know you have no reason to trust me, but I want the same thing you do." I doubted it and let my silence speak for me. "Um, we both want Decker's mum's killer brought down, right?"

"Um, hmm, and you've been quite helpful to this point." My snark was not lost on her.

"I deserve that. I just…didn't think I could trust you guys, and it turns out, I was halfway right."

"Halfway?" She'd piqued my curiosity.

"That dude who was Decker's friend…Piedmont or whatever…he's bad news."

"Logan? He's an officer of the law," I replied.

"Doesn't mean he's above it. I've met his type before," she

paused before adding, "In fact, I've met him before, though I'm sure he didn't bother to tell you that."

"Actually, he did."

"I'm not ashamed, if that's what you were thinking."

"I wasn't."

"Well, that was the past, anyway. And though I've done a few crappy things since, that one's has never changed his spots."

"How so?"

"For starters, did you know he's been following you?" she asked.

"And just how would you know that?" I wasn't pleasant, but she definitely had my attention.

My reward was a harsh laugh. "Because I've been following him, of course." She continued to chuckle. "Oh sure, I started following you, but once I realized the two of us were doing double-duty, I got curious and shifted gears. You'd think he'd be a bit smarter for a cop. Then again, I don't recall him being all that impressive the first time around. Other than being easy on the eyes, that is." She released a bout of amused piggy-snorts.

I paused to ensure she'd had her fill be responding. "Okay, let's say you are right, and Logan is following me…why does it have to be for some nefarious reason?"

"Nefarious? Yeesh. If it were me, I'd be a little freaked if some dude who was jonesing for me suddenly turned into a stalker."

Logan…a stalker? Perhaps she was watching too many of those mystery series on the Hallmark Channel. I didn't say as much.

"So Logan has been following me. Big whoopie. Has it occurred to you that he might be keeping an eye out for me, because of you?" I responded.

More snorting ensued. Perhaps it was a condition.

"Because of me? Please. Besides, he wasn't acting like he was concerned for your safety. Seemed to me like he wanted to keep tabs on you, see what you were doing, based on how he was lurking around and stuff," she replied.

"Tell me. If you were following him, where did he follow me?"

I heard her blow out a breath. "Oh, gosh. Since the hotel? Well, actually, that's where it started. Right after that big dude hauled you into the SUV."

"Wait…you saw that?" My mind was reeling.

"Yeah, what was up with that? You were in there for a bit—who was in there, anyway—the Pope?"

No way was I going to reveal that nugget until she offered up what she knew. "Never mind that. Where was Logan during all of this?"

"In the lot adjacent to the hotel, behind some trees."

"Hmm… And you?"

"Let's just say I was in a position to see you both and leave it at that," she replied, a terseness entering her voice.

"Ok, so he stayed nearby while I was in the room collecting my things."

"And witnessed his girlfriend getting manhandled by a Cro-Magnon." Her tongue made a sharp clucking sound in my ear.

"Not his girlfriend. Moving on," I prompted.

"Touchy subject…okay. Today, he followed you to Newport Beach…to Auntie Mae's. That was a nice move you made, by the way, even if you did lose him."

"Whatever," I snapped, tiring of the direction this conversation had taken.

"You still haven't caught up with him, have you?" She chuckled.

"You already know the answer to that," I grumbled.

"So, you believe me?" Despite all her crowing, she sounded relieved.

"That someone was following me? Yes. That Logan was the person following me? Possibly. That he's stalking me? Doubtful."

"Suit yourself. How is Auntie these days, anyway?"

It gave me no pleasure, but she deserved a quid pro quo. "Seems to be doing well. Lovely house and gardens. Prime ocean view."

"Yeah, I'd heard she'd done well for herself," Danielle sounded amused. "And before you ask, it's been a while since I've chatted with her. A long while. Though I'm sure she already told you that."

"Your decision? Or hers?" I asked, genuinely interested.

"Does it matter? That ship sailed a long time ago," she replied. "Did you get the information you were looking for?"

"I spoke to her at length, and while her recall is exceptional, she didn't have any insights that were new."

"Meaning she couldn't point the finger of blame at the person who killed Ellen? Not surprising. She wouldn't have, even if she'd had the silver bullet." Her tone had turned prickly.

"Why is that?"

"Auntie Mae doesn't do anything that doesn't serve the greater good." This time, Danielle sounded bitter—where had that come from? She confirmed my assessment by huffing out, "And by 'greater good,' I mean her own."

"I thought you and your sister liked Mae?"

She hacked out a laugh. "She was my mother's friend. Not mine. I'll let Larissa speak for herself."

"But you spent time with her, at her house?" I prodded, determined to get some insight into this animosity.

"Like I said, the woman didn't do anything that didn't benefit her. We were a means to an end. And that's all I'm going to say about that."

I nodded to myself. There was something I'd forgotten that perhaps Danielle could shed some light on.

"When I was chatting with Mae, a man dropped by. I didn't see a vehicle, so perhaps he was a neighbor?"

"Yeah, I saw him. And his jogging ensemble. But I didn't see which direction he came from, though he definitely did so on foot." Danielle's response seemed sincere.

"You didn't recognize him, though?" Perhaps I was overly hopeful.

"Nuh-uh. Never laid eyes on him before. And walking in the way he did? Either he's a nosy neighbor, or he's getting busy with Auntie, though the thought of old people doing the nasty kinda creeps me out."

I shook my head and face-palmed. Only Danielle could take things to that place. I switched gears. "It was a long shot, anyway."

"What are you going to do about Officer Piedmont?" she asked, catching me off-guard.

Honestly, I hadn't thought that far ahead, and considering my concerns had been stacking up prior to this call, Danielle's claims —though unconfirmed—definitely added kindling to that bonfire.

"I'm…not sure."

Danielle huffed. "Either you're not as smart of a chick as I thought you were, or you're blowing smoke where you have no business to."

"I guess you'll find out," I sniped.

She chuckled. "There's hope for you yet. See you on the flip-side, Arianna Jackson. I know you don't give a squat about me, but don't you dare let Kelly Decker down."

And for the second time in less than an hour, the party on the other end of the connection abruptly disconnected.

I didn't like my odds.

CHAPTER TWENTY-TWO

Before I'd even had the conversation with Danielle—as bizarre as it was—I'd decided that I need to put some space between Logan and me. Weirdly, I believed her—even if she'd admitted to following me—but I wasn't buying her rationale for calling me. What she'd said about Mae seemed to be just as valid for Danielle —she didn't do anything that didn't serve herself.

Still, I had to admit—her timing for reaching out was spot-on and helped bolster my decision. Now, I just needed to put it into action.

It seemed as though it took forever to make my way to Logan's—chalk it up to L.A. traffic—but I heaved a sigh of relief when I finally arrived, carefully parking a safe distance away. After letting Nicoh out to stretch his legs and do all things doggy, I glanced over my shoulder to see whether any familiar vehicles were lurking. Satisfied I was momentarily in the clear, I used the key Logan had lent me and hustled into the condo.

If I could just collect my things and get the heck out before confronting the man himself, I'd give myself bonus points. I was in a bit of a mood, however, and would have welcomed the opportunity to have a little chat with Officer Piedmont.

As I tossed my belongings and Nicoh's toys into their prospective travel bags, I fought the urge to turn the television on to catch the latest on the investigation into Edwards' attack, and of the eyewitness' description of the possible perpetrator of the crime. "Person of Interest"? Riiight.

I wasn't touching that with a ten-foot pole. Or any pole, for that matter.

Glancing around to ensure I'd grabbed everything, I started to leave Logan's key on the kitchen counter, realizing that doing so without a valid explanation would only raise his coply suspicions. I dug in my bag and pulled out a notepad that Leah had snuck in there months ago. I smiled at the "USE THIS!" scribbled at the top of the page in her big loopy handwriting.

Flipping to a blank sheet, I quickly wrote, "Logan—Sorry to bail. Something has come up; gotta go. Thanks for the place to stay." I was careful not to mention a time to catch up later or how or when to address Decker's case. Besides, "something" could allude to anything—home, work, etc., so there would be no reason for him to assume he was the cause of my hasty departure.

Other than a guilty conscience.

I didn't have time to think about that now, as I placed the key on the note and hauled my bags to the vehicle. A hint of color caught my eye after I'd tucked them in the back. Careful not to stare, I pretended to wipe my hands across an invisible spot of dirt on the side, noting that the vehicle parked across the street on the opposite side just a half a block up. I could see a frame hunched down behind the driver's seat and given its size, confirmed it likely belonged to the male species.

Warmth filled my cheeks as I fisted my hands at my side and a slew of unforgettable adjectives swirled through my head. Before I had a chance to weigh the consequences, the naughty devil on my shoulder whispered in my ear, something that cannot be repeated in mixed company, causing me to charge in the direction of my "stalker" as Danielle had aptly called him. I must have caught him off-guard because as I pounded my fists against the passenger side window, I found a familiar face staring back.

Fuming, I gestured for him to roll the window down. He frowned but complied and I leaned it, clasping my hands together to prevent myself from punching him in his ugly mug and demolishing those snazzy wraparound sunglasses.

"What? Nothing to say?" I ground out. "Guess you're not so tough without your boss around." I received a healthy frown for my efforts, causing me to hack out a laugh. "By the way, it seems like someone's going to be looking for new employment. Good luck getting that letter of recommendation."

"Get in," Thuggy replied, his tone gruff as my sarcasm fell flat. "Unless you want the neighborhood watch to tattle on us."

"Well, unless you want the law enforcement officer who owns the condo I just left to join us, I suggest we move this little chat elsewhere."

"You did seem to be in a bit of a hurry—lover's spat?" I noticed he hadn't reacted to my mention the nature of Logan's employment, so he probably either knew, or just didn't care.

I jutted my chin out and garnered him with a stare that could have defrosted a snowman in a Minnesota winter. "You buy those glasses in bulk, or what?"

Thuggy grunted. I belatedly realized it was his form of a chuckle. "There's a place, not far from here. You game?"

"If you promise not to ditch and run," I retorted.

"I don't run. From anyone," he replied.

"Whatever, Thug—err, where is this place?"

He relayed the directions, the parking lot of a nearby shopping mall.

Busy, easy to go unnoticed, easy to get mugged, I noted to myself before solidifying my fate.

"Five minutes. I'll be following you. No funny business."

Another grunt ensued, this one not of humor. Just as he started to roll up the window, I added, "By the way, you got a name?"

"Wendell." The window popped, and he pulled away from the curb.

Wendell? Thuggy's name was Wendell? I decided I liked the name I'd graced him with better as I raced back to the vehicle.

Thankfully, I managed to keep up with him while glancing around for signs of Logan, but as we reached our destination, I felt confident I hadn't been followed. After nosing into a space and ensuring that my snoring beast was indeed sleeping and not faking it so that he could commandeer my seat again, I hopped out and walked over to Thuggy's SUV. After settling in, I couldn't let it pass.

"Dell for short?"

He shook his head.

"Wend?" Given the man's girth, I didn't dare venture into the female variation associated with a famous fast-food chain that jumped to mind.

Again, he shook his head.

"Okay…gotta first name?"

He didn't remove the sunglasses, but the set of his mouth suggested he was glaring at me.

"Nevermind," I murmured, before getting down to business. "So, what's up, Wendell? Last time I saw you, you were hauling me into a meet and greet with your boss. Now an eyewitness has fingered someone who coincidentally looks somewhat like me for attacking him. Anything you'd like to share regarding that? Like, where were you when it all went down?"

He shifted in his seat and turned away. I raised a brow. Had I struck a nerve so soon? Surely, the big guy wasn't the sensitive, sentimental type?

Fighting a compulsion to blurt out something that would prompt him to speak, I waited him out.

After a few moments, he swiveled his head in my direction. "Against my better judgment, Mr. Edwards directed me to follow you."

"And?" I prompted.

He frowned. "I was not present when the unfortunate event occurred."

"Hmm. So, you were following me as instructed at the time of Edwards' attack. What exactly did that yield you? And, just how far did you take it—the tailing part, that is?"

He nodded. "After you left, I quickly realized I wasn't the only one following you," he paused to offer what I assumed was his version of a smirk, but it translated into a creepy snarl. "It seems you have quite a fan club."

"Describe the vehicle." I wasn't about to offer up that, according to Danielle, both she and Logan had been on my tail. And, I didn't care what Danielle said, by default, she was following me.

"One was an SUV like this one, though it was a bit older of a model," he replied. "The other, or others, were all old hunks of junk, but considering their size, none of the drivers could have been all that big."

"Not as big as you, you mean?" He shrugged. "Could they have been female?"

"Possibly," he replied, scratching his chin. "It was odd, though."

"How so?" I prompted.

"At first, I thought they were following you but it seemed like they were following the SUV."

I withheld my commentary, even though his observation lent credibility to Danielle's claims. "Could they—or rather the random set of vehicles—all have been the same person?"

"Could be," he shrugged before adding, "They weren't my main priority."

"Mmm, how fortunate for me." Even behind the shades, I knew the sarcasm was not lost on him. I was pretty sure he was deciding whether this had been a bad idea, and it was just time to off me.

"You asked about the other vehicles. Do you already know who the driver of the SUV was?"

"Meh, I have my suspicions." I waved a hand and moved on. "So, just how far did you follow me?"

It was his turn to play it off. "Yesterday, just to the condo. I didn't have all day to wait around to see whether you and your boyfriend would emerge all kissy-face. Or tramp after you to the nail salon." I subconsciously tucked the tips of my fingers into my palm. They were nibbled to the nub—an old habit that had recently reared its ugly head again.

My response caused him to shake his head and scoff. "Anyway, picked you up again today, and during that time, everything hit the fan."

The last bit came out a bit wistful, if not self-admonishing, and had he not been part of Edwards' world, I might have had a bit of sympathy for him.

I grimaced. When had I gotten so jaded?

"Not that I'm a fan of your boss', but if he sent you to follow me, then what happened to him wasn't your fault. It may have happened regardless, whether that day or another." Thuggy grunted and shook his head, frowning. "Whatever. Edwards probably had it coming to him for some time, so it's no wonder he's on the threshold of the fiery gates as a result. He put himself in that scenario long before you came along—so if I were you, I'd make peace with what transpired and move on."

The frowned deepened. "Why are you so quick to judge the man so harshly? Have you never stepped outside the lines to do what you thought was right?"

I scoffed. Surely he was talking about himself and not his employer?

"We're not talking about me and my morals this round, *Wendell.* You think I'm judging him harshly, but why are you so quick to give the man the benefit of the doubt? You work for him every day and have witnessed first-hand what he's capable of." I paused, noting the rigidity of his demeanor.

Interesting. Had I overlooked the obvious? Time to poke the Thuggy—see if I could get to his tender, squishy parts. Or to the meat of this thing…whatever it was.

"Just what does he have on you that…inspires such loyalty?" Thuggy frowned. "Come on, spit it out, mate. I haven't got all day." I mimicked the sarcasm in his earlier remark.

He huffed out a breath. "Alright, but this stays between us. I'm also working under the assumption that you are willing to keep an open mind." He thrust a meaty hand at me, and I stared at it for a moment before grasping it and nodding, its firmness as surprising as the gesture.

"I grew up in a time when the streets of L.A. burned, and anarchy reigned. And the colors you wore defined your loyalty. Rather than turn out like my father—who my mother said was nothing but a sweet-talking thug with a nice ride and a lousy bedside manner—I was shipped off to live with some cousins in the Midwest.

"In the years that I was away, Mums got hooked on the pills and a dude that was worse than a bad rash—and the result was a younger brother. But, rather than pawning him off on family like she'd done with me, she kept that poor kid close. I think she was using him in a delusional attempt to keep the baby daddy, who was also her feed bag, on the hook. Didn't quite work out that way, though." He shook his head. "Looking back, after hearing the stories, it was amazing that she never made it onto the Child

Protective Services' radar. Then again, it was a pretty common situation, so they were probably inundated with cases as it was.

"The long and short of it is that my stepbrother, despite his circumstances and the environment in which he lived, was not only smarter than he let on, he was an exceptional athlete, too. According to his coach, he could have had his choice of colleges, and probably gotten both a football and an academic scholarship, had he applied himself. It all started well enough but peer pressure, coupled with repeated injuries…" His voice trailed off for a moment, and though he was too tough to wipe away tears, had there been any, he cleared his throat a couple of times before continuing, though his voice was raspy.

"Unfortunately, before long, he took the route he believed offered him the easiest path and fell in with a crowd that chose the lifestyle of the streets. Soon, gang-banging turned to drugs—which only fostered the escape from a world whose pressures he deemed unfathomable and thrust him into another, where he would never escape.

"Of course, his coaches, teachers, and counselors could only do so much—there were other kids in the same predicament and if he wasn't willing to meet them halfway, they had to move on. I can't say I blame them. In fact, I wish I could say all of it wasn't the same trite cliché, but we've all heard the same sad story over and over."

His lip curled as his voice got higher as he mimicked some unknown source. *"But he was such a good kid."* He sneered. "I call bull on it. It is what it is. People gotta stop blaming others and own their crap. All the excuses—and the whining—make me sick. People make choices and end up in situations as a result. Period. So shut the heck up and get on with it."

You would have thought that he'd sound bitter, but Wendell's tone suggested he had resolved his words as truth. Still, I wondered how Edwards fit into all of it, but let him tell the story at his pace.

"Anyway, bear with me. I do have a point here." He shot a sunglassed glance in my direction, as if sensing my desire to spur the conversation toward the matter at hand.

"Speaking of choices, by the time I turned eighteen, I decided college wasn't for me, and as my uncle had drilled into my skull, my remaining choices were to either work for him in his feed store or to enroll in the military. Having my fill of the prior, working for him every day before and after school and on weekends, the latter was an easy decision. Best one I ever made. Who knows where I would've ended up...probably back here. Dead." He paused to release a low rumble that slightly resembled a chuckle.

"Obviously, I did eventually end up back here, but that was two tours and what felt like several lifetimes later."

"Is that when you started working for Edwards?" He gave a curt nod. "Why? You had experience provided by the military. Surely—"

He raised a palm to intercept me. "Like I said, when I came back, it felt like several lifetimes later. I wasn't just talking about mine. My brother had started working for a bad, bad dude. Doing bad things. Found himself locked up for a few murders that I have no doubt he was responsible for." He ground out the last bit, clenching the steering wheel tighter with each syllable.

"Turns out, little bro was not only smart, but crafty and had quickly bypassed others who'd been there longer as he worked his way up the ranks. The boss man was impressed and, before long, came to rely on him and even treated him like kin.

"Unfortunately, the boss man's notoriety had not gone unnoticed by law enforcement, and as my brother was a known associate, they were well-versed on the group's ruthlessness in dealing with those who crossed them—an area of the enterprise in which my brother excelled. So, when he got tagged, the boss man quickly realized that having his prized possession rotting behind bars for eternity did not serve him well, so he called in a few favors, which included the assistance of one equally notorious high-powered criminal defense attorney."

I groaned. "Terrence Edwards."

He nodded. "He got my brother off on a technicality, and though I don't condone what my brother did—on a social or moral level—I felt that I owed it to the woman who raised me. And the brother I was never there for."

"And so you went to work for him." My voice sounded hollow, as was the sentiment behind it. It was not lost on him, and after contemplating me for a bit longer than I was comfortable, shrugged. "And were they…grateful?"

"My mums and stepbrother?" He grunted. "Doubt gratitude ever entered into it. My mums died of an overdose shortly after he was acquitted. And my brother, well, a month later, his body was found by some hikers up by Big Bear. His throat had been slit, his eyes gouged out and his tongue…well, they never found that. There were a few rumors it had been a rival of the boss man, but more likely, it was done by the thugs that he'd stepped over on his rise to the top."

"I'm sorry," I replied.

"Don't be. It was better it turned out like that. Before—" He shook his head. "Anyway, you wanted to know how my loyalty for Mr. Edwards came about, and that's how. It didn't matter what my stepbrother was, Mr. Edwards tried to do the right thing, hoping once he got out he would realize he'd been given a second chance and take the better path. And just because he didn't, doesn't mean the gesture wasn't genuine. So while you may not get it, I owe him for the opportunity he afforded him, when I couldn't have done the same."

I think Wendell had taken the honor crap a bit too far when it came to Edwards' intentions, but it wasn't my story, and my judgment had no bearing on its outcome.

My concern was finding the man who had killed Decker's mother, and if I proved that to be the truth, whatever altruistic thoughts Wendell had about him would need to be tossed out the window.

"So…how long does this indebtedness to Edwards last?" Apparently, I was getting started early on that notion.

"As long as it takes," he replied.

"Takes?"

He shrugged. "I'll just know."

"And then?"

"I plan on opening my own security business." I'm not sure what he saw in my look, but he felt the need to add, "A legit security business."

"Careful, Wendell. You're true feelings surrounding your boss are starting to show."

His lip curled. "Guess you're rubbing off on me."

"So, what will you do in the meantime?"

"Today? I'm talking to you."

I release a fake sigh. "If or when Edwards recovers?"

"I'll do what I do best."

"For Edwards?"

"Of course."

"Until you open your security firm."

"Are you making fun of me?" His mouth formed a cryptic curl.

"Not at all. I think it's a nice…goal."

"Meh, you're just saying that because I'm helping you."

I shook my head and looked at him straight on. "I mean it. It suits you. Wait—you're helping me? Why?"

"Same reason I told you that lengthy backstory. We're both lost." I opened my mouth to protest, but he held up a hand. "Go ahead, try to deny it, but I've been following you. I've watched your actions and noted your reaction and body language and you've got nowhere to go. Neither do I. We may not see eye to eye, but we want the same thing."

I raised a brow. "Higher thread count in our sheets?"

Wendell just shook his head and rumbled out a laugh. "Justice."

I leaned back and put up both hands. "Hold up. We're talking two different sides of the coin here."

He tilted his head. "Are we?"

"You tell me…if I prove your boss killed Ellen Decker?"

"You won't." No snark behind that response. Only confidence. Who knew that could be blind, too?

"Let me rephrase that. If I prove it…will you see it as justice?"

"*If* it's true—yes." No hesitation.

I nodded. "Okay, then. If we remove my side, exactly how do you get justice out of it?"

"Once we figure out who killed Ellen Decker, we'll know who attacked Mr. Edwards."

"You think they're linked?"

He shrugged. "Makes sense to me. None of this started until you showed up, and I don't think that is a coincidence." He paused for a moment. "I don't like coincidences. And judging your expression, neither do you."

"Let me ask you something, Wendell." I paused, and once he gave me the head nod to proceed, I continued. "When all is said and done, if it turns out you are wrong, and Edwards is on the hook for murdering Ellen Decker, will you renege and slink home to papa? Or will you put your big boy pants and do what's right—and put justice above loyalty?"

Wendell hacked out a laugh, which on anyone else would have seemed like a lung was coming up. "You're blunt, Arianna

Jackson, and I like that." He scratched his chin and was silent for a moment.

I let it stew, unsure what his response would be. Perhaps he'd just kill me now and be done with it, but I didn't think so. I chewed the side of my cheek while I waited.

Finally, he spoke. "I say let the gates of Hell open and expose this demon, whoever he is. I'll deal with the fallout after the fact, whatever the consequences."

I nodded but wasn't sure about eliciting anything from Hell. I noticed his gaze had fallen upon me as he went silent. I stared back, sensing the other shoe was about to drop.

"But, to be fair, I've gotta ask, if *you're* wrong and he's innocent, are you prepared to do the same?" I shrugged, garnering a scoff. "I figured as much. Before we shake on this deal, there's something you should know."

I sucked in a breath but gestured for him to proceed.

"Edwards knew his attacker."

"How do you figure?" I shifted in my seat.

"He let them into the vehicle—he would have never opened the door otherwise," came the reply, and my mind began to swirl as he added, "but that's only half of it. Not only did he know his attacker, there's evidence something went wrong with their plan —he fought back, they were interrupted…whatever. The point is: they didn't get a chance to finish the job."

"Meaning…"

"As long as he's alive, they're at risk."

Not that I was feeling particularly sympathetic toward Edwards, but we couldn't overlook the contrary—as long as he was still alive and could identify the person who'd tried to end him, he was the one whose life hung in the balance.

CHAPTER TWENTY-THREE

I digested that statement and wasn't quite ready to put a label on the emotions it tapped into, so I put a pin in it, though I knew it would change everything moving forward, regardless of how I felt about it.

It was probably for the best if I kept my attitude under wraps, considering I needed whatever information Wendell was willing to provide. I took in a deep breath as he watched, sucked up my Edwards spitball, and focused on the matter in front of us.

"If he knew this person—which one of them would have had the cojones to plan and execute an attack?" I was guessing the list was long and moved on. "What makes you think it had to do with Ellen's murder? It's been more than twenty years—why now?"

"You ask me that, and yet you are here for impossible answers to the very same questions." Wendell shifted in his seat so that we would have been looking eye to eye had his not been hidden. "Not to mention that your name could easily have been added to that list."

I shook my head. "But I didn't beat him within an inch of his life, though, did I?" I raised a brow, considering Wendell had been tailing me when the attack had occurred.

As per standard Wendell, his body language revealed nothing.

"Fine. Don't answer that. Why do you think the attack ties into Ellen Decker's murder?"

"Why now…is the better question," he replied. "Think about it. You turn up, start asking questions about a twenty-year-old murder, and hours later, my employer is attacked." He waved a hand, prompting me to fill in the blanks.

I shook my head. "Decker…err, Kelly Decker, Ellen's daughter, had already gone down this path. Just like her father before her. It was already out there."

"But neither got that far, did they? The killer is still out there." His tone was more reflective than taunting; otherwise I would have probably done the unthinkable and slapped him upside the head.

And dealt with the consequences later.

"Perhaps not, but both of them had knowledge, resources, and experience I don't. Plus, they had a lay of the land, the surroundings, and the players. Years of it, in fact."

Wendell grunted. "Some of that is true. But, you have one advantage that neither Max Decker nor his daughter possessed." He paused to ensure that he had my complete attention. "Perspective. A point of view they would never have—you're on the inside looking in."

It sounded suspiciously like the lyrics to a song—one that the Red Rocker had belted out in the 1980s. I bit my lip. "I'm not sure that constitutes an advantage."

"I disagree. Your vision isn't clouded with judgment, other than those formed by your interactions and conversations." He paused when I crossed my arms. "Admit it. What Kelly and her father accomplished equated to nothing more than repeatedly tromping around a dust bowl, grabbing at straws at every turn, and the more time that passed, the less credibility their claims had. Especially when they weren't backed by evidence. Case in point: Why is your view of Edwards' tainted? Can you truly say your opinion was formed because you'd gotten to know the man on a personal level? Or because of what you've been told?"

I bristled at his reference to "personal." Any sentence pairing that with Edwards' name activated my gag-meter.

"Just so you know, I did meet Edwards before our get-together in the SUV, if that's what you're asking, and while it was a memorable experience, the man himself wasn't all that special."

Wendell raised a hand, as though circumventing my intention to keep moving that train rolling down the tracks. Yeah, I'm cagey that way.

"I'm well aware of that occasion. I was in the parking lot of Stanton Investigations." When I cast him a questioning glance, he added, "I was his driver that day. His relationship with his son Blaze had been tenuous over the years at best, and when he suddenly called out of the blue, requesting his father's assistance, Mr. Edwards decided to take precautionary measures in case the situation escalated."

Situation? Blaze had erroneously thought his father could be of assistance after his best friend was murdered and he was considered the prime suspect. It had been my first introduction to the senior Edwards and had not ended well—Edwards had been granted the last word, which had left a lasting impression.

"Anyway, there were extenuating circumstances on that day— and given the heightened emotions of all parties—you formed an opinion of Mr. Edwards based on the experiences of others, did you not?"

"True," I said slowly, "but he was very much true to form on our second meeting, which only added to what opinions I may or may not have formed due to outside influences."

Wendell nodded slowly, then tilted his head. "Was he…true to form? What if you hadn't been involved in that prior meeting or been supplied with other perspectives?"

"I still would have thought he was a pompous, entitled donkey's butt." I deadpanned.

"Surely, in your line of work, that could be said of any number of people? And yet, it does not mean they are murderers."

I huffed out a breath, frankly tired of the discussion. Edwards, murderer or not, would never rank high on my list of people I'd like to sit down with to share a meal. Plus, he'd already gotten more air time than he'd deserved.

"Are you suggesting that Decker injected thoughts into my mind and is controlling me from beyond the grave?"

He shook his head. "Not at all. She also had been given the false sense of the situation based on the things her father had shared or left in his files."

"Okay…but if it all comes down to perspective, then why do others not involved with Kelly Decker or her father, including his own son, have a similar opinion of the man?"

Wendell's mouth formed a pucker. "I'm not talking about 'others.' I'm simply suggesting that *you* keep an open mind."

"Fine," I snapped from behind gritted teeth, "but Edwards' attack doesn't automatically link to Ellen Decker's murder." I paused to give him time to reflect, before adding, "Even if they were connected, it still doesn't explain why you think he's not responsible? You were a child who lived out of state. How could you possibly know what he was capable of back then?"

Wendell tapped his head with his index finger. "Come on, Arianna. Think. You've seen Terrence Edwards. Regardless of the company he keeps or the opinions people have formed about him, do you really think he's the type who is willing to get his hands dirty?" He snickered when I failed to mask a smirk, which quickly turned into a grimace when I rallied back.

"By 'dirty,' I assume you mean brutally attacking a woman to the point of death before gutting her?" I'll admit, the phrasing was harsh, but if this guy wanted to plead his undying loyalty to Edwards, I was gonna make him squirm.

"You didn't answer my question."

I sighed. "I think that any person, given the right motivation, is capable of just about anything, especially when they are about to get knocked off their high horse. The up-and-coming version of Edwards would not have stopped at anything if it meant keeping the truth from coming out and his career from being destroyed."

"You're referencing Ellen Decker's unborn child."

I nodded. "In addition to Ellen and the way the child was conceived." I gave him a pointed stare but his expression never wavered and still, his body language revealed little to nothing.

"I'll admit, there were several rumors about him fathering a child."

Yup. Edwards had gotten him one cool cucumber for a thuggy.

When I hacked out a laugh, his lip curled at the corner, increasingly so when I responded with overt finger quotes. "'Fathering a child?' We both know Edwards had quite a reputation for getting his way when it came to the ladies and what that translates to, no matter which pretty words you choose to phrase it."

He shook his head. "Never to be proven, and you know it. Regardless, that's quite a stretch to murder."

I hated to admit it, but part of what he said was true. "Okay, then let's run through possible suspects for the attack." When he opened his mouth to respond, I raised a finger. "And, what ties them to Ellen Decker's murder."

"You're talking about motive."

"That would be a good start," I replied. "So, you work for Edwards and are familiar with his routines, who he interacts with, blah, blah, blah. Who's on your highlight reel?" When he remained like a marble bust for a moment too long, I smirked.

"What? Not up for a game of I'll show you mine if you show me yours?"

Wendell shrugged. "Sure, if you go first."

I hacked out a laugh. "Nice try. How about a little prompt: has he been receiving any threats or been in any heated altercations recently?"

"You mean other than the one with you?" When I huffed, he chuckled but then turned serious. "In his line of work, there are always choice words exchanged and innuendos tossed about, but if I parsed through all of them in search of someone who would act on them, I'd say it would be a stretch. And, even if they had, those parties would have made sure they finished the job."

Having heard of some of the unsavories that Edwards defended or had ongoing dealings with, I didn't doubt that statement. I also knew that was as far as Wendell would go in divulging specifics about any of them. Besides, if he was right, and there was a connection to the murder, we'd be hard-pressed to find a tie in with any of them.

"What about on a personal level? Anyone that might have harbored resentment or felt as though Edwards had crossed them? Business partner? Disgruntled employee? Family member? An angry husband?"

Wendell chuckled at the last one, but cut it short when he took in my glare. "Again, no. Sure, there are always skirmishes, employees who'd gotten too big for their britches and said so, whatever. But none that would have resulted in an attack."

I noted this time around, he didn't seem all that convinced but was holding things close to the vest. Whether out of loyalty or something else I was sure. Could he be protecting someone? Someone other than Edwards?

"How about you?"

I started. "How about me…what?"

"Who's on your hot sheet?"

The hamster on its wheel in my noodle gave her little legs a workout trying to determine how much to divulge, especially after he'd failed to share anything substantial, including any names, for his part of the trade. What if he was meeting with me at Edwards' behest? Perhaps Edwards sent him to get a leg-up on what I was doing so that he could intercept and deal with the person himself. Or cover his trail.

It didn't help that Logan and I had gone sideways—could I even trust my own judgment? Admittedly, I was gaining very little traction on my own and spending more time dodging Decker's bestie than finding evidence on her mother's killer. Sighing, I nodded. My consternation was not lost on him as he surprised me by patting me on the arm in a buddy-buddy gesture, though I still wasn't stuck on the idea that the person who had attacked Edwards was the same person who had murdered Ellen Decker.

Wendell had done little in the way of altering my mindset. Instead, I focused on the prior for the moment, hoping that by offering a bit of goodwill, I'd get something out of the big guy in return.

"What do you know of Danielle Reynolds?"

Wendell shook his head, so I pulled up a picture that I'd secretly snapped at the hotel. It wasn't her best look, but it would have to suffice.

"She's young," he mumbled and, after a moment, shook his head. "But she looks like a lot of girls her age, so I can't say I'd recall her, even if I'd seen her. She's definitely not someone my employer has done business with."

"What about Maria Reynolds?"

"Considering the similarity in the last name, I'm assuming there's a tie-in to this young woman?"

I nodded. "Her mother, who was formerly employed by Edwards' wife as a personal assistant of sorts."

"Hmm…not ringing a bell. Sounds like it was before my time. Gotta picture of her?"

I shook my head while suppressing a frown. He was right, Maria had worked for the Edwards' family long before he arrived on the scene, though I'd hoped the scuttlebutt had made its way through the staff, especially ones who'd been around the block for more than a hot minute.

Wendell dashed my hopes, even though what he shared came as no surprise.

"No one lasts long with the missus. Most are lucky if they make it through the probationary period—a week or less, in case you were wondering." I couldn't see his eyes, but he tilted his head, and I caught a glimpse of the arc of one of his brows above the shades. I nodded my understanding and gestured for him to continue. "Contrary to what you probably believe, Mr. Edwards doesn't require as much assistance as his wife and isn't nearly as…" He worked his mouth and seemed to struggle to conjure the right word.

"Hysterical?" I attempted to mask a grin.

"That's actually a bit kinder than the word that immediately popped into my head. Anyway, those of us who are employed solely for the purpose of working for Mr. Edwards tend to stick around a little longer. And before you ask, I'm the one with the longest tenure, so there's no way to backtrack and compare notes. If Maria left her position, though, it wasn't of her own doing. Of that, I'm sure."

This time, I didn't bother suppressing a frown. It definitely made things more challenging.

A thought came to mind.

"I hear what you are saying. Maria may very well have been let go at some point, but in this scenario, it seems as though Edwards would have had some say-so in the subject, especially when a revered member of the community referred her. At that point in his career, he certainly couldn't afford to lose face in the event word of her…separation from her position made its way back to this man, especially considering she was a single mother with two children to support."

Wendell swiveled in his seat. "Wait—are you talking about Babbo Santini?"

I wasn't sure about the Babbo a.k.a. dad reference but continued. "You knew him?"

He released an exasperated sigh. "Everyone knew him. He served as both a father figure and a leader that spanned generations. You either wanted to be him or be in his presence. You see that park across the street?" He pointed over my right shoulder to an outcropping of trees. Without waiting for my response, he continued, "*He* made that happen. He's also responsible for the one on the west side and most of the community centers that span the area. Before him we had nothing. And the fact they are still standing speaks volumes."

"A testament to his legacy," I murmured, to which Wendell offered me a nod. "I'd heard that he did the same in his own backyard, quite literally, and that his house became quite the revolving door for the neighborhood kids."

He shrugged. "I wasn't here at the time, but I wouldn't doubt it. The man was a force. "

"I heard he had some involvement with one of the local baseball teams, but other than that, never really got a sense for what his profession was, though I didn't get the impression that he a particularly wealthy man."

"He wasn't wealthy in the financial sense, but he'd made valuable connections over the years. His loyalty was rewarded in a variety of ways." He pressed his lips together. Apparently, that line of questioning had come to an end.

"I…see," I replied. "So we can agree that he was very well connected."

Wendell shrugged and turned to gaze over at my vehicle, where two pointy ears had popped up in the backseat. "He gonna be okay?"

"Yes, he'll probably fall back asleep. It *is* nap time," I added when he returned his gaze to me. "If you're concerned, though, I can bring him over."

He raised a hand. "That's okay. I'm sure you're right."

"Not a dog fan." I chuckled when Wendell's mouth worked too hard formulating a response and reached over to pat him on the leg. "It's fine. It'll be our little secret."

Wendell grunted. "So, getting back Maria Reynolds. How does Babbo Santini fit in?"

Dog issues, indeed. "His daughter, Mae, was best friends with Maria."

"Is that so?" He shifted in his seat. The movement was slight, but it was there.

I surveyed him for a minute, but when he offered no more, I continued. "Yeah, there was a group of neighborhood kids who hung out together at the Santini house. From what I've heard, the place was a revolving door. Everyone was welcome, whether it was for a meal, a reprieve from their own home life, whatever. It was a safe haven."

"Sounds like Babbo." Wendell nodded. "I wouldn't be surprised if some of those kids stayed more than others."

I shrugged, Mae had alluded to the same. "Max Decker was part of Maria and Mae's circle."

His mouth opened, closed. "I had no idea."

"Small world, huh?" My voice was thick with sarcasm, though Wendell was not taking the bait.

"Certainly seems that way. So, Maria Reynolds got her post with Mrs. Edwards because of Babbo."

"Because of his *connection* to Edwards, yes." I grabbed the opportunity to toss that bit out.

"Probably because of his daughter's influence," he added.

"Do you know her?" A thought occurred to me.

He shrugged. "Can't say that I do." I wasn't convinced but tucked it away for later as he continued. "But I can see what you're saying about Mr. Edwards' possible concern over his wife having dispatched her."

"Not good for business, you mean." It was not a question, and either he did not take it as one, or he ignored it, so I added, "Then again, neither is murder."

He chewed on that for a moment before responding. "Quite a coincidence that these people all knew one another and their lives were either deeply intertwined or connected by circumstance." He paused to glance at me. "I've never been a fan of coincidences."

I shook my head—neither had I. He gripped the steering wheel with his meaty claws and released it, only to repeat the exercise. I wondered how many he'd replaced and was giving that some consideration when he huffed out a breath, leaving his voice ragged as he spoke.

"Someone's gotta be lying. Question is, which one has the most to hide? And lose?"

I wasn't sure if he expected an answer, though I knew he wouldn't take kindly to my response. Instead, I bit my tongue until blood crept over my bottom teeth, and the metallic taste filled my mouth, which was the only thing that prevented me from pointing out that his employer was a key factor in solving that equation.

CHAPTER TWENTY-FOUR

We sat in silence. Until I couldn't stand it any longer.

"Wendell, what made you reach out to me?"

"Despite what you think about the man or the blackness of his heart, Mr. Edwards is innocent." He turned to gaze at me. "And I believe deep down, you think so, too." It was the only time I would see Wendell's eyes, as he tipped his shades down to reveal an intense shade of hazel, with flecks of yellow rimming the pupils. Before my mouth could drop open, he pushed them back up with a meaty knuckle.

I shifted back my seat in an attempt to put some distance between the question and Wendell's ploy to distract me.

Finally, I managed to conjure a coherent response as I shook my head. "Nice try, Wendell. It's more than that. Guys like you don't come out from behind the Wizard's curtain simply to have a chat with mere mortals like me."

His massive frame shook the SUV as he chuckled. "Touché. Then tell me how a nice girl like you got herself involved in this mess."

I sighed, then told him about Decker's request after her death. Wendell nodded when I finished, a broad grin spanning his face.

It wasn't quite as creepy as I'd pictured, but it did hedge toward the list of things that kept me from falling asleep at night.

"*That*, Arianna Jackson, is why I emerged from beyond the curtain to chat with a mere mortal like you. And the reason I'm entering into this arrangement to work together." I squinted, not quite capturing his point, causing him to hack out a rough chuckle. "It's about respect. And loyalty. What you're doing for Kelly Decker—that's righteous in my book."

I shrugged. "Guess you just caught me on a good day."

I had more to ask but knew that I'd squeezed all the juice from that orange. Wendell and I parted ways with a loose agreement that we'd touch base when we learned something that could benefit the other. I hoped that he'd been truthful when assuring me he had no intention of running back to papa to share the details of our discussion.

I slid back into my vehicle, cursing when I noted the messages that had piled up in my absence—Logan; Ben Jennings, the apartment manager; Larissa; Danielle—when had I gotten so popular? The irony was not lost on me as I reflected on the fact that I had been chatting up Edwards' henchman. I hated to admit it, but the guy was growing on me.

I bypassed Logan's message in favor of the one left by Ben— the only one of my callers who had not annoyed me in the last forty-eight hours.

I sighed, listening as Ben prattled off who he was in detail, despite the fact we had just spoken a few hours earlier. It wasn't until he got to the reason for his call that my spidey senses started tingling.

"After you left, I relayed our conversation to the wife. She reminded me of something I'd forgotten—probably because it was third party information—which I don't put much trust in. Anyway, here goes: according to one of the neighbors—Frank Powers was his name, been gone eight or so years now—he and another resi-

dent had to break up an argument between the gals the night Ellen was murdered. Fortunately, they were able to do so before things turned physical, and the little ones got involved—they were up in Ellen's apartment, blissfully unaware and deep in their own play—but not before Frank overheard some less than savory threats being bantered about.

"The missus couldn't remember the exact dialogue that Frank had relayed—and truth be told, I'm glad for it. The man could get a tad colorful with his adjectives—but she did recall that the argument started over a man. From there, a variety of accusations were tossed out—fighting words—which, no matter who the 'he' was, it didn't sound to Frank that it bode well for the man in the end.

"Frank and the other resident told the police all of this and it never amounted to anything, so I guess it doesn't really matter now. Just thought I'd let you know so that you'd have a different frame of reference, especially if you'd been left with the impression that everything was all puppies and rainbows back then. They weren't, for whatever it's worth." Ben hacked out a chuckle that was laden with sadness before bringing the message to its conclusion.

Or so I thought.

"Darn it, I almost forgot. A friend of yours stopped by after we chatted. Said his name was Hogan...Brogan or something like that. Nice young fellow—perhaps your young man? Said he'd been delayed and after I told him that he'd just missed you, we had a quick chat about what you and I'd discussed. Figured I'd save you the trouble of having to repeat everything."

I gritted my teeth while pinching the bridge of my nose as he rattled on.

"You can thank me later, but he's up to date on everything— except for that last bit the missus just drummed up. Anyway, you

*can give him heck later for having to put up with me on your
own.*" He released a rumbling chuckle before signing off.

I saved the message so that I could listen to it again and fully
digest it. I wasn't sure how I felt about Logan and the fact he
knew I was aware he hadn't actually been to Decker's old apartment building. Perhaps he was curious why I'd checked up on
him. If he was angry—too bad. His tongue-lashing would have to
wait—and even then, it would pale in comparison to the choice
words I'd be sharing with him.

Right now, I needed to ruminate on Ben's last tidbit, though I
knew all it offered was more questions. Why were Maria and
Ellen fighting—and about who? Could it have been a possible
connection to Edwards? And, if there had been trouble, to the
point of violence, why had Maria left her child with the woman
she had just argued with? Surely if the argument had taken a
violent turn, the last thing she would have wanted was the other
woman watching over her child? Had Ellen found out about
Danielle's paternity? If so, how? And why would it have caused
two friends to turn on one another?

I shook my head. We'd never have answers to those questions,
as Maria's mind would remain static, forever a locked vault.

Moving through the messages, more to distract myself from
Ben's than anything, I received a reluctant "just checking in"
from Larissa, a hang-up from Danielle and a terse "Call me. We
need to talk" from Logan. Oh, how things had changed. I'd
initially trusted him, based on his relationship with Decker, and
had even grown to like him after she'd passed. But even she
would have raised a brow at his recent behavior. I doubt she
would have condoned it and would have demanded an explanation. Or put him in the ground herself.

If I could just channel her bravado.

I sighed. Sooner or later I was gonna have to rip the band-aid
off. I searched through my phone's contacts and stabbed an index

finger on Logan's number. He picked up on the first ring—there went my shot at changing my mind.

"AJ." His voice was ragged. Perhaps all that running around trailing me had left him breathless.

"Just curious—did Ben manage to get his clothes dry before his wife found out?" I asked, smirking when I heard him suck in a breath. It was time for Officer Piedmont to receive a dose of reality.

Mine.

"That's right, Logan. I know you had your little chat with Ben *after* I was there. Imagine my surprise when he informed me that I had been the only other person, since Decker, to discuss her mother's murder with him."

I paused to let that settle but not long enough for him to form a response. "So while I realize you can't be in two places at once —I'm sure following me up and down the coast can be quite a chore—what's got me scratching my head is that you used your *job* as an excuse when your employer isn't expecting to see that sweet lying face any time in the foreseeable future."

I'll admit—the length of silence I received was satisfying.

Once the beast was unleashed, it was hard to rein it in, but I managed to temporarily keep the clawing and gnashing under control.

Finally, my efforts were rewarded.

"You've been busy." Logan's voice was flat. At least he had the good sense not to deny it. As uncomfortable as it was, I sat with the silence. "Listen, about the job—"

"Later," I huffed out. Silence was no longer a path to least resistance. "I'm sure you've got your reasons, but while we've all been following each other's tracks and running around in circles, we are no closer to bringing Ellen Decker's killer to justice, as Decker asked us—me—to do. That is, unless you've got something compelling to share."

"I don't." He sighed, sounding wearier than my aching bones and wonky brain.

"That's too bad. Well, at least there's one pinprick of light in these otherwise inky circumstances—I don't have to rehash everything Ben told me during our visit." I laid into the sarcasm, which he ignored.

"Mmm, hmm. Yeah, unfortunately, there was nothing new there."

"Says you."

Against my better judgment, I shared the information that Ben had provided after Logan had left the apartment complex. Perhaps in hindsight, I should have held off until he could explain himself, but my exhausted brain was acting a bit hinky, and I think the part that handled rationalization had gone off to take a siesta. Or a margarita, followed by a siesta.

"Well, that's a new wrinkle. Why would Maria allow Danielle to stay over after having a heated argument with the woman who was watching her child?"

"My thoughts exactly." I paused, chewing my lip as I parsed everything I'd learned. "Which brings me to another question: how did Max Decker conclude that Edwards was responsible? We initially thought it was related to one of the cases he'd investigated where Edwards had been involved, where the two had crossed paths and butted heads—payback, or that sort of thing. But, when you think about Edwards, can you really see him getting his hands dirty?"

Perhaps some of what Wendell had pointed out had sunk in and forced me to look at the reality of the situation. Sure, Edwards had been decades younger then and been an up and comer—aggressive, assertive and arrogant, yeah, but a cold-blooded murderer? I had my doubts that the man had shed his shark skin with age. If anything, it was a much better fit.

"Anyway, I guess what I'm trying to spit out is that he's not really the type to burden himself with such laborious details. His clients, sure. But none of them would have gone out on a limb for their lawyer, no matter what he was doing for them. And Terrence Edwards doing the deed himself? I just don't see it."

"You're suggesting Edwards is just too high-brow—and fussy—to commit murder."

I made noises that suggested he had gotten the gist of my assessment. I expected a snark that didn't come. Instead, Logan sounded…contemplative.

"You're proposing that while he may not be willing to get his hands dirty, he wouldn't be opposed to the notion of murder itself, if it served his greater good. Meaning, murder's not outside the realm of possibility where his moral flexibility is concerned, as long as he doesn't have to concern himself with the implementation."

He wasn't off-base, but it sent shivers up my spine.

"Maybe. Yeah. Yeah." I nodded as I sucked in a breath. It was time to own what I'd just put out into the universe. "Ellen's murder was so up close and personal. I'm just not sure when you take a step back and look at the events of that day, that Edwards was ever a viable candidate."

"You've certainly changed your tune."

"I've just gained a bit of perspective. On all counts," I replied through gritted teeth. Even though we were having a civil conversation, it didn't mean that Logan's actions no longer had my toes curling.

"Whatever. Your perspective has merit." He'd elected to ignore the elephant that was stomping on his foot.

"Gosh, Officer Piedmont, I appreciate your vote of confidence." Yeah, the childish devil on my shoulder still felt a few digs were warranted.

Logan cleared his throat. "Sorry. I meant your intuition wasn't completely off."

I made my best huffing sound. "And this is making things better...how?"

Discombobulated and tongue-tied, he attempted a few starts before his mouth finally relinquished the reins and let a bit of common sense slip in, along with an exasperated sigh.

"Let me back up. I reviewed Max's files again, and based on what Ben told you, a few things started making a bit more sense, including other motives behind the murder." He paused and then continued, almost speaking more to himself than anything. "I'm just not sure why Max didn't see it."

"Earth to Logan. Care to expound?" I interjected.

"Sorry, sorry," he huffed. I think I was starting to wear him out. The thought almost made me smile. Almost. "According to Max's files, his sights were set on Edwards after receiving an anonymous tip."

I rummaged through my internal database. "The person who claimed they saw someone who looked like the Edwards leave the complex shortly after the murder?"

"Yeah. Convenient how this case—if you tie the two events together—seems to be getting its fair share of anonymous witnesses, isn't it? The first puts Edwards leaving the scene of the crime, and the second, we've got yet another anonymous witness claiming to have seen a woman matching your description in the vicinity shortly after he was attacked."

"Hey. Wasn't me."

Logan clucked his tongue in my ear. "Of course not. No one could blame you if you smacked that smirk off his arrogant, self-righteous face, especially after having his thug drag you into his lair so that he could school you."

I pulled my phone away and squinted—I didn't recall Logan being there, yet here he was, offering up a side-commentary when he should have had my back. I was about to point that out when I realized he was still talking.

"No matter how you look at it, there seems to be a couple of people out there who are trying very hard to divert our attention elsewhere—whether they're working together remains to be seen."

I nodded, belatedly realizing that he could not see me.

"According to Max's notes, someone he refers to as 'M' confirmed that Edwards knew his wife. As it turns out, Edwards first laid his eyes on Ellen when he was asked to speak on ethics and the law—if you can believe that—at the college she was attending.

"She just happened to be in that class, sitting in the front row as she typically did, so Edwards' beady little eyes zoned in on her. He asked around and learned that she was looking for a part-time entry-level position in the legal field to help her get her feet wet as she worked to get her degree. She'd had dreams of becoming a legal assistant."

"It's sad that her dreams were ripped from her," I murmured.

"Heartbreaking," Logan replied, his tone solemn. "Of course, you probably won't find it surprising that he just managed to find a spot for her in his firm. Max didn't note the specifics, other than Edwards went out of his way, and that there were rumblings about why and how he'd made it happen so quickly."

"Are you thinking that this 'M' was involved somehow or overhead something?" I asked.

"'M' could have recommended her in the first place. Assuming this person is Maria, she would have known that Ellen was looking for a job."

"Riiiight. Just a typical casual conversation in the laundry room. I can see it now." I cleared my throat to prepare my best Edwards' imitation.

"'Hey Maria, have you seen my silk boxers? No, not those, the ones with the little sharks on them. It's gonna be one of *those* days in court. By the way, my office could use some sprucing up, if you get my drift? Of course you do. So, what do you say? Got any friends that are as fine as you that could work for me? No pun intended.'"

I finished by releasing an Edwards-worthy laugh before adding, "Of course, there's that whole baby daddy thing, which would have totally inspired her to recommend her childhood friend's hot wife." I followed it up with a faux retching sound.

"You about done?" I noticed he didn't really allow me time to collect myself much less respond. "She may not have recommended Ellen, but there is a reference to her in Max's notes. Maybe she overheard Edwards talking about it on the phone… whatever…it doesn't really matter, 'cause Decker—our Decker— was able to confirm it."

He'd put a tack in my balloon, and if his pregnant paused suggested he was reveling in the moment, my response put placed it on his highlight reel.

"What?" I squeaked. "How?"

A low chuckle emitted from the other side of the connection. "According to Decker's files, initially she backtracked her father's notes and reconfirmed everything she could—his tips, leads, the case file, the detectives who worked it—anything and everything, just in case someone had forgotten a detail the first time around—"

"Or purposely left something out," I added.

"Exactly. And after she did that, she started over again, at the bottom of the food chain."

"I assume you're referring to Danielle?" Logan made a grumbling noise that ended with some colorful language.

I wondered if he ever just let his preconceived notion of Danielle go. She had been a different person—heck, we all had— and if his best friend had faith in her word, why couldn't he bury the hatchet with her?

Mind you, I didn't like her much better, but I was at least

trying not to let it get in the way of solving this case. Just as soon as the thought entered my mind, I wondered if I could do the same for Logan, as I'd allowed my current feelings about his actions to cloud my judgment.

He was no Danielle, though perhaps I had expected…more.

In looking at my own life, who was I to pass judgment on others, whose lives I couldn't even begin to understand, and who I could not ask the same in return?

Perhaps somewhere in there was the answer.

"Anyway, Danielle told Decker that her mother was the one who told her about the connection."

"And Decker believed her." I came off sounding more judgey than I had intended.

"Well, she did, when it confirmed what she found in Max's notes." When I started to interject, he quickly added, "Keep in mind that Decker never mentioned anything about it to Danielle."

"So, you're saying that Danielle knew about the encounter at the university and then how Ellen went on to work at Edwards' firm?"

"No on the latter. I failed to mention that Ellen never ended up taking the position. Instead, she opted for another, working on the staff of one of the criminal court judges."

I whistled. "Criminal court. How ironic. What I don't understand is why Maria would have told her daughter about any of it. Danielle was already out of the house. Then Maria had a stroke. How and when did the topic even come up?"

"I honestly don't know any more than what we have in the notes." Logan sounded somewhat deflated. I couldn't say I blamed him.

"At least we know the connection between Edwards and Ellen."

"That is true. Interesting how all of this seems to lead back to Max's 'M,' who could easily be Maria. Unfortunately, we're not going to get any more from under that rock, given her current condition. I wish we had one more shot at finding out what she and Ellen fought about the night Ellen was murdered."

"I guess it was just convenient that I happened to stop by and have a chat with Ben then, isn't it?"

"Listen, AJ—"

"Later, Logan," I snapped. "Not everything is about you."

"Point taken." If he was caught off-guard or felt slighted that I continued to prevent him from pleading his case, his tone bore no indication, so I took it as a sign that I could proceed without rehashing it. For the time being.

"Our problem is this: both Max and Decker went down different paths and ended up coming to the same conclusion—that Edwards was single-handedly responsible for Ellen's brutal murder. But what if—and this is in no way a dig on either of their investigative skills—both of them were working on false truths to begin with?"

"Then both of them could've arrived at the same wrong conclusion." His voice was barely a whisper, but he spoke as though the idea was growing on him.

"Big words, big man. But yes, and I think we both have our *feelings* about Edwards, but as I've stated before, the probability that he killed Ellen with his own hands is not likely."

"Still, he could have ordered it." This time, there was no conviction behind his words.

"I agree that Edwards is capable of delegating many things. A lot of them reprehensible. But this murder was personal. Whoever is responsible would have wanted to inflict the fear, terror, and horror themselves. They wouldn't have gotten the full benefit of the act if they had delegated it to another."

"Okay, if not Edwards, then who?"

"And that's the real question, isn't it?" I paused for a moment to let that settle. "All this time, we've been going off what Decker told us, while the killer has hidden safely in the shadows. No, the real question is: who wanted—or needed—Ellen dead, and had the capacity to do it?"

"So basically, we're starting over," Logan grumbled.

"Glass half-full, half-empty perspective." He made another noise, and though I wasn't sure what it was, he didn't sound convinced. "Cheer up, Logan, all is not lost."

"Two idioms in three seconds. Impressive, AJ."

"Cool it, Officer Piedmont. You're on thin ice as it is." More grumbling ensued, followed by silence. I let it sit before proceeding. "What I'm saying is that while it may seem as though we're starting over, it doesn't mean that we're starting from scratch. There has to be some truth buried in there. Both Decker and her father were excellent at what they did. The nature of what they were investigating was just too close for them to gauge things from an unbiased, impassive perspective."

"Okay, so they both arrived at the wrong conclusion. That's a huge help."

"Hear me out. Not *arrived*, Logan. What if each was carefully, masterfully led down that path?"

"Are you suggesting that Danielle is masterful?" Before I could respond, he continued. "Not likely. Besides, when Ellen was murdered, Danielle was a child. As for Maria, she couldn't have overthrown Ellen, much less inflicted that kind of…injury. It had to be a man."

"True. But what if neither were the original source of the information given to Decker and her father?"

"Someone else manipulated the situation and fed Maria and Danielle the precise details they wanted, knowing they'd eventually get passed on."

I nodded, though he couldn't see me. "Classic misdirection."

Identifying the method of the madness may have fallen under the category of "good to know" but it was a far cry from helping us determine who the murderer was or what had driven him to end Ellen Decker's life.

All we knew was that he was comfortable doing his own dirty work and had no bones about pulling any necessary strings. And while he had more than twenty years to become a master of his craft, he'd failed to remove Edwards as a loose end and, in doing so, had raised the stakes.

CHAPTER TWENTY-FIVE

We didn't have time to reflect, as my phone buzzed. It was Wendell. "Uh, I need to take this. Can I put you on hold?"

I realized Logan had disconnected when he was staring at me from the passenger side window, gesturing for me to unlock the door.

Rising above the shock, I cast him a "what the heck?" look, releasing the child locks while trying to catch Wendell's call before it disappeared into the voicemail black hole.

"Someone just tried to kill Mr. Edwards," Wendell growled before I had an opportunity to utter a salutation.

Tried, as in they didn't succeed? I wasn't sure what to do with that question that bubbled up from who-knows-where. Thankfully, I hadn't said it out loud, collecting myself enough to babble something along the lines of "What? Who?"

Logan stared at me with a cross between venom and disgust—I had inadvertently put the call on speaker—as Wendell growled, "That…girl. The one you asked me about. Danielle. She tried to inject something into one of Mr. Edwards' tubes, just as he started coming to."

"No," I whispered, my mind scrambling. What had driven her to attempt to kill a man she'd never met?

A mix of exasperation, frustration, and worry filled Wendell's voice. "He recognized her—heck, the way Mr. Edwards told it, they had an entire conversation. I arrived just as she was slipping out of his room. She looked like she belonged—a nurse's uniform, badge—how was I supposed to know? Mr. Edwards was uncommonly flustered, and despite his weakened condition, attempted to rip out his IVs so that he could go after her. I calmed him down before he set off alarms, but he was adamant that I find her and bring her back. My preference would have been to dangle her out the window by her feet." Wendell released a growl that made me shudder, causing Logan to roll his eyes.

I shot him a warning look. One didn't need an ejector seat when they had an Alaskan Malamute who could pounce on command ready and waiting behind me. Glancing back, I realized that the only thing Nicoh was ready and waiting for was dinner. Sighing, I returned to glare at Logan and drew a zipping motion across my mouth to remind him to keep his thoughts to himself as Wendell continued.

"When I couldn't find her, Mr. Edwards insisted that I not mention it to anyone. I was collecting the syringe just as the staff came in and checked him out. I was asked to leave, but once they confirmed he was stable, he demanded that I be allowed to stay— the man tends to get what he wants. Anyway, against their policies, procedures, and all their rigmarole, they conceded.

"Once Mr. Edwards was satisfied we were alone, he told me that he was being blackmailed, and when he refused to pay, he was attacked the next day."

"By Danielle?" I managed to squeak out.

"That's what I thought, too, but Mr. Edwards said no. The blackmailing had been going on for more than twenty years, until he decided it was time to put a stop to it," Wendell replied, exasperation filling his voice. "He did note it was coincidental that Danielle appeared shortly after to finish the job."

"How so?" I glanced at Logan, frowning at the phone while he worked his jaw. Was it possible that Danielle and the blackmailer were working together—and playing us all?

Wendell blew out a breath. "The blackmailer threatened to expose the girl's paternity. What I'm about to tell you remains between the two of us." When I agreed, he continued. "Mr. Edwards confirmed that this girl, Danielle, *is* his daughter, conceived with his wife's personal assistant. He's not proud it happened, and said it had occurred at a difficult time in his life, both professionally and personally." When I didn't respond, he added, "You already knew…about the girl."

I glanced at Logan, who nodded. "I did. But it wasn't my information to tell."

Wendell grumbled something unintelligible before huffing out a breath. "Fair enough."

I shook my head. "You honestly had no idea?"

"I did not." Wendell's frustration had morphed into resignation.

"What about the blackmailer?" I pressed, eager to identify the source of the extortion and the person who had gone out of their way to make me look guilty of attacking their money bag after he'd reneged on their agreement.

"A woman."

I frowned, noting that Logan's expression mirrored my own. "He wouldn't say who?"

"He doesn't know, for sure."

"But he suspects."

"He suspects," Wendell replied in a clipped tone that suggested he wasn't pleased with his employer's secrecy.

"And Danielle?" I prompted.

"I'm still looking."

"Keep me posted."

"You do the same, Arianna Jackson." If it hadn't been for the circumstances, I would have thought he sounded amused.

For some reason, a moment of weakness came over me. "I'm glad your boss is okay, Wendell."

He paused, surveying me before he responded. "That must have hurt."

"More than you possibly know."

* * *

I held up a finger as Logan started to speak and punched at a name on my phone's contact list.

She picked up on the first ring. "Why the hell didn't you tell me?"

"Listen to me, Danielle—"

"No, you listen! Why didn't you tell me that arrogant jerk Terrence Edwards was my father? And don't tell me you didn't know, because I know you did."

I heard a slamming sound before she released a string of choice phrases directed at yours truly. Finally, after running me through some extended expletive thesaurus, her voice lowered an octave, though the venom remained.

"I almost killed my father, Arianna—my *father*! One minute, he's all pathetic and tubed up—and I think this *monster* deserves what he did to Decker's mom. He destroyed my family and my life, just as much as he did hers. I lost my best friend and my world in one night, and as I'm the only one left who's got the guts to do anything about it, I decided it was time he paid for what he owed me. What he owed all of us.

"Everything that brought him to that point made it perfect—the attack gave me a way to access him. I didn't even care if I got away with it, as long I scraped every ounce of him from this earth. I was reveling in the moment, plunging the syringe into his IV, when he woke up and called me by name!"

"What happened?" I managed to eke out before she shrieked, and more slamming ensued.

"I dropped the damn syringe, that's what happened! And, I came to my senses—I almost killed another human being!" Her voice shook. "I turned to bolt when he called out to me and pleaded for me to stay. Terrence Edwards...*pleaded.*"

"And that's when he told you?" I prompted, keeping my tone even to avoid more verbal and physical abuse to whatever she'd been pummeling.

"If you're asking if that was when he told me he knocked my mom up and left her to fend for herself, then yes," she snapped.

"He said that?"

She hacked out a harsh laugh. "Of course not. The great Terrence Edwards would never cop to anything so lowly. Whatever," Danielle sniffed, before adding, "at least the man proved useful."

"Because you found out who your father was?"

She tilted her head, studying me before doling out the sarcasm. "No, because I found out before I made good on my plan to end him."

"Edwards may be okay, but don't be surprised if the police come looking for you. Then again, you could beat them to the punch and turn yourself in." I shrugged when Logan squinted at me. I was hoping she might be more...cooperative if she thought her world was closing in, and I could be a means of helping her out.

"Sorry, babe. Not a chance," Danielle snickered before

adding, "at least not until I confront that backstabbing liar. Looking back, it makes sense. We all got played. And now it's time to call that hand for what it is—a bluff."

"Wait—what makes sense? Who—"

My query was met with a dial tone.

CHAPTER TWENTY-SIX

"I need to call Larissa." Logan nodded and gestured for me to proceed.

Once the niceties were out of the way, I got down to business. "I know this sounds like it's coming out of left field, but how much did you know about Danielle's father?"

"Honestly, our mother never told us anything about him," she replied, "and the subject was off-limits, punishable by grounding for life."

"Who else could have known?"

"No one that I know of. Mother was far too proud for that and besides, not long after, she had the stroke which affected her mentally—"

"Hold up—'not long after' what?" I rasped out.

"After Ellen…died."

"Wait—I thought the stroke happened decades after the murder?" Belatedly, I realized that Larissa wouldn't relish reliving that night. Even though she'd been at her father's, Ellen's murder had impacted her life, too.

Larissa sighed. "That was the second stroke—the one that

finally broke my mother and stole her from us…forever. And now, there's no chance we'll ever get that answer."

"I'm sorry…I didn't mean—"

"No, there's no way you could have known. If Mae hadn't found her that day—the first time—and done what she did, my mother would have died. But the damage was done—many of her memories were lost and those that remained…were questionable. Funny, other than some minor motor control issues, anyone who met her from that point forward would hardly have known. It was those of us who knew her that realized how much she'd lost that day. Still, thanks to Mae, she was alive. More alive than she is now, anyway."

Sadness consumed me like a tidal wave, while guilt pulsed through every pore for reopening her wound.

"So, Mae saved your mother's life?" I asked as gently as I could.

After a few sniffles, she responded in the affirmative. "Mae had recently completed a nursing program and gotten a plush job in one of the local hospitals. She happened to be dropping off some things we'd left at her house when she found my mother. If she hadn't spotted the symptoms and known what to do—my mother would have died."

I attempted to hide an audible gasp before responding, "Oh my, I had no idea. Mae…never mentioned it when we talked."

She released a sad chuckle. "Not surprising. Mae never did care much for the limelight where her nursing career was concerned. I think she secretly aspired to bigger things but was always stuck in the shadow of her father."

"I would have thought that he would have been proud that she'd not only chosen such an admirable career, she'd used it to save her friend's life?"

"I'm sure he was proud of her accomplishments, in his own way. The man was larger than life—everyone he came in contact with was family—though sometimes I think his own took a back-seat and were given whatever leftovers remained after he served the masses."

"I see." My tone might have been laden with sarcasm, which had been unintentional.

"Goodness, I didn't mean to speak ill of the dead. He was a good man. A good provider and an integral part of the community. He just allowed his cup to get overfilled at times. Of course, I'm repeating this secondhand, but it's what I gathered from hearing Mother talk about him." She chuckled lightly but there was sadness behind it, perhaps thinking of her mother and the memories of the stories she'd once told.

There was a moment of silence before Larissa cleared her throat. "Sorry, having a moment. Not sure why it's been getting to me more lately, but I find myself welling up over the dumbest things. You know what I mean?"

Thinking of my parents, her grief cut me to the core. "I do, and I'm sorry for the pain that this situation has drummed up."

She made a tsking sound before responding, "My mother is still alive. Danielle is still alive. I'd rather feel these things while they are with me, in whatever form, than live a lifetime wondering 'what if.'" She sighed and paused for a moment before continuing, "It's interesting, though. The passing of Mae's father might have been a blessing in disguise. After his death, Mother said that Mae got her brother back. Apparently, the two picked up where they had left off in their younger years and were as thick as thieves."

"Mae has a brother?" I glanced at Logan, who shrugged, apparently, this was news to him as well.

"Oh, yes. But Matteo and his father fell out when I was very young, which is why I didn't remember him."

"'Fell out'?" Friends could fall out. Families? Blood was

blood, and in many cultures, it would require an apocalyptic transgression to be cast from the tribe.

"According to Mom, Matteo was disowned for lacking moral fiber and tarnishing the Santini name. Initially, it was rumored that Babbo had heard rumblings on the street that Matteo was Danielle's father. Granted, the lot of them were once close, but both Matteo and Mother denied it, and frankly, both were embarrassed and incensed that he'd believed it could be true."

"And after Matteo was disowned?" I prompted.

"From what I've heard, he wanted to become an entertainer, and after attending one of the more notable drama colleges in the country, he changed his name to Antonio Santini—Mother said he thought his middle name would look better on a marquee than Matteo—and ended up getting some work on Broadway. Why do you ask?"

"Just curious," I replied, fighting the desire to dig into that goldmine a bit more. I needed to stay focused on the challenge I currently had in front of me, however, and shifted the subject back in that direction. "Continuing that curious streak, has Danielle been in contact with you?"

"No. Why?" Larissa's tone was a mix of hopefulness and hesitation.

Whoops. Wrong Move. "Um. No reason. Chalk it up to lack of sleep," I replied, reddening at my misstep when Logan face-palmed.

"Ah…okay," she replied as though I'd deflated her tires. "I've gotta run, but you'll keep me posted?" Still hopeful, so thankfully, I hadn't punctured all four.

"Of course." I blew out a breath, having averted a possible crisis. Logan peered at me from behind splayed fingers but shook his head. "Oh, and Larissa?"

"Yeah?"

"Don't worry, this will all work out." The words sounded so

hollow the minute they exited my mouth, I immediately regretted them.

Larissa released a sad chuckle. "If only that comment made me feel better."

Once she disconnected, I turned to Logan. "I think Mae Santini left out some of the good parts when I talked to her. What did she have worth peeking at that she didn't want me to see?"

"It certainly makes you wonder," he replied, drumming his fingers on the dashboard.

I was equally impatient with these people. "How is it possible that this brother's name never popped up before now?"

Logan squinted. "It is strange. Decker never mentioned it, and there's no reference in Max's notes. Do you think it's relevant?"

I understood his hesitation. Was it a shiny object or something worth pursuing?

I answered as honestly as I could. "Heck if I know. I guess at this point, it is until it isn't."

"Very reassuring."

It was okay. I came prepared for his snark.

"Yeah, seem to be getting a lot of *reassurance* myself today."

Logan tilted his head. "Aren't you are the one who said you didn't want to talk about it?"

"I am. And I still don't," I replied in a tone that was perhaps a bit too clipped. Still, the point was transmitted. Which suited me fine.

"Got it. So, what do you want to talk about? I've got time."

"I'm not sure you want to know." I hacked out a laugh as he shifted the farthest distance he could put between us without jumping out of the vehicle. "Don't worry, you and your buffoonery are the last things on my mind at the moment. But if you must know, I'm rummaging through some pretty dark thoughts, and am worried about saying them out loud."

"Because it will make them real?"

"That, and if I'm wrong, I will have put some bad juju out there. And we all know what happens once it's *out there*." His face remained passive as he studied me. "What's that look about?"

"Just thinking that it can't be any worse than what's been running through my mind lately."

"Such as?" I prompted.

Logan shook his head and chuckled. "Nice try. You brought it up, you finish it."

"Fine," I huffed, "but you can't hold anything I say against me."

"That goes both ways."

"Err… Let's get one thing straight. I'm referring to this case. Specifically."

"Chicken."

"Realist."

Logan bowed his head and laughed. "Whatever, AJ. Lay it on me while I'm in a good mood."

It was my turn to hack out a chuckle. If he wanted to compare moods…meh. Another day. Another time.

"Okay. You asked for it. A couple of things I find odd. The first is that Mae was present when Maria suffered a stroke. Her first stroke."

"I'll bite. Go on."

"Why is it that no one knew about her medical expertise? Neither Max, Decker, or even Ben mentioned it. And, for a woman who has never been married and seems to have retired early—well, let's just say I've seen her home, and she done quite well for herself somehow."

"Maybe she's living off her father's inheritance or sold his home…whatever. It's possible she didn't need to rely on her income," Logan replied.

I nodded. "Right. The inheritance. What do we even know

about that?"

"Based on your friend's idolization of Papa Babbo and his vast endeavors, perhaps he can give you the inside scoop." When I gave him a deadpan stare, he added, "Fine. I might know someone who can give us a more unbiased answer."

He ignored my snide, unladylike remark, and made a quick call, looking pretty satisfied with himself upon its conclusion. At least he had the good sense to wipe the smugness from his face before making his announcement.

"Mae's father left everything to various charities, which was dispersed according to his wishes by an executor—who was not Mae."

"Okay," I replied slowly, "and his home?"

"Upon his death, it was turned into a halfway house for paroles of lesser crimes."

"So, Mae was evicted."

Logan nodded. "Though she was not specifically mentioned, the official documentation referenced 'current inhabitants.'"

I blew out a low whistle. "Harsh. And an interesting tie-in to the second thing I find odd—the reemergence of this brother after their father's death. Hinky."

"Very hinky. If that's even a word," Logan replied.

"It is."

"I guess I'll take your word for it. And you can take that pun however it's intended." He offered me a devilish grin, followed by a wink.

Before I could inject a few more bits of snark, my cell buzzed again. Glancing at the screen, I noted it was Ben Jennings and immediately answered.

"I just wanted to check back and make sure you got my message. I don't really trust those machines or voice messages, or whatever they call them."

"I don't blame you, Ben. Too much technology, not enough

face-time, right?" After I'd earned myself a chortle, I continued. "And yes, I did receive your message. I appreciate you sharing your wife's recollection from that day. Even if it was third party, any information we can gather is helpful, though I'll admit I was surprised to learn that Ellen and Maria exchanged some words, especially considering Maria was leaving Danielle in her care."

Ben cleared his throat. "Pardon my hearing, but come again?"

"Um, in your message, you mentioned that a couple of the residents reported seeing Maria and Ellen fighting the day of her murder."

"Oh, goodness, no. Ellen wasn't fighting with Maria. I don't think a harsh word ever passed between them. Not ever." He paused to cluck his tongue and a hint of disdain slipped into his tone. "No, it was Santini's girl who started the whole thing."

I glanced at Logan, and suddenly something shifted into place.

And it all started with Mae.

CHAPTER TWENTY-SEVEN

"Mae? Mae Santini was arguing with Ellen on the day of her murder?" I managed to reply, as Logan's brows raised and his mouth opened. And closed.

"Yes, indeed. Though the missus didn't say as much, I'm sure the Santini girl was the one who started it because Ellen Decker didn't have a mean bone in her body or a negative word for anyone. Can't say the same for the other one. Poor Babbo Santini had no good apples falling from that tree." He paused to scoff. "As for Maria, she was at work long before the row occurred, but honestly, Arianna, why would you think a hard-working single mother like that that would leave her daughter in the care of someone she'd just had it out with, even if that had been the case?"

An incoming call from Wendell saved me from having to answer that, though I'd wondered the same thing. I quickly thanked Ben, mentioning the need to take an incoming call and scrambling to catch Wendell before it rolled to voicemail.

"We hit paydirt, kiddo. Your girl Danielle is on the move."

"What? You tracked her down?" I thought once she'd

succeeded in evading him at the hospital, it would be fruitless trying to locate her. Unless she wanted to be found.

"Did I wake you from a nap or something?" Wendell grunted. "Of course I tracked her down. Got a guy following her now."

"How? And wait—what guy?"

He sighed. "I pulled the video from hospital exits. Saw her slink out an employee exit. Captured her license plate. Called a guy who owes me a favor—"

"Hold up—the hospital just handed the video over?"

I was met with silence.

"Err, yeah, right. Edwards and his clout thing…blah, blah, blah. But this…guy—"

"Don't worry, he's trailing her—from a safe distance—on the Pacific Coast Highway. No idea where she's heading, but at last report, she doesn't seem all that worried about getting snagged by the highway patrol."

I had a sickening feeling I knew Danielle's destination. Question was—did I tell Wendell?

My prolonged silence and perhaps the unintentional "hmm" tossed in there precluded me from having to ponder that any further, as Wendell drew his own conclusions.

"What? You don't trust me to pick *a* guy?" Wendell made a point of enunciating each word into my ear.

"No, it's not that," I sighed, not wanting to make an enemy when he'd extended a branch.

Granted, it might have been from a lemon tree, so I hoped it wouldn't be wrapped in contingencies down the road, as this was one situation where I knew the price would be too high.

Especially where Edwards was concerned.

After filling him in on the latest Ben-o-gram and allowing him a few of his own random external thoughts on the matter, I added, "So to answer your question, yes, I trust you. I just want to know who I should be looking out for so that he doesn't end up getting caught—or killed—in the crossfire. You know, when the doggie doo-doo gets stepped in."

Wendell hacked out a chuckle that probably would have scared my Chuck Taylors' off, had I not met the man in the flesh.

"You're a freaky one, Arianna Jackson. In a good way. Sometimes, I have to wonder if we were separated at birth."

"I very much doubt that, Wendell," I chuckled. "Take my word for it, and you should be happy about that."

Another cryptic laugh resounded in my ear. "See, I knew we were kindred spirits."

"Mmm…like that makes me feel better."

"Come on, admit it—in another lifetime, we might have even been friends, or however that saying goes."

"Ditch Edwards, and we'll talk. When all of this is over."

This time I was rewarded with a snort. "Later, Ms. Jackson. I'll see you on the flip-side."

Wendell abruptly disconnected, which was probably a good thing, because while I enjoyed the random *Boondock Saints* reference, it troubled me that he was familiar with them.

Logan had the good graces to sidestep any awkward commentary and suggested we make that call to Mae as he presented me with her number from one of his mystery sources. After receiving a continued ringing with no connection to a voicemail or answering machine, I turned to him.

"Are you sure this is the right number?"

Logan rolled his eyes. "Of course it's right." When I arched a brow, he added, "Let's just say that I trust this source. And no, you are not allowed to ask questions—whether who it is or how they acquired it. I'm not Wendell."

I punched in an alternative number.

"Who's that?" he asked, leaning over in an attempt to catch a glimpse.

"Danielle," I replied, snatching the phone from his view. It immediately went to voicemail. "Crap. Crap. Crap!" I pummeled the steering wheel, causing Nicoh to release a howl.

"We're heading to Mae's." Logan had drawn the same conclusion. When I nodded, he placed a hand on my arm as I started to turn the key in the ignition. "Mind if I drive?"

"Be my guest. You don't happen to have one of those coplylight things, do you?"

"Sure, I always keep one handy in my back pocket," Logan replied, chuckling. "You know, life isn't always like you see on TV, AJ."

"No, I suppose not," I replied, my tone dry. "Otherwise, there would be a pop-up coming out of my head that reads, 'Don't blame me for Stupidity' with an arrow to the right."

I expected a snarky comeback, but Logan focused on the road, and except for my occasional request for updates, we settled into our thoughts as we headed into the unknown.

Danielle was a wildcard, and if her previous actions were our only gauge, we were in trouble.

I mulled over everything from the day Logan had relayed Decker's request to this moment. After several sidesteps, near misses, and epic fails, it had come down to Danielle nearly killing the man who'd fathered her to crack open a lie that could be the key we'd been searching for all along.

It was also the piece to the puzzle purposely hidden from Max Decker and his daughter.

But how was that possible? Had Max readily believed the lie as easily it had been spun? Or had he been unable to corroborate it as one and before long, it became the truth that he could put some teeth to—even hold onto—in the dark hours when the silence allowed his thoughts to consume him?

Decker then picked up where her father had left off—though it had always been part of her life. Her mother's death was part of her story. And while she hadn't taken all of his conclusions at face value, she'd done her due diligence to prove and disprove them.

Still, she'd ended up on the same path, hitting a blockade when it came to proving that Terrence Edwards had killed her mother, just as her father had. That seed had been sowed and harvested so many times that its origin was known only to those who would not, or could not, reveal it. And the truth of what had transpired that night, and by whom, was safely buried.

Until now.

Somewhere along the line, someone hadn't thought things would progress as they had, assuming perhaps, that things would be forgotten over time. Or that the lies would eventually become the Truth.

One thing they failed to take into account is that there is no statute of limitations for those whose deaths were at the hand of another, leaving justice to the loved ones they'd been forced to leave behind.

Enter Danielle.

What was it that made her react with such fury? Learning that Terrence Edwards was her father had built the fire, but something else—something that had once been elusive and unattainable had lit the match. Was it unraveling that lie that had led her down the path of all other lies?

Allowing Logan to drive failed to calm my nerves as I gnawed what remained of my fingernails, cursing as I repeatedly called both Mae and Danielle and received the same result.

"Best not to run your battery low," he murmured.

"Yeah, well, it's either punch the 'Redial' button or bite my fingers to stumps," I snapped.

I waited for a retort that did not come, and using my peripheral view to gauge his demeanor, found him to have been unmoved by my sudden outburst.

"Sorry."

"Don't be." When his eyes met mine, I knew he meant it.

I nodded. "This request of Decker's…it's taken some unexpected turns."

His gaze shifted back to the road. "Something tells me we've barely tapped into this one."

"I'm worried that the truth may not be worth the cost." I hunched in my seat and stared out the passenger window at the changing landscape, figuring that would be the end of the conversation.

"Thinking of Decker?" he asked after several moments had passed.

"I am," I replied, continuing to watch the shapes, images, and colors whiz by without digesting them. "And I have to wonder…"

"Decker didn't always get things right, AJ. Just because she did everything two-hundred miles per hour without regret doesn't mean there was never a cost." He paused for a moment too long —perhaps choosing his next words. "She wouldn't want her request to place you in harm's way. Or force you to risk your life." The last part was barely a whisper, and though I knew the sentiment had been Decker's, it was Logan who'd given them life.

I turned to look at him. "Are you asking me to bail?"

"What? No!" Apparently, my response had caught him off-guard, as he struggled to find the appropriate words.

I gave his inner thesaurus a rest and offered him a life preserver. "Good, because I'm pretty sure we've had this conversation before, and my answer is still the same."

"So it's settled, then?" His voice had quieted again, and there was no confusion.

"It is. Settled," I replied.

We rode the rest of the way in silence, except for the snores of our canine passenger, whose legs occasionally spasmed against the backs of our seats. He'd gotten uncommonly quiet after Leah's departure, and I wondered if he thought it was his fault, or he blamed me for causing her to leave. Either way, I would need to make it right—with both of them.

First, I had to honor my commitment to Decker and see this through, even if the outcome was not one she or her father would have found closure in.

The scenery changed as Logan moved off the freeway, and we transitioned from concrete and the glory that was the Pacific Coast Highway to the residential flavor of Newport Beach.

"Don't park too close."

I noticed Logan shaking his head and mumbling.

"What?"

"Not my first rodeo, Jackson," he replied with a bit more emphasis than I thought was warranted.

"Yeah? Well, hate to mention it, but you have a habit of letting the wily ones out of the corral," I replied, injecting all the smugness I could muster.

"What does that even mean?" he huffed, squinting as he avoided my gaze.

"It means that your tailing skills could use some work. I saw you from a mile away the last time we ventured this way."

"If you say so," he grumbled.

I noticed he'd ignored my reference to "we" even though the two of us hadn't been this way together. Instead, he focused straight ahead as we entered a familiar neighborhood—one that he amusingly hadn't needed directions to.

"No idea what either Danielle or Wendell's guy is driving, so I'm hoping this turns out to be just another friendly pop-in to chat with Mae."

Logan nodded. "You think she'll buy it?"

I swiveled in my seat and pulled my sunglasses down. "I don't know, Logan. When was the last time your charm didn't work on a woman?"

His eyes widened just a tad, and though he fought a snicker, managed to form a response to my proposition. "I see. I'm just the eye candy of this operation."

"Make that a side of man-candy, and yes, I plan on asking her some follow-up questions but may need your…special charms to obtain her compliance."

Logan scoffed. "Whatever, AJ. What would you have done if I hadn't commandeered your vehicle and gotten us here?"

"Nicoh would have been my first choice," I sniffed, "but since you are available, awake, and somewhat less smelly—" I cast a glance back at the beast, whose fours were up in the air as he showed his goods to the world, emitting a snore that only a mother could find adoring—"you might as well pull yourself to good use."

"Glad I could oblige," Logan mumbled.

"That's the spirit." I punched him in the arm and was rewarded with a dark look.

"Sorry. Bruise easy?"

He returned his gaze to the road, pulling off on an adjacent street and parking behind a nondescript minivan sporting stickers of the "Best Glamma," "My Grandson is a Star," and "Back off this Glamma's ride" variety.

"Don't ask," I snickered when I caught him mouthing "Glamma?"

"How do you want to play this?" I asked after hopping out and scoping out the scene.

Nothing appeared out of order at the residence in question.

At least, not from the outside.

"*Now* you want input?" Logan tilted his head, his mouth quirked up at the corner.

"As good a time as any, I suppose," I retorted, waving a hand in dismissal.

"Fine," he grunted. "What about him?" he nodded at Nicoh, who was far from rousting from slumber.

"Him? He's the getaway driver." When Logan frowned, I added, "There's a cat on the premises."

His mouthed formed an "o" as he nodded in understanding.

"Let's proceed as you planned—one side of man-candy coming up."

If anyone had overhead us, he or she might have found our banter too jovial, but we were both well aware of what was at stake. If my gut was right, Danielle would rather chew her toenails than spend a day driving so that she could merely bask on a crowded beach. No, the girl was on a mission. I just hoped we weren't too late.

I offered him a curt nod and started walking, each step more cautious as I listened for signs of unrest. All appeared as it should, from my limited perspective, though I did not miss Logan sliding a pistol into his waistband. His face was void of emotion as he squinted at our destination.

As I stepped onto the first step, it was clear we should have hashed out Plan B.

"Did you seriously think you would get away with it?" Danielle growled, her voice coming from somewhere in the back of the house, perhaps on the covered porch looking over the sea. "I trusted you, and you did nothing but use me and ruin my life!"

I looked at Logan, who shook his head, mouthing "backup" before hunching down as he texted some unknown savior. I bit my lip as we inched forward, still eavesdropping on a conversation we had no business being privy to and yet, could lead us to the answers we'd been seeking.

"I wasn't the one jamming drugs into your veins." Mae's voice sounded oddly...amused.

"Your hands are far from clean in this, *Auntie*," Danielle snapped, the sarcasm as thick as the L.A. smog during rush hour.

"Aww, and here I thought I was your fairy godmother." The laughter that echoed was not quite right.

Danielle must have caught it, too, as her voice amped up a notch. Anywhere else, you would be worried about the neighbors overhearing. "God. Look at you. You don't even have the decency to deny it."

"Why should I?"

"Why? Why did you do it...to me?"

There was a loud sigh, followed by a slow, raspy chuckle. "Oh, Danielle. After all these years, everything is still about you, isn't it? I'd almost forgotten what a little brat you are."

"Was I part of it, Auntie Dearest? Were you trying to make me forget?"

"*It?*" If I were Mae, I'd lose the smugness. Provoking Danielle was possibly more dangerous than poking a stick at a bear.

"What happened that night? And don't bother asking me *what* night," Danielle growled. "We both know you're way smarter than that." The beast was so very near the surface now. "Tell me, Mae...what part did you play?"

"Me? What could I possibly have to do with Ellen's murder—that is what you're fuming about, isn't it?" There was a moment's silence before she added, "Regardless. I barely knew the woman."

"That girl, Kelly's friend from Phoenix. She and that cop who busted me, they *know* things." When Mae rolled her eyes and shrugged, she added, "I've been keeping tabs on them."

"Whatever makes you happy, Sweetheart—"

Danielle cut her off. "I followed him, following her *here*, Auntie. To. Your. House. You didn't think for a moment that her arrival was odd?"

"Not in the least. We had a nice chat. She was quite forth-coming about why she was here. And I was equally forthcoming in my responses. I wanted to help, after all. Such a terrible thing."

I audibly scoffed, causing Logan to place a hand on my shoulder. He cast me a dark look and shook his head. I made an overt zipping motion just as Danielle responded.

"Murder is a terrible thing? Is that all you've got to say?"

"My conscience is clean, Sweetie. I'm sorry that Kelly and her father and, of course, your poor mother, suffered as a result of the loss."

"'The loss'? Ellen lost her life. Kelly lost her mother. Max lost his wife and Mom, she lost a beloved friend."

Mae laughed. "Beloved friend? Your mother was a glorified housekeeper. She was never in that woman's league."

"Is that what this is about? Ellen's…class?" Danielle sounded both incredulous and doubtful.

"The only reason she agreed to watch you brats was because Max asked her to."

"Careful, Auntie. The green demon is showing her talons."

"Hardly," Mae snapped. "That woman thought she was too good for the rest of us. Had ambitions for a career and a family, and while I don't begrudge her that—female power and all—it was that it was a step toward moving her husband and child out of what she believed was an unsavory environment.

"Well, it was good enough for me, Max, your mom—so excuse me if I'm offended. Green? No. Incensed? Hell, yes." She was in a rolling boil, and still, Logan shook his head, even as she grounded out, "And look where that got her, Danielle. Good and dead. Obviously she crossed someone who thought she needed to be knocked off her high-horse."

Danielle shook her head. "Just because he didn't want you and couldn't have her doesn't make him a killer." There was a pause as she hacked out a wicked laugh. "What? Afraid to say his name? Or too bitter? That's right, Auntie. I know that your beloved Terrence Edwards is my real father. I also know that he didn't kill Ellen. And that you know it, too."

And that's when the floodgates opened, and everything went sideways.

CHAPTER TWENTY-EIGHT

Glass shattered overhead, and the sounds of grunting and scuffling echoed.

"Forget the backup—they won't make it in time!" I ground out in a hushed tone, crouching low as I moved toward the source.

I glanced back at Logan, watching his frown deepen as he assessed the situation, before his eyes met mine, and he pointed up. The only way to intervene was by scaling the exterior of the deck.

Spiderperson, I was not.

I gripped the first joist and pulled myself up, working hand over hand. Granted, we were talking feet and not stories, but the effort was still sizable, especially when adding in the constraint of time, which was not in our favor.

And so, we climbed.

It would be nice to believe we were stealthy in our advance, but using one's body weight to scale the side of a structure was a whole lot harder than it looked in the movies. Finally, we reached the deck. I was hoping to get a vibe on the current situation before we made our move when I heard an amused cackle. I glanced at

Logan, the muscles in his face twitching as he glared over the ledge and his body went rigid.

I shifted my position and squinted between the bars. Danielle had Mae straddled on the floor, a wild, exhilarated expression spanning her face. That's when I noticed the zip tie cinched around Mae's neck, the ends whimsically positioned between Danielle's fingertips.

"Look familiar, Detective?"

Outed, we climbed up the remaining rungs and flopped ourselves over, until we were at eye-level, sitting on the deck with Danielle and her captive.

"You're not the only one with connections or tricks up his sleeve." Danielle pulled a tablet from her lap, which showed our toil up the side of Mae's house. I was humbled to admit it had seemed more impressive of a feat than it looked.

"We don't want any trouble, Danielle." Logan held both hands high where she could clearly see them, though I knew he had a plan.

Didn't he?

"Smart move, Officer. Didn't think I remembered you earlier, did you?" When he shrugged, she scoffed. "I remember every-thing. Isn't that right, Auntie?" She pulled on the zip tie, causing Mae's eyes to go wide as her fingers scraped at the pressure against her neck.

"Ease up, Danielle," I snapped. "You can't afford to kill her— she has the answers you need."

"Come on, Arianna. Don't you mean the answers that *you* need? That Decker needed?"

"At the end of the day, aren't they the same?" I replied.

Danielle shrugged. "You've got the floor, Babe. Ask away. We've got time." She waved her free hand, giving a tug with the other as she chuckled.

I glanced at Logan, but he refused to capture my gaze. I was hoping his plan—this backup—was going to buy us the time we needed.

"Err, okay, but you're gonna need to let her breathe," I paused to nod at Mae, whose eyes had closed, her body slumping awkwardly against Danielle, "because I think you're gonna wanna hear this."

"Have it your way." Danielle made a show of releasing her grip, but Mae didn't budge.

"Mae? If you're conscious and can hear me, why were you and Ellen fighting the day of her murder? Was it because you thought she was sleeping with Terrence Edwards?"

All eyes shifted to me, including Mae's, who'd apparently not been in as bad of shape as I'd initially thought, as her eyes widened, and she attempted to use one of her hands to ward me away from the subject.

Of course, Danielle's sharp little eyes caught the gesture. "Answer her!"

After a moment, Mae responded in short, raspy breaths. "There were rumors that you were my brother's spawn," she paused, her eyes tearing at the effort and the strain, "I only found out later, from your mother, how wrong I was about that. And about *her*."

Still under duress and she couldn't bear to utter the dead woman's name.

Danielle cinched the restraints. "What did you *do*, Auntie?"

Mae pounded her hand on the floor, and Danielle finally eased her weight off just enough to allow her to speak again. I glanced at Logan, but he shook his head, his eyes focused on the pair.

"I did nothing to that woman," Mae croaked out.

"'That woman' had a name—Ellen," Danielle hissed, leaning in so her lips almost grazed the other woman's ear. "For some reason, you seem reluctant to share your story, which leads me to believe that while you may not have wielded the knife that killed her, your hands are still filthy.

"And once she was dead, you still weren't satisfied, were you? What was it that caused the confrontation that followed the murder—the one that caused the rift between you and my mother?"

Mae shook her head, wincing at the movement. "Your mother learned about our argument from one of the neighbors and confronted me. And when I told her about my suspicions—how Ellen had cheated on Max to get herself a job with his firm and an heir she could hold over him—she angrily informed me that I was wrong. Ellen had not only turned the offer down, she had shared her pregnancy news with Maria before Terrence had even laid eyes on her. She was never involved with Terrence." Mae paused to catch her breath. "Of course, by then, the damage had already been done."

Danielle narrowed her eyes, her voice husky as she growled, "'*Damage*'? That's easy to say when you've lost nothing. Ellen's murder sentenced Kelly and her dad to a lifetime in Hell."

Mae mumbled something I didn't catch, though it caused Danielle's frown to deepen.

"What did my mother reveal that was so horrible...for you?"

"That she'd had a brief affair—with him, years earlier," Mae whispered, pressing her eyes shut.

Hearing that her mother, like Mae, had relations with a married man did not seem to faze Danielle. She had bigger fish to fry and was just throwing logs on the bonfire in preparation. "Wow. You truly believe everything revolves around you, don't you? If you want something, it should go without saying. Is that it?"

"You are so naive," Mae sniffed.

"Try me."

"Terrence was mine, you fool! And your mother threw herself

at him." Mae's lip curled into an angry snarl, her constraints causing her to wince.

Danielle threw her head back and hacked out a laugh. "Yeah, that sounds *exactly* like something she'd do. Not. So. Much."

"Well, not now, she wouldn't. But back then?" Mae lifted her shoulder. "Thankfully, she's not a problem for me anymore."

Danielle's demeanor shifted, and her body went rigid as recognition dawned. "What did you do to my mother?"

"Nothing she didn't have coming." There was no hesitation or regret in the older woman's voice, but a glint of satisfaction flickered in her eyes.

"My mother is in a borderline vegetative state," Danielle spat. "A woman of your own age with nothing. No dreams. No memories. All of it…lost."

"Perhaps it was karma," Mae replied, her voice scratchy and without a hint of emotion.

Mae was testing the limits where Danielle was concerned, though I didn't follow her logic, as Danielle still controlled the reins—no pun intended.

"Not sure it was as much karma as it was that green-eyed monster Danielle mentioned," I injected.

Mae's eyes shot to me, and in that moment, I saw her for what she was. She knew it too, as her mouth formed a cruel smile, creating an image that mirrored a creepy circus clown.

Danielle caught a side-glimpse, then looked at me before tightening her grip on the woman. "I'll ask you one last time. What. Did. You. Do?" Each word was enunciated with a progressive tug, causing Mae's eyes to bulge and her mouth to open, though the sneer still lingered.

I glanced at Logan and found his eyes trained on Danielle. I was about to warn her not to take her frustration out until Mae had a chance to respond when a figure emerged on the deck.

No one could forget those cheekbones. Or those eagle-sharp

eyes, as soulless as they were dark. His hair was slicked back with enough product to cause an oil baron to get a kink in his neck doing a double-take.

Mas had swapped his charcoal running suit for a crisp white button-down paired with slate trousers and highly polished loafers with tassels. He straightened the knot on the eggplant cashmere sweater that was draped across his shoulders as he assessed our group and frowned.

In my experience, most people would have cut and run after seeing their neighbor wrangled flat, straddled by stranger garroting her with a zip tie. Yet Mas wasn't fazed.

"What's going on here, Mae?"

"Take a seat, Fancypants," Danielle replied, looking bored.

"Mae? Who…is this? And why are you on the floor?" Still no mention of her air supply being cut-off while being held captive, or the fact Logan and I were present. Then again, it was hard to tell, as his face had yet to catch up with whatever he had going on inside his head.

Mae cast her eyes away, and for a moment, I thought I saw a bit of dampness at the corners.

Mas caught it, too. "Oh, dear sister, what have you gotten yourself into this time?"

Everyone bobbleheaded in his direction. It was Danielle who spoke first. "*This* is your brother? The guy you thought was my dad?"

I almost laughed as Mas pressed a hand to his chest and attempted to look aghast, as it didn't quite translate to his face.

Mae tilted her head and coughed out, "Come on, Danielle. From what you just said, could it be any worse than the truth?"

"That truth with a capital "T" being Terrence Edwards, of course," Danielle replied, her tone droll. "Big whoopie. I don't even know the man, and now that I've met him, I'm not sure what the big deal is." She scrunched her nose, shaking her head. "He's done nothing for me, and I'm guessing, based on his rep, that he got exactly what he wanted from my mother when he wanted it and not the other way around. Can you say the same, Mae? Sounds like you were handing out the milk for free, and still, nobody wanted it."

"At least I have something to give. Unlike your poor mama, sitting in her chair with her mouth hanging open," Mae snapped, her voice straining under the restraints.

Mas pursed his lips as he crossed his arms and shook his head at her.

Harsh. Even for a brother.

Danielle responded by tightening her grip on the zip tie, causing Mae's eye to bug. The rest of us didn't budge. Mae had walked into that one on her own.

"Speaking of my mother and her condition—what did you do? And don't bother denying it. I know you were there."

"If you really want to know, fine," Mae rasped, her eyes watering. "Yes. We fought. Yes. I was angry. Embarrassed. Enraged. And when her mouth was a flappity-flappin' with all kinds of innuendos—how she was going to tell everyone what he'd done to her, and that he was her daughter's baby daddy—I snapped. So yes, when the opportunity presented itself, I decided it was time to shut her up."

Mas stepped closer, his brows furrowed. "Mae, you keep quiet."

She glanced up at him. "Why? What do *you* care? You've lost nothing." Even the bubbles forming on her lip from the strain of talking under duress seemed pathetic.

Danielle gave him a single headshake when Mas attempted to move closer. He complied, but his gaze remained on his sister.

"What are you talking about? I lost *everything* because of our father. So you keep quiet. Or you'll know what it's like to lose everything, too," he ground out between clenched teeth.

Mae's eyes flashed to him, and her mouth opened but Danielle beat her to it. "What the heck are you talking about? I swear the two of you are completely mental," she growled. "And here you thought *I* was the one with daddy issues?"

I'm not sure what compelled me to respond, though Logan stiffened when I did. "Their father gave everything to charity. Despite all that he had acquired throughout his life, he left them with nothing. Not even their family home."

Mas gave a nod in my direction while Mae gaped, perhaps appalled that I'd pulled her socks from the laundry basket. Danielle, on the other hand, looked interested, if not amused.

"Don't know about this guy," she tilted her head toward Mas, "but Mae seems like she did okay for herself." She waved her free hand around, nodding toward the beach.

I feigned a laugh. "Blackmail goes a long way, doesn't it, Mae?" I gave her a pointed stare and was surprised when I received a confused, open-mouthed expression in return.

"I don't… What?" she stuttered, looking from me to Mas.

"That's enough, Mae," he huffed. "You don't owe these people any explanation."

"'These people'?" Danielle raised a brow. "Just who are you to tell us what we do and don't need?"

Mas gave her a tight smile. "I'm the owner of this property. And all of you are intruding."

And with that, he pulled a pistol from his outfit and shot Danielle, hitting her in the shoulder and causing her to release her grip on Mae, who slumped forward and choked. In hindsight, one might have made a pretty good argument that he'd actually been aiming for his sister, because a shot that good…well, none of us saw it coming from this guy.

Logan reacted, pulling the weapon from his waistband and got a shot off before Mas fired two directly into his chest. Logan fell, and his head connected with the railing as he went.

I covered my head and crouched behind an Adirondack as Mas chuckled, tapping the pistol against his thigh. "Your finest performance, Sister. Sadly, I think I could have done a tad better." Another laugh erupted as he did a little jig with his gun raised over his head. Wyatt Earp, he was not.

Realization dawned. "It was you."

Mas regarded me for a moment, clucking his tongue as he assessed the position I'd placed myself in, barely concealed by a patio chair—obviously, I was no threat—before responding, "Another performance. Another time."

"Performance?" I nearly fell on my behind, and awkwardly gripped the back of the chair for support. "In what society are murder and mutilation considered performance art?"

He frowned and wiggled a finger. "Don't be crass. Who are *you* to judge what constitutes art?"

Mae groaned as she eased herself into an upright position. The zip tie still dangled and while there was a crimson ring around her neck, it didn't appear to have cut into her skin. I couldn't say the same for Danielle, who whimpered as she pressed a cushion against her wound. Logan was silent.

"What the hell is she talking about, Mas?" Mae rasped.

"Your brother murdered Ellen," I replied, when it was clear Mas had chosen to ignore her.

When he gave me a bored stare, almost goading me to continue, I did.

"Likely because he believed she was pregnant with Edwards' child."

"Wasn't she?" Mas asked, though I doubted either answer would have changed his decision at the time. His flinty eyes had been on a bigger prize.

"A delusion. One that your sister created in her mind. Only when she found out that Maria had been cornered, and that her daughter was living proof of the demon that was Terrence

Edwards, her anger was not at her lover. No, she blamed the woman who had been her loyal friend since childhood—deeming Maria a temptress and a thief of something that never belonged to your sister in the first place."

I turned to Mae, who refused to return my gaze. "I'm betting that your theatrics aren't what sent Maria into her first stroke, are they, Mae? You were a nurse, after all. How hard would it have been to subdue a small woman like Maria and induce stroke-like symptoms?"

Mas' head whipped between his sister and me. "What did you do, Mae?"

"What did I do? What did *you* do?" she replied, her eyes as big as extra-large chicken eggs.

"I did what I thought you wanted me to do." What he lacked in sincerity, he made up for in arrogance.

"You…murdered…Ellen Decker?" Mae's lip quivered as she struggled to speak. "You mutilated that woman…murdered her unborn child and defiled her…in front of children!"

"Anything for my beloved sister." Mas' reply was heavy on the sarcasm as he offered her a smug smile and brushed a casual hand through his sculpted locks.

"Yes, I orchestrated the whole masterpiece—plucking a few of your boyfriend's hairs from your brush when he was over for one of his weekly trysts was the easy part. It also ensured he would pay the consequences for my handiwork. Of course, I didn't realize this one—" he tilted his head toward Danielle, frowning "—would be such an annoying little sneak—snatching my carefully planted evidence. And before you bore me with questions, yes, I know about that. No matter, it worked out in my favor.

"Before I indulge you with that, however, there were the anonymous calls. Again, child's play, but they were still an opportunity to show off my talents. First, there was the concerned neighbor, who reported seeing a man matching Edwards' description leaving the apartment building on the night of the performance."

His eyes were bright as he paused to give us a playback, transforming his voice into a middle-aged woman, speaking in an anxious, rushed tone, before gracing us with his other atrocities.

"And of course, just in the past few days, I crafted the good Samaritan, calling in the description of a possible perpetrator leaving the scene of the crime, after painstakingly morphing into a twenty-something female with a mediocre physique, an abysmal haircut, poor posture, and all-around bitchy disposition to effortlessly dispatch that pig you call a lover." While he'd been describing me, Mae looked none too pleased with his embellished storytelling.

"But getting back to the pièce de résistance—the premier on the night of the main event, so many lovely years ago. I slipped unnoticed into the building, up the stairs and slid right into the apartment. One would think a P.I.'s wife would have been a bit more careful. Unlocked doors, even back then?" He clucked his tongue. "She was sleeping when I found her, so I woke her so that we could play."

I pressed my eyes shut when he released a maniacal laugh.

"I cannot reveal all of my delicious secrets, my adoring fans, though I can give you a tease—while the human body is a thing of jaw-dropping wonder when you dissect it section by beautiful section, the mind is simply perfection when it's tweaked, ever-so-slightly and the right…stimulation is applied.

"When it came to the pod she had growing in her disfigured belly, she mutated into a beast. Sadly, I was forced to end our play to exorcise the demon and its spawn so that she could have a peaceful ending, one filled with calm and serenity." He looked off in the distance, at no one in particular, his mouth opened, almost salivating with delight as he relived the moment.

I couldn't look bear to look at Danielle or Mae. I could barely contain the disgust I felt as it was.

Mas' brow furrowed as he returned to the present, turning into a scowl. "It was only later that I learned about the adolescent demon spawn hiding in the closet, and their insolent meddling in my careful preparations, otherwise I would have dispatched them in the third act." Just as quickly, his disapproval slipped away, replaced by a lunatic's sneer.

"No matter. The encore turned out even more fortuitous as a result, as I shifted course and elected to make your boyfriend pay in an entirely more satisfying manner. All in all, it was a brilliant performance." An elated chortle escaped his lips.

Mae's face twisted, and when her mouth couldn't seem to find the words, I stepped in, despite the fact her brother represented everything I despised in human nature, and that frightened me to the core. That a man could embody the pure essence of evil chilled me to the bone and put my every nerve on alert.

"The encore he's referring to started after Ellen's murder. When he realized his 'careful preparations' wouldn't result in Edwards' demise, he resorted to extortion. Edwards thought his blackmailer was a woman, but like the anonymous calls, Matteo Antonio Santini, the wannabe star, made that easy work. Also known as Mas, for those of us who've been a bit slow to the game." I tilted my head in his direction.

"Last time you barged in, I thought you were just a nosy neighbor. It's quite the clever nickname, really. Perhaps you would have had more luck seeing it up on that Broadway marquee," I paused, giving his current act an exaggerated once-over, before adding, "Then again, probably not."

Mas ignored me, focusing instead on his sister and her reaction, which was a mixture of shock and repulsion as she paled, and her mouth dropped open.

While they were distracted with one another, and Danielle

glared at them while tending to her wound, I elected to continue, while inching toward Logan and the railing.

"All this time, she thought you were making money from your acting gigs. Broadway didn't quite turn out that way for you, though, did it?" I paused, but he refused to acknowledge me or offer a response, which was fine by me, as it allowed me to close the gap between me and my prone, unconscious friend.

Don't die on me, Logan! I plead silently over and over, my heart thudding against my chest with each repetition.

I continued, hoping I could draw out the truth while keeping the attention off me. Mas may not have agreed with the conclusions I'd drawn, but he hadn't denied anything either.

"Instead, you found a way to put your skillset to good use, where the pay was much better. And guaranteed. Until recently." I turned to Mae. "For a smart woman, you sure couldn't see what was in front of you all along. Then again, I don't think you wanted to. I'm betting you didn't realize your brother was also the person who attacked Edwards."

"Why? Why would you do that?" Mae pleaded with her brother, but he held his ground, almost mesmerized by her outcry.

I rolled my eyes. "Because the cash cow decided that he'd been manipulated for long enough. The crap was going to hit the fan sooner or later, with us digging into his past. He wasn't about to continue being extorted on top of it."

"Is that true? Is…all of this?" she wailed.

"Yup, everything here was bought and paid for by way of Terrence Edwards," I responded, nodding as I glanced around. "He's got good taste, I'll give him that."

Finally, a crack in the armor emerged as Mas turned to me, balling his free fist. "It's mine, you twit. He owed me!" he spat, forgetting his beloved sister in the process as the truth came tumbling out.

My sarcasm hits some people like that. Fortunately, it was a good thing this time, as his outburst was enough to knock some sense into Mae.

"You didn't do this for us! You did this to get back at our father for what he did to you, casting you out for your lifestyle and choice of careers. You saw Terrence as an easy mark, and you used my feelings for him to orchestrate it.

"How could I have been so stupid? You came home—I had missed you for so long, I welcomed you with open arms. But our little heartfelt reunion was all for show, wasn't it? I was merely your way to make a quick buck.

"And the murder, it was because you just couldn't stand me attempting to have a life of my own, after both us of lived in the shadows of that man."

"Listen to you, 'a life of my own'…what a crock!" Mas raised the gun and shook it at her, enunciating each word as she shrunk back against the floor. "You're referencing this precious life of yours that involved throwing yourself at a man that belonged to someone else? Did you even love him? Or was it the challenge of taking something from someone else, because you could?"

"What do you know about love? About loyalty? You split the minute things got rough, leaving me behind to deal with that man," she cried, though her words were angry.

Mas scoffed. "I know that neither involves attempting to kill your best friend. Twice. Yeah, don't forget you invited me to that party the second time around. I know all of your little tricks."

Mae cast him a deathly glare, gritting her teeth. "You swore you wouldn't breathe a word of that, ever, Brother. You haven't changed at all."

Mas cut her off, laughing harshly. "Don't fool yourself, Mae. We are no different. We're products of the same environment, after all."

"Don't say that! I could never…murder…" Tears streamed

down her face as she struggled with her words, finally biting out, "You're a butcher!"

"That's all you've got?" he snipped. "Dad was right. You're weak." He scrunched his nose in disgust when her cries became audible.

I touched Logan's immovable form, but there was no response, though he did still have a pulse. Danielle was weak, and her eyes were half-closed but she, too, was alive. As there was nothing I could do for either of them under these conditions, it was time to move things along.

"I hate to interrupt this family get-together, but you both have some serious issues," I replied, turning to Mae. "You see what he's doing here, don't you? He's gonna set you up for killing us, and then he'll take you out. Your father was right. Leopard. Spots."

"Shut up, whoever you are. You have nothing in this game." The gun was suddenly aimed at my head.

"Actually, I do. Kelly Decker—"

"Screw the Deckers. They're dead. All dead," he screamed, his face morphing into a crazed Chucky doll.

"Well, you did have a hand in that. I'm just here to clean up your mess," I replied, my tone even and calm, despite the fear that raged through me.

"My mess?" He raised a brow, his tone still on the edge of hysterics.

"I'm going to make sure you get judged by a jury of your peers, and you never see the light of day." I raised an angry finger and pointed it, noting the tremble of the barrel that was milliseconds from ending me.

"You are in no position," he snapped.

"Maybe. But I've always gotta Plan B. And in this blueprint, it says that you're finished."

"Shut up!" Mas' eyes went wild as he shook the gun.

"Or what?" I tested fate and lost, as he shifted it from my head to Logan's.

"Or I'll put a bullet in all of your brains, starting with your boyfriend here. Wakey, wakey, Prince Charming." He stalked over to Logan and gave him a solid kick to the ribs. And still, Logan didn't budge. "Come on, Pretty Boy. Don't think I don't know you're playing possum. Those bullets hurt, but that jacket I just kicked surely protected that steroid-induced chest of yours."

I blinked. Logan had been wearing a vest this whole time?

At that moment, Mas kicked him in the head.

"Stop!" I screamed.

Mas turned the gun on me. "I told you I'd put a bullet in your brain if you didn't shut up."

Out of nowhere, Wendell stepped through the door and placed a sawed-off shotgun against the base of Mas' skull.

"Not before I put one in yours."

CHAPTER TWENTY-NINE

"Did you bring the cavalry?" I rasped.

Wendell deadpanned, even behind the shades. "I *am* the cavalry."

He scanned the room, glancing first at Danielle, who glared at him with gritted teeth. The cushion she'd pressed against her wound had bled through. After moving to Logan, who remained unconscious after the damage Mas had inflicted, he turned to me. "What exactly are we working with here?"

"Both need an ambulance. Danielle was shot in the shoulder. Logan took two in the chest, but was wearing armor."

"Good man. And the trauma to his head?"

"That…was compliments of this guy," I ground out, nodding at Mas.

"Kicking a man when he's down. Weasel move, little man," Wendell growled.

When Mas frowned and opened his mouth, Wendell tapped the base of the man's skull with the pistol he'd removed from his hand without incident, "Don't. Speak," he said calmly, before turning toward Danielle. "Lift that cushion, and let me see."

"Is this considered bedside manner?" she snapped, conceding when he gave her a "move it along" gesture.

"Looks like it went through. Continue applying pressure. You'll live." Danielle's eyes widened, but before whatever retort she'd conjured could escape, he added. "You can thank me later, and I'll take repayment in the form of a favor."

He shot a wink at me, noting my open mouth. "How's that for bedside manner?"

"Riiight. Getting back to it. Logan called for backup, but we've not heard a peep from them or your guy until you arrived," I replied.

Wendell pursed his lips. "Do I look like a peep to you? Nah, I entered with a BOOM." He chuckled when Mas jumped. "This guy, who only attacks when he knows his prey can't fight back, enters with a peep." His lip snarled as he leaned toward Mas' ear as he whispered, "You make me sick."

He leaned back, and with his free hand, made a call. He wasn't a man of many words, but from what he did say, I assumed help was on the way for Logan and Danielle. When he finished, he gave Mas' head a quick tap, probably just to mess with him, before turning to me.

"About that backup. My guy's job was complete when Danielle stopped here. As for your friend's backup—it appears they've been delayed." He shook his head when he caught my expression. "You can stop giving me that judgey look. According to the scanner, there was a pile-up on the 101, as well as a possible leak of a toxic variety in one of the nearby neighborhoods."

When that judgey look transitioned to doubt, he muttered, "I *might* have had something to do with the latter." A small smirk escaped before he added, "Let's just say I know a guy who owes me a favor that owns a portable toilet business...if you get my drift?" He chuckled at his own joke, even though no one else followed suit.

When I waved a hand, prompting him to move the subject along, he turned serious. "Fine. So what's the deal with these two? Is she the blackmailer?" He tilted his head at Mae.

It was Danielle who answered, and though her voice was as weak as she was pale, there was a hint of bitter amusement in her tone. "No, this one's just a harpy. Isn't that what they called woman like you in your day, Auntie?" She nudged the older woman with her knee, causing Mae to grunt in pain. "Nah, Fancy-pants, here is your blackmailer."

Wendell looked from Danielle to the back of his captive's head. "Interesting. What are you, a falsetto? Mr. Edwards was sure his pickpocket was a dame."

Mas rolled his eyes. From where Wendell stood, he couldn't see it, and I was glad, not wanting to be splattered with the brain matter of this vermin. "I'm an *entertainer*."

"Whatever. Not impressed," Wendell hacked out a laughed as Mae shifted.

"I can't believe you blackmailed Terrence, for this?" She waved a hand around as she sobbed, an emotion so contrived we all looked like we'd eaten bad sushi.

Danielle scoffed. "That's rich. Murder. Mutilation. Death of an unborn child. Not to mention attempted murder—twice—of your best friend. And *blackmail* is what gets under your skin?"

"Whoa!" Wendell glanced at Danielle, who nodded, silently affirming her declaration. "You two have a seriously messed-up sense of family."

Mas ignored both of them and sneered at his sister. "The best part is that it's all in your name, so it'll trace right back to you if your lover digs hard enough." Mae cast him a seething look that could have created icicles in the heat of an Arizona summer, but Mas ate it up, giggling in an ear-splitting, high-pitched rhythm.

"Just a little insurance, in case you didn't see things my way. You were always a bit of a Daddy's girl, after all."

Mae released a wail as her brain caught up with her mouth, but Wendell held up a meaty hand.

"Enough with the family squabble! Let's talk about this murder. You—" he jerked his head toward me, "explain."

And so I did, as quickly as I could, all while receiving expressions that ranged from disinterest to disgust and hatred from the peanut gallery. Personally, I wanted to vomit, right after I punched Mas in the throat and slapped his sister upside the head.

When I finished, Wendell was the only one to offer commentary. "So nobody would mind if I blew his brains out into the Pacific." As usual, I couldn't see his eyes, but his expression made me wonder.

"Actually, it might traumatize the sea life. And piss off the Environmental Protection Agency, as well as everyone in the vicinity." There was zero sarcasm in my tone.

Wendell nodded. "He does seem a bit...toxic. Meh, maybe a stint with the prison gangs will do him some good." He nudged Mas with his gun. "What do you ya think, Fancypants? It'll give you a chance to practice that act. I'll warn ya, though, they're a tough crowd."

Mas grimaced while Wendell rumbled out a full-bodied chuckle.

I was about to expound on a few of the finer details that Wendell had missed out on when a familiar sound snapped my attention toward the inside of the house. "What the—"

"Oh yeah, forgot to mention. Saved the neighborhood from this guy." He thumbed behind him, "Thought he could check things out inside. You know, do his doggy thing while I dealt with this mess." I gave Wendell a head shake. "What? You said he was trained."

Before I could utter a syllable, Alabaster skidded out of the house, fur on end, claws out with Nicoh hot on his trail in full howl.

"Cat!" Danielle yelled while Mae's eye widened in horror as she whimpered his name.

Someone was screaming like a small child as Nicoh barely missed snatching the cat as it dove off the deck.

Turns out cold-blood murderers can be quite the sissies, given the right incentive.

Nicoh panted, whipping his tail in delight, looking at each human to determine who would be giving him scratches, and of course, treats.

Mas squealed, catching us all off-guard as he hyperventilated and pointed in the direction the cat had launched himself.

"What? I'm sure it's fine," Wendell responded, leaning away from him so that he could catch a better glimpse off the deck, causing Mae's brother to amp up the screeching and nonsensical muttering.

The rest of us winced. It was pretty over-the-top, even for an entertainer. It wasn't until his lip quivered, then curled up ever so slightly on one side that I realized that's all it had been.

An act.

Mas had used the spat between Nicoh and Alabaster as a distraction.

When Wendell's focus shifted to the cat's suicide dive off the deck, he moved away from the man, allowing him an opportunity to extract a knife from his waistband. Spinning on his heel, Mas slashed Wendell's midsection, forcing him to stumble backward. Wendell was still holding the gun, but as he glanced down at the wounds, his foot caught the corner of one of the patio chairs, and he started to tumble. Mas advanced on him, slicing down and knocking the gun away as I looked on in horror.

Wendell got his own jabs in, but the knife came at him again, this time slicing his good arm. Danielle struggled to push Mae off her but the woman, frozen in disbelief or shock, pressed into her trying to put as much distance between her and the battle. On my knees, I scrambled toward the gun, just as Mas shoved the knife at Wendell's carotid artery.

"Don't. Even. Try." He looked at me calmly, his tone even. And that's when I saw what was truly behind those cold, dark eyes.

Evil.

I skittered back on all fours and nodded, shoving my hands up in the air.

Mas snarled out a harsh laugh. "Surrender so soon?" He swiveled the knife against Wendell's neck as though it was a harmless plastic toy. "What would your precious Kelly have to say about that?"

My mouth worked, but as frustration and anger flooded me, I struggled to formulate the words, causing him to sneer. "What? Cat got your tongue?"

I'll admit, it was cliché, even for a zero-talent, washed-up entertainer, but it did the trick. Nicoh took his cue and charged toward the man—thinking it was all part of the fun—knocking him to the ground, then standing on his back, all while howling with delight.

The knife wriggled free, and I rushed over, kicking it in the opposite direction of Mae and Danielle, who looked on in surprise and relief. After picking up the gun, I pulled a treat from my pocket and tossed it at Nicoh, who happily snapped it up and crushed it in one bite, his paws still firmly planted on Mas' spine.

"Should have warned you, Fancypants—never utter the 'C' word around an Alaskan Malamute."

CHAPTER THIRTY

Of course, I happened to be the one brandishing the weapon when Logan's backup finally arrived and found myself face down on the patio before I could plead my case.

I was just fortunate that neither Danielle nor Wendell had passed out. Who knows what kind of tale Mas would have spun. Then again, after scanning the expressions of the law enforcement present, Mas' squealing was getting on their nerves, so they may have arrested me, too, just to get him to shut up.

After I'd safely handed over the gun, I corralled Nicoh so that the cops could secure the scene, and emergency personnel could tend to Logan, Danielle, and Wendell.

As I relayed my account of what had transpired, from the embarrassing tale of how Logan and I had ended up on the deck, to Mae's confession of the attempted murder of her best friend and finally, to Mas'—a.k.a. Matteo Antonio Santini's—unabashed revelation of the night he murdered Ellen Decker and her unborn child.

The details surrounding the blackmail were a bit more delicate, and Wendell shot me a look of warning as I connected the dots to Edwards, simply relaying that Mas had bragged about extorting money from him for years under the veil of undisclosed threats and admitted to attacking him when he'd refused payment.

Outwardly, the officer remained neutral, but a wave of skepticism flowed from her as I concluded. Finally, she nodded, and after confirming my contact information, handed me her card, "should anything else come to mind."

Nicoh and I made our way through the house, emerging to see a semi-conscious Logan and a fully-conscious, furious Danielle, sharing some colorful opinions with the emergency medical staff as each was loaded into an ambulance. Mae cried as officers handcuffed her to a gurney before she was placed in another.

It must have been quite a show for the neighbors, who huddled and whispered as Mas was also handcuffed and escorted to an awaiting cruiser. Before the officers could thrust him into the back, he sent air kisses to the onlookers, as though they were his adoring fans.

I shook my head, thinking I'd seen it all—until I realized someone was noticeably absent.

After scouring the surroundings—squinting when I thought I'd caught a glimpse of his lumbering figure tucked behind a delicate rose bush—I had confirmation.

Wendell was gone.

CHAPTER THIRTY-ONE

I could have left it at that and gone back to the life I had waiting for me in Phoenix. I missed my bed and plain-old-Jane routine—clients, dog training—just normal, everyday stuff, without any murderers, blackmailers, or other unsavory types lurking in the shadows.

Edwards still lingered in the latter category in my book. He had not murdered Ellen Decker, and though his limited association with her resulted in her murder and brought Decker and her father a lifetime of heartache and missed memories, he, too, had been a victim.

At last report, he continued to improve and demanded to be moved to a more suitable location for recovery—some ostentatious penthouse sweet atop one of the city's most coveted hotels.

Danielle and I had reconnected shortly after she was released from the hospital. Still simmering over being shot, she expressed her desire to have five minutes alone with Mas and Mae and didn't seem to care whether it meant taking them on together or separately.

Five minutes would be enough, she figured, to unleash Hell

on both of them and ensure they never hurt anyone again. She didn't believe that the district attorney could file enough charges against them to justify what they'd done—and though I tended to agree—I didn't need to throw any more fuel onto that fire.

As for her relationship with her father, she was more than happy, now knowing who he was, to leave things "as is." Her life was complicated enough, she reasoned, without including the BS that epitomized Terrence Edwards.

The only time during our chat that she paused for air was when I mentioned Larissa and her mother, and the possibility of a reunion. At this, she became contemplative, and to my surprise, not only took her sister's contact information when I offered it, she called later that day.

At last word, they were making in-roads on repairing their relationship, and Larissa was hopeful Danielle would eventually venture home. If there was a silver lining to come out of this situation, perhaps this was it, even if it was a bit tarnished.

"I don't care how she shows up, just that she makes an effort," Larissa said in her message on my voicemail, the emotion snagging her voice the more she spoke. I can't say I was dry-eyed by the end of the replay.

Logan, too, would be okay, physically, and that was a harder sit-down than the prior.

We'd come together to do what was necessary to bring Decker's last request to fruition. Her mother's killer had finally had gotten his due, but at a cost.

Logan had manipulated and lied to me but felt I owed him a chance to explain, even if it was solely out of respect for Decker and their lifelong friendship. Besides, what he needed was not my forgiveness, but the opportunity to openly and honestly purge whatever monster was raging inside—whether fury, guilt, remorse or despair—so that he could eventually forgive himself.

And so we sat, somewhat awkwardly at a diner not too far from his condo. I'd dropped Nicoh off at a nearby groomer for a little post-excitement TLC. It was the least he deserved, considering he'd saved us from what would have been a dark ending at the hands of a killer who had no bones about doing it again.

Plus, I wasn't going to ride home with him smelling the way he did after his skirmish with the cat, followed by that "puppy moment" when he'd unleashed his stellar dance moves once he hit the sand—by that point, I think he was just showing off.

Anyway, it gave me a couple of hours with Decker's best friend. If what we needed to say to one another couldn't be said in that amount of time, it never would.

"When we started this, I asked you if you would help me, and you said you couldn't, yet your tune changed when I came back—and while I'm appreciative—I want to know why. Why did you decide to help me, only to undermine me? You lied about where you were and what you were doing. And you followed me after we agreed on a plan. Why?"

Logan winced as he bent his head. Apparently, the injury he'd sustained from Mas' kick was as painful as it looked, though I wondered if he preferred that agony over having this conversation.

"Do you find me untrustworthy? Unskilled, I get, but I thought that I laid everything on the line when I came here, and when you agreed to assist, I thought we were on the same page."

I opened my hands to him, pleading.

"It's not that." His brow furrowed, his eyes cast downward. "When Decker died, I thought I would eventually be okay, and the pain would lessen, but it didn't."

I leaned into him, placing a hand over his and found them shaking. "It hasn't been that long, Logan. The grieving process is different for everyone. Believe me."

He nodded slowly. "I know. I just thought I could beat the curve. Instead, I fell under it." It came out in a whisper, but the emotion behind it spoke volumes.

"At first, it was little stuff. I'd forget a meeting at work or arrive late. When I did show up, I was distracted, and it translated to my job. I started slipping up—making rookie mistakes. And while the guys tried to be sympathetic knowing I'd suffered a loss, I was putting their lives on the line, too. A few of them tried to talk to me, even urged me to seek professional help, but I just brushed it off. And bottled it up. After a while, all that pent-up emotion turned to anger. And as things escalated, rage."

"What happened?" I asked softly, noting he'd pressed his eyes shut.

"It's started as a minor disagreement. I won't go into the particulars, but it was fairly routine, something we encounter every day. My partner got the commanding officer involved, and I lost the upper hand. And then, I lost control. Broke my partner's nose—have known the guy since high school—and shoved my superior hard enough that she fell. Hard. She was pregnant." He shook his head as his voice cracked, and I fought back my shock. "The baby is okay and she's okay, but there was a moment..." His voice trailed off as his body shuddered.

"And that's why you haven't been on active duty."

He nodded, shifting his hand from beneath mine so that he could push away the wetness threatening to fall from the corners of his eyes. "My superior could have done a lot worse, but she took pity on me and gave me the choice."

"Not pity, Logan. Compassion. There's a big difference, and your superior did you a favor." I clutched his hand again when he refused to meet my gaze. "Logan, look at me. You lost your best friend. Tragically. It's okay to grieve and still be overwhelmed by emotions that continue to manifest. It's all part of the process, but we can't do it alone. And there's no shame in admitting you need help."

"I am…getting help. It's slow-going, but as you said, it's all part of the process. I guess."

I bobbed my head. "Yes. And we all hit different bumps on that path, but there will be better days. Not perfect, but better than the day before."

"I guess I've been hitting all the bumps lately, potholes and all." His eyes glistened as he peered at me beneath those unfairly long lashes. Still, I knew that he was not only seeing me, he was hearing me.

I patted his arm with my free hand. "All at our own pace."

"The pain never fully goes away, does it?"

I shook my head and gave him a sad smile. "No. But it becomes more manageable. And the memories, they're what keeps her spirit alive. And will keep you going."

"Yeah, she'd probably come back just to kick my butt if she saw the likes of me now." He chuckled.

"Most definitely." I laughed.

"So, about Mia…" he bit his lip and cast me a nervous look. "I wasn't doing so hot. Neither was she. And at some point, I felt that if I couldn't help myself, how could I help her? I felt like it bordered on neglect. Not the physical kind, but I just wasn't present for her, if you know what I mean."

I nodded. "I do. Where is she now?"

"With a friend. The woman who had Mia's mom actually. She regularly works with an animal behaviorist and a trainer, and together, the three of them help dogs who have had sustained some form of trauma, whether physical, psychological, or emotional."

I nodded, having met a few individuals in the field, I'd gained an enormous amount of respect for their work. "How's she doing?"

"Great. I visit her almost every day. And when we're both… better, we may start integrating into each other's lives, though a bit more slowly. We were unprepared the first time around, and I made a lot of bonehead mistakes."

"Not mistakes, Logan, opportunities to learn. View it as a work-in-progress."

"Kind of like you and me?" He glanced at me, and though there was a playful tone in his voice, his eyes searched mine. "That's why I did what I did, you know."

"Because of boneheaded, manly-thought processes?" I replied, a tiny smile teasing the corner of my mouth.

"Something like that." He chuckled, but then his brow creased, and seriousness slipped back in. "I was afraid. I'd lost Decker and I didn't want to lose you, too. I know it sounds weird, you'd just come into my life, whereas Decker…" He shrugged and I gently caught his chin and tilted it toward me.

"Stop. It's not weird at all, it's just life." When he nodded, I gestured for him to continue.

"I allowed the idiot brain to take over and thought by staying one step ahead I could keep you safe, but I should have come clean and shared my concerns, rather than doing what I did. Even now, I realize how ridiculous it was."

"Hey, girls always like the knight swooping in to help her in a pinch, but circumventing her efforts and stalking her movements? Kinda creepy." I shrugged.

Logan pursed his lips and nodded. "If you can give me some time, I'd like to start our friendship over." His look was so sincere, and yet so filled with sadness, my heart hurt for him, and all I wanted to do was reach out and pull him close. But that was about me.

"No," I replied, watching his face morph from sadness to surprise. "While I can give you time, I can't take this friendship back to zero and pretend it meant nothing. I can, however, agree that—as friends—we will continue our journey, wherever it leads, and be there to support one another through good times and bad."

Logan gave me a small smile and nodded. "A work-in-progress."

This time, I did pull him in for that hug.

"That's right, *my friend,* a work-in-progress."

CHAPTER THIRTY-TWO

And then there was Wendell. One might have found it strange that out of this cast of characters he'd been the most unlikely ally, yet turned out to be the most reliable.

I still didn't care for his boss much, but everybody has a calling in this world, and if serving as Terrence Edwards' right-hand and bodyguard was Wendell's, who was I to cast him in the same light as I did his boss? My issues were not with Wendell. Those were about me and my "stuff" and I had no right to place that in someone else's court.

We sat side by side on the bench outside the Puppy Palace of Pawfection, awaiting the beast's session with the masseur to commence. Even though he'd acted entitled after his grooming, thanks to all the pampering he'd received, I figured a bit more wouldn't hurt and certainly couldn't pay him back for helping to ensure Mas hadn't put a bullet in all of our skulls.

Having said that, I was happy to pay the exorbitant L.A. prices, as there was no amount of gratitude that made me want to spend my days personally massaging his tender tootsies or spritzing him with Zen Doggy aromatherapy mist.

"Back to business as usual in your neck of the woods." It

wasn't really a question, and the big guy, impeccably dressed like his boss and still hiding behind his customary shades, simply grunted.

We sat like that for a moment in comfortable silence.

To my surprise, he broke it first. "He…um…is appreciative of what you did. He knows that he's not your favorite person, and still, you followed the path to the end. He wanted to offer you something in return, but I told him that would be overkill."

And awkward, I thought. "Much appreciated."

"Maybe now you owe me instead." His voice rumbled though he was fighting to contain a laugh.

"Not on your best day, though that was nicely played. I do appreciate the fact that you spared a word with his Holiness on my behalf."

"It was a pretty big word." Wendell feigned a mock sniff before turning serious. "Still, it was a relief to have his black-mailer and attacker identified and in custody."

"Plus, a huge weight lifted, no longer having the question of his involvement in Ellen Decker's murder looming," I murmured, shaking my head.

Only Terrence Edwards would put the focus on himself first.

Wendell tilted his head. Perhaps my tone broadcast my feel-ings. "It weighed on him more than you know. He intimated that he wished Max Decker and his daughter were still alive to see the murderer brought to justice."

Intimated? "To get them off his back."

"I see he still hasn't won, even by concession, in your book." I noted that Wendell wasn't posing judgment, and actually seemed to be reflecting on the subject.

"Nobody won in this scenario. My book was a moot point."

"True." He appeared to have something on his mind as he folded his hands in his lap and stared into the chaos that was the world in which he lived.

"Tell me, Wendell, what does life look like for Edwards' thuggy these days?" I asked after several minutes had passed,

He chuckled. "Back to the status quo, thank goodness. I know this seems trite, considering the circumstances, but I've missed my shows for the last few days, which are a huge source of decompression and relaxation for me."

I quirked a brow. "Shows?"

Wendell shifted and puffed out his cheeks. "Don't judge, but in my line of work, I need something that helps me feel as though my life is normal. Compared to non-thuggies, that is," he replied, breaking into a rare grin.

It was good to know he actually had teeth and not the razor-tipped throat-ripping gnashers I'd envisioned.

I leaned over and gave him a mock-punch in the arm. "Come on, spill it."

Of course, Wendell was too much of a tough guy to feign injury. And apparently, just as serious when it came to his shows.

"Real Housewives."

I fought to keep my body language in check as I took a moment to formulate an appropriate response, which turned out something like "Um. Okay? Which one?"

His head swiveled—probably a BS check—and apparently satisfied with what he saw, responded, "Have seen them all, and I'd have to say New Jersey."

"You can't be serious," I scoffed.

"Like I said, I pick 'em based on the normalcy they bring to my own life."

"I see." I didn't agree but could see it from his perspective.

"I used to favor others—which shall remain unnamed—but when a lot of the women all started having that surprised expression whether they were happy, sad, or ripping out a chick's weave, I bailed on those. And the dialogue—I can get my fix of soap operas elsewhere, if you get my drift."

I was thinking more along the lines of a horror movie but kept my trap shut, not wanting to offend him after he'd finally opened up and shared something personal.

"If it makes you feel better, my homey refuses to watch anything but those Beverly Hills gals. He likes sparkly things." He shrugged.

I swiveled on the bench to face him. "Homey?

Wendell pulled out a new cell phone—a model I'd heard of, but knew it hadn't been released to the public. Apparently, the privileges of being associated with Terrence Edwards had a far reach. He noticed me staring.

"A thank you for my service."

As I nodded, he scrolled through pictures, smiling again as he settled on one and turned the phone so I could view it.

I absorbed the captivating eyes behind that disinterested look and the bored, leisurely posture. And gasped. "Is that…Alabaster?"

"Big guy needed a home," he replied, rather matter-of-factly.

"Who knew you were such a softy?" I grinned. Or a cat lover, I thought. Nicoh would be bummed.

"Don't you go ruining my rep, Arianna Jackson," he rumbled, but when my eyes snapped from the phone to his face, found him withholding a chuckle.

"Yeah, your rep. Seriously? With a name like Wendell?" I teased.

"What? It's all in the delivery." He offered me a knowing nod, puffing up his already mighty chest.

"Whatever you say," I laughed. "You do have a last name, right?"

Wendell chuckled, slapping a beefy hand on his thigh. If we had been in a different neighborhood, residents would have been ducking for cover at the sound. "Wendell *is* my last name."

"And what, your first is a matter of national security?" I was only half-serious.

He sighed, shaking his head. "It's Titus."

"Titus Wendell?" He nodded. "And you chose *Wendell*?" When he shrugged, I was compelled to add, "Can I call you Titus?"

The smile fell away. "Absolutely not."

I was about to add some churlish comment when my phone rang.

"Uh oh, I knew this was coming." Wendell a.k.a. Thuggy a.k.a. Titus glanced from me to my phone as I checked the contact information. "My P.I. friends, the Stanton brothers, probably calling for a play-by-play and a bit of razzing for not reaching out while on their turf. Their associate, Anna, is engaged to Edwards' son."

"Yes. I know." Duh. Of course he did.

Wendell waved a hand, gesturing for me to answer.

I snickered as I took the call. "Was just getting ready to call you—"

"Later." Abe, the elder Stanton brother, interjected in an uncharacteristically harried and clipped tone. "When did you last talk to your cohort?"

"Leah? A few days ago, when she packed up and headed to L.A. to work, for you."

There was traffic noise in the background when he responded, forcing him to yell. "What? I don't have any cases requiring her skillset at the moment."

My stomach started churning. Something was off in La La Land, and it wasn't the smog. "No long-term contract? One that required her to move?"

"AJ, I honestly have no idea what you're talking about. None of us have talked to her in weeks," Abe huffed.

"That's not possible," I whispered, feeling Wendell's meaty grip on my arm.

"I was afraid of that," he replied. "We gotta call from your ex, Ramirez. Purely courtesy. He knew you were out here—to our surprise and disappointment—and asked if we could pass a message onto you when we saw you."

"Just tell me, Abe." My voice had a disembodied quality to it.

"Her car was found at Phoenix Sky Harbor Airport in long-term parking."

"Okay?" That didn't sound so bad.

"Not typically a problem, but security was making the rounds and saw something dripping under the backside of the car. Under closer examination, they noted it appeared to be blood or a blood-like substance, so they called the cops, who had probable cause to pop the trunk."

"Nooo…" I wasn't sure I'd said it out loud until I felt the heat from Wendell's frame and his arm circling my frame in a protective hug.

"She not only never got on any flight, all of her possessions—her luggage, laptop, notebooks, purse and all of her identification—were still there."

"And Leah?" I whispered.

"It's time for you to go home," Abe replied in a somber tone. "And prepare for the worst."

~ The End ~

ABOUT HARLEY

Harley Christensen lives in Phoenix, Arizona with her significant other and their mischievous motley crew of rescue dogs (aka the "kids").

When not at her laptop, Christensen is an avid hockey fan and lover of all things margarita. It's also rumored she's never met a green chile or jalapeño she didn't like, regardless of whether it liked her back.

For more information on the author and her books, please visit her at www.mischievousmalamute.com.

OTHER BOOKS BY HARLEY

Mischievous Malamute Mystery Series
Book 1 ~ Gemini Rising
Book 2 ~ Beyond Revenge
Book 3 ~ Blood of Gemini
Book 4 ~ Deadly Current
Book 5 ~ Gemini Lost
Book 6 ~ Fatal Bonds
Book 7 ~ COMING SOON!

Six Seasons Suspense Series
Book 1 ~ First Fall
Book 2 ~ Winter Storm

www.ingramcontent.com/pod-product-compliance
Lightning Source LLC
Chambersburg PA
CBHW071750190726
48292CB00003B/928